WHAT REMAINS *of* LOVE

Suzanne Trauth

Willow River Press is an imprint of Between the Lines Publishing. The Willow River Press name and logo are trademarks of Between the Lines Publishing.

Between the Lines Publishing
9 North River Road, Ste 248
Auburn ME 04210
btwnthelines.com

First Published: July 2022

ISBN: (Paperback) 978-1-950502-98-1
ISBN: (Ebook) 978-1-950502-99-8

Library of Congress Control Number: 2022939719

WHAT REMAINS *of* LOVE

What's past is prologue…

– William Shakespeare

For Helen

1

Lloyd Davis sits with splayed fingers in front of him, covering a sheaf of papers as if they needed protection. He motions to a water pitcher perfectly centered on the conference table. "Perhaps a glass of water might help?"

"No thanks," DJ says.

Lloyd is looking his age. Mid-eighties. He'd been Dad's best friend for, what, seventy years? That long. Since he is still the senior partner in the law firm that handled all of Dad's legal work, sitting in this room makes sense. He pours a glass of water and takes a sip. His office, high above the streets of Manhattan, is a refuge from the noise below. There is no extraneous sound and muted lighting. Like Lloyd, the place is appropriate and tranquil. When DJ and I were kids, Lloyd was always around to help manage family crises and offer advice, legal and otherwise. When I was younger, I thought his high forehead, aquiline nose, and sensuous lips made him appear almost cruel until he smiled.

Stop gathering wool; Dad would have said. I push myself upward against the cushy back of the office chair. I need to stay focused. I *was* gathering wool, letting my mind unravel into fuzzy thinking about when I was a child, and Dad patted my head and whispered some piece of advice to me. Until Lloyd drops a bombshell. It will take more than a glass of water to absorb the contents of a codicil to Dad's will.

"Kate?" Lloyd asks.

"I'm fine." Three weeks alternately awake and dozing in an oversized hospital chair witnessing the life ebb from Dad's fragile form has left my body aching and my spirit dulled. For the last few days, my on-again, off-again insomnia has kicked in. *I miss him.* I pull a wad of tissues from my jacket pocket and blow my nose in a futile attempt to stop the burning behind my eyelids, the catch in my throat, the tears on the brink of spilling out. Could I still have fluid left in my body? And now this. I need to distract myself.

"I don't understand, Lloyd. What does it mean?" I ask.

During the past week, Lloyd had spent most evenings at the Whitman house in New Jersey, offering his condolences, suggesting solutions for the kinds of problems that emerge before, during, and after a funeral. I have never seen Lloyd lose his equilibrium. Until now. "Exactly what it says."

"How long have you known about this?" DJ asks. He stands behind a chair, frowning down at the two of us as if he was our parent and we were misbehaving kids. His expensive, pin-striped, black suit nicely covers the bulge at his middle, but DJ's puffy face gives him away: too much food and alcohol as antidotes for his stressful life.

Lloyd catches DJ's eyes over the rim of the glass. "Your father wanted it this way," he says, skirting DJ's question and glancing at me. I am tired and confused, at a loss for words.

"But when did he change his will? He could barely get out of bed the last couple of months. Was he in his right mind?" DJ walks to a corner window of the room that faces Park Avenue and leans his head against the glass. He looks as lost as I feel – like I am falling down a black hole. Like I am wandering in a wilderness of grief.

"This wasn't a recent decision. As his executor, and friend, I need to honor his wishes." Lloyd pauses and sets his glass on the tray. It had angered DJ that Dad had made Lloyd his executor. He felt that as his oldest child, Daniel Whitman, Jr., he was entitled to the position. I hadn't thought much about Dad's decision one way or the other.

"Kate?" Lloyd places his hand lightly on my arm.

"I don't know what to say. Who is this woman? Why would Dad leave her so much money?" And why have I never heard of her?

"My point exactly," says DJ.

Both of us know that isn't DJ's point at all. It's the money, plain and simple. It doesn't matter how much Whitman Textiles grosses or what percentage DJ personally pockets; it never seems to be enough.

"Who is she, Lloyd?" I ask again.

"I don't know much about her." He hesitates. "She was a friend of your father's, an artist, someone he met during the war."

I knew he had been a medic in Europe in World War II, though he'd never talked about it. Once, when I was ten, I rifled through an ancient army trunk in the attic and discovered his mothballed uniform, ribbons—including a combat medic badge—still pinned over the left breast. When our brother Billy had tumbled off his bike and broken an arm, Dad's splint and bandage stabilized the break until the emergency room doctor was able to apply a hard cast.

"I don't get it." DJ interrupts my reverie. "Why don't we know her?"

"Dad obviously knew her," I say. My words hang in the silence, begging anyone to contradict them. "Lloyd?"

Lloyd examines the palms of his hands. "A few years after your mother passed away—"

"We're talking twenty years ago?" DJ asks, unbelieving.

What would Mother have thought of Dad's generosity?

Lloyd continues without missing a beat. "...Daniel told me he wanted to change his will to include this bequest. He didn't offer an explanation, but he was firm." He fixes his eyes first on me, then on DJ. "You know how your father was when he made up his mind about something."

Dad defined "gentleman" as he was considerate and polite to a fault. But there was a stubborn streak that occasionally surfaced when he insisted on getting his own way: vacations at the Jersey shore instead of Myrtle Beach, which was what Mother wanted; Columbia University instead of the University of Miami, which was what I wanted.

"I still don't understand why I wasn't consulted," DJ says.

"It's Dad's will." Even though I have as many questions as DJ about the bequest, I can feel the old tightening in my chest that starts whenever DJ and I disagree. At times like this, I especially miss Billy, the family buffer. He had often stepped between DJ and me, preventing a scrap of a spat from exploding into a major conflagration. He had Dad's personality and easy charm, but since Billy's unexpected, permanent move to the Alaskan wilderness ten years ago, the tension between us had worsened. Billy's presence in New Jersey the week of the funeral forced DJ and me to call a truce. He'd left before the will was read; Billy had little interest in the family business. Or the material world, for that matter.

"But it's my...uh...our money," DJ says, sliding his eyes in my direction. "It affects the business. I'm the one who kept it going these last twenty years. Not Dad." DJ visibly tries to contain himself. "He should have consulted me."

"Not really," Lloyd says. "It's part of his personal assets, not part of the corporation."

"This makes no sense." DJ unbuttons his jacket and throws himself into a chair across the table from Lloyd and me. "You think I'm going to 'okay' a gift of a quarter of a million dollars to a woman I've never heard of? Who the hell knows what could happen. What if she demands more?"

"DJ…" Lloyd starts.

My head pounds, my face is warm. I'm trying to be patient—DJ has a point.

"Is she even alive? This entire thing could be a dead end," he says.

"According to your father, this is her address." Lloyd removes a pale blue envelope from a file that lay on the table. It is addressed to "Daniel Whitman," at his New York City address, from "Emilie Renault, L'Avigne, France," with "Par Avion" printed in the top left-hand corner. The writing is precise, with flourishes decorating each capital letter. "This was all he gave me." "She's French," I say in surprise. Why am I surprised? Dad was stationed in France for a period during the war. He was happy when I decided to major in French in college and then, eventually, teach it.

I had settled on studying French as my foreign language in middle school because my best friend had chosen to study it. To my amazement, I learned quickly and relished the feel of the language in my mouth. At Christmas time, when the French Club baked a *bûche de noël*, I was the primary chef. I was a star pupil and stuck with it in high school. By then, I knew I planned to make French my career. Dad was enthusiastic; Mother thought other fields would be more appropriate, but I was insistent. When I resolved to spend a semester abroad at the Sorbonne, he supported me, and she, initially, opposed my plans.

DJ glares at me as if I'm a traitor. Being connected by the language is enough to make me guilty. I pick up the envelope, turn it over, and see a decorative stamp of Santa Claus in a sleigh with "l'Association

5

des Paralysés de France" written in script at the bottom. She sent Dad a Christmas card.

DJ's cell phone clangs and splits the air. He studies the caller ID. "I've got to get to the office. Let me think about it." He rebuttons his suit jacket as he strides to the door.

"Nothing to think about." Lloyd slips the envelope back into the folder. "I've already written to her."

DJ whips his head around, sputtering. "This is not over," he says and slams the door as he leaves.

I wince, and a bulb blows out in the chandelier above the conference table. I stare at the darkened lamp. Is it an omen?

"I'm sorry for all this..." Lloyd's voice trails off as he waves a hand, indicating that he means everything—the bequest, DJ's anger, and Emilie's appearance in our lives.

"I'll talk to him," I say. I'm not sure I'm telling the truth. "Let me know if you hear from Emilie Renault." I stand up and chuck my bag over my shoulder. I'm not bothered by the money as much as I am by Dad harboring a secret relationship.

"Sure."

We hug good-bye, clinging to each other for a bit.

Once on Madison Avenue, I walk a block over to Park Avenue. The March air is brisk and damp, and the sidewalks are covered with a layer of melted snow mixed with street dirt. Bits of snowy slush cling to the soles of my shoes. The most unpleasant time of the year to walk in New York City is late winter, early spring. This year winter has gone on and on, cold and relentless. I pause in front of an ornate, turn-of-the-century building. Dad had bought an apartment here many years ago for overnight use by himself or family members working or entertaining late in the city.

The doorman steps in front of me, his eyes sad. "Miss Whitman, I am so sorry about your father," he says and touches the bill of his hat.

"Thanks."

"If you need any help..."

I nod and cross to the elevator, hesitating before pushing the button. Riding to the sixth floor is uncomfortable, and I have a knot in the pit of my stomach as I confront the entrance to the apartment. I have to clean out his clothes and other personal items sooner or later. Still, while ostensibly a practical visit, coming here is also a chance to feel close to him, to feel his presence lingering. For the moment, I usher all thoughts of Emilie Renault out of my mind.

The moment I open the door to the apartment, I get a whiff of cigar smoke mingling with the essence of Old Spice aftershave. Cigars were the one vice Dad allowed himself, but only here in New York, not in New Jersey. It's been months since I've been here. There is a layer of dust everywhere. The Polish cleaning woman, who normally kept the place presentable, had returned home to Warsaw, and I had yet to replace her.

I drop my coat and handbag on a chair in the foyer and walk to the spare bedroom slash office that was his personal and private domain. The master bedroom and living room were open territory for anyone staying overnight, but "the office" was his and his alone.

While I was a graduate student at the University of Illinois, I stayed in the apartment a few times on visits home. When I returned to New Jersey and began teaching, I found myself using the apartment once a month, particularly when I needed to escape my marriage. After the divorce, it was a good place to bring dates or throw a little pre-theater party.

Dad's scent had permeated everything in his closet. I touch a brown wool sweater that he loved to wear on cold winter nights, a birthday gift from Mother many years ago. There are a couple of suits, a favorite charcoal gray one that he used to wear to work, and a royal blue sweat suit barely worn, a Christmas gift from three years ago. The sight of them starts the stinging behind my eyes. I have to begin in safer territory.

In the kitchen, two coffee mugs are in the sink; the insides are stained dark brown. A dead bouquet of baby roses sits in a vase on the counter – a get-well gift from Whitman Textiles employees. On the refrigerator, I find a picture of Dad and me, taken at Tavern on the Green at Easter, and a photo of him with Nate and Drew sitting in a golf cart. Neither of his grandsons comes across as too thrilled, but Dad smiles broadly, in his glory, sharing the game he loved. I remove the picture of us from the refrigerator and tuck it into a pocket. A pair of reading glasses, one of many that he left lying around the house or stuffed in his pockets, rests on the glass kitchen table.

I open the refrigerator door and laugh. I am my father's daughter, all right. Both of us see the refrigerator as a way station, a place to keep the basics. For him, that meant olives to grace his perfect martinis, maraschino cherries for the odd Manhattan he was required to serve, part of a bottle of Chardonnay I'd left months ago, peanut butter, moldy cheese, and a pint of half and half now soured and reeking. What does amaze me is a nearly empty jar of hot fudge tucked into a corner of the bottom shelf. Dad disliked sweets; at least that's what I thought. I wash one of the mugs, pour the bottle of wine, and gulp it down. The gentle buzz gives me the strength to get back to work.

I confront the closet once again, folding the sweater, the sweat suit, the charcoal gray three-piece, a few shirts and slacks, and tuck them into a shopping bag. DJ might want these. If not, I'll give them away. I'll keep the sweater anyway. Dad lived simply: for a wealthy man, his material interests were few. By the daybed, there are *Complete Works of Arthur Conan Doyle*, old issues of *Photography*, and a *Bible*. I might as well leave them here for now.

I move to the master bedroom and debate with myself about stripping the bed and changing the sheets when my cell phone dings signaling a text. I keep the phone in my pocket, a habit I developed during Dad's final days when I needed to be available to DJ, or his wife Nancy, at a moment's notice. The text is from Cheryl, my colleague in the French department and a good friend. Questions: "How are you? Where are you? Will I see you on campus tomorrow?"

I lie down on the bed and curl up into a fetal position. I gaze at the photo from Tavern on the Green and cry, "Did I even know you?"

2

I should be grading papers. I should be writing thank you notes for the flowers and thoughtful expressions of sympathy. Instead, I'm sitting in the middle of campus, with the sun warming my face and my arms spread over the back of the wrought iron bench. I could float away as though I'm unmoored. An hour and a half before French II. I might fall asleep. With any luck, no one I know will see me, though the odds are not in my favor. Dunham University is a small, private college. Barely two thousand students wander about the picturesque Victorian grounds and buildings.

"Hi. Thought we were meeting in my office at noon?" Cheryl's voice tugs me back to the present, and I open one eye. She pushes a wisp of gray hair off her forehead and studies me, concerned as only a best friend can be.

"Sorry," I say, forcing myself back to Earth.

"Are you all right?" Cheryl sits down next to me, and I make an effort to scoot over.

"How about some lunch." Cheryl is gentle with me, treating me like fine china that might crack if it's squeezed too hard.

"I'm not really hungry."

"You've got to eat anyway." I know she thinks eating is a partial solution to most problems, and it's beginning to show in her waistline. "At least have some coffee to wake you up."

I drag myself to my feet and follow Cheryl to the faculty dining room. "Coffee sounds good."

The salad bar is brimming with pasta, mixed greens, assorted veggies, toppings, and dressings. As a rule, I would gorge myself, filling a plate to overflowing and coming back for seconds. But today, everything is unappetizing, picked over, and lifeless. I pluck some greens here, carrots and peppers there, a few bean sprouts, and dressing.

"Is that all you're going to eat? Take a little pasta." Cheryl loads up her own plate.

"Will you stop?" I can feel the blood rushing to my face. It's not her fault I am irritable and defensive.

Cheryl pauses, serving tongs poised above the celery. "I'll meet you at the table."

Most days, we sit with other faculty from foreign languages, chewing over each other as well as the food. It's politically important to lunch with colleagues, if only to avoid being the topic of discussion. Today I can't handle it.

I move to a corner of the dining room circuitously, avoiding potential contact with other faculty. Cheryl plops down into a seat opposite and lays a napkin across her lap. "Sorry I couldn't make it to the house after your father's service. Holly had a half day of school and Paul had to get back to the office."

"No problem." Cheryl's life is totally hectic: two pre-teens and a husband who works twelve hours a day.

"How was it?" asks Cheryl.

"Fine. Exhausting. Beautiful. Endless." I study my salad as if preparing to make a surgical incision and then stab a carrot. "Lots of lovely tributes but by the end I was so tired I almost fell asleep on my feet. Then I went to bed and was wide awake mulling things over."

Cheryl put down her fork. "I know this is so tough. You and your father were close."

I focus on the bean sprouts and chew, nodding.

"I envy what you shared with your dad. I've never had a personal conversation with mine. The last time I remember talking with him longer than fifteen minutes we discussed actuarial tables and the likelihood I'd outlive Paul. I don't even know my father at all and I usually see him every week. Fifty years and he still feels like a stranger," says Cheryl.

"I thought I knew my father, inside and out. Especially the last few years. After my mother died...not at first, but later, after I took the job here, he started depending on me. We confided in each other. Like his fear decades ago of transferring Whitman Textiles into DJ's hands and my paranoia about getting tenure." I bite into a piece of pepper.

"And?" Cheryl waits.

"It's just that I figured I knew all there was to know," I say. "We felt like friends instead of father/daughter. At least I did."

"There's something you didn't know?"

"I think he had a fling during the war that no one was aware of. A French woman."

"Before your parents were married, right?" Cheryl stops eating.

"True. Still..."

"How did you find out about her?"

"The first I heard of her was in the lawyer's office last week." I lean back in my chair and frown.

Cheryl takes a sip of iced tea. "What does the lawyer have to do with it?"

"She's probably still alive and she's in his will. My father left her money."

"How much?"

"A quarter of a million dollars."

Cheryl's jaw drops.

"I feel like Dad kept something important from me and DJ's been fuming since we found out."

"Wow."

"I want to find out more about her. Our lawyer sent a letter and he hasn't heard back yet," I say. "Why wouldn't he mention her to me? We talked about everything." I know I sound like a petulant child.

Cheryl waits for me to say more.

"There were times when Dad was off in his own world. We'd be watching television and his eyes would drift to the window. I'd ask myself 'what is he thinking about?' It never occurred to me that his world was any wider than the one we shared."

"You feel left out?" she asks.

"I guess so."

"It's been a lot of years. She might not be alive."

"That's a possibility." I glance at my watch and wipe my mouth. It's getting late, and class would soon start without me. I canceled it two days ago. I had to make this one.

"Though it would be interesting to know why he left her all of that money," Cheryl says.

Laughter erupts from the table next to us, and I steal a quick glance. I couldn't wait to laugh like that again. "Yes, it would."

3

"I learned to putt with this." DJ taps a golf ball just enough to send it rolling into a coffee mug that serves as a hole.

I sit on the living room floor of the carriage house and survey the clutter surrounding me. "Why don't you take all the golf things?"

DJ is more a hindrance than a help. We start to make some progress on Dad's clothes or photographs or even furniture, and he gets distracted and hits a golf ball or reminisces about camping trips with Dad when he was eight or nine.

There are four rooms in the carriage house: a small kitchen, a bedroom, a living/dining area, and a bath. Dad had managed to fill every space. He had moved out to the cottage behind the main house the year after Mother died and offered the Whitman home to DJ and his family, dividing his time between here and the New York apartment. Stuff bulges out of two closets – suits he'd bought and never worn, years' worth of *The New Yorker*, two sets of golf clubs, three pairs of golf shoes, and a drawer full of golf shirts still in their plastic wrap. The condition of the carriage house was nothing like that of the uncluttered apartment. Where the latter was neat and formal, the former was a charming bungalow that looked lived in and loved. Dad's collection of photographs and prints covered every wall.

"I have my own set of clubs. Two in fact." DJ takes aim again.

"It might be nice to have some of Dad's things. I'll take the recliner, unless you want it."

Late evenings and early mornings the last few months, when Dad couldn't sleep, the two of us had stayed up, watching old movies on cable and ESPN updates on sporting events. We sat through infomercials selling lint brushes for the dryer vent or satellite dishes that promised hundreds of channels ("Who needs hundreds of channels?" Dad had asked). Sometimes I placed a TV table between us and dealt a few hands of gin rummy. He always won. The recliner was his usual seat.

"Nah, most of this will have to go." DJ swings, and the ball rolls under the sofa. He swears under his breath.

"What about the photographs?"

DJ shuffles his feet. He had always seemed ambivalent about Dad's artwork.

Thirty years ago, Dad had begun snapping pictures on trips to upstate New York. The early ones were amateurish, sometimes out of focus, but eventually, he developed a real knack for capturing the essence of a pattern of moss on a fallen tree trunk or the startled expression of a doe before she darted to safety.

DJ's patience with emptying the house is rapidly coming to an end. He tosses the putter onto the pile of golf equipment and scans the worn furniture and the stacks of photos and prints.

"I feel him here," I say.

DJ nods. For a moment, we are just siblings sharing a terrible loss—no competition or tension between us.

"What about his clothes? I'll take care of them unless you want something?"

"I'd never fit into them," DJ says, patting his belly.

"All right, I'll do the clothes and photographs and you can take care of the furniture. Except for the easy chair."

I take a picture of a lone flower blooming by the side of the road off the wall while DJ stands in the center of the room, hands jammed in his pants pockets, as though he can't quite figure out why he is here and what he is supposed to do next. I want to say so much to him, but I've learned to be careful. As kids, it felt like we had always been at war over Dad's attention and Mother's discipline. But we are adults now. Still, it is difficult to talk about family or feelings. DJ is like a powder keg waiting for a spark to set him off. Maybe things will change with Dad's passing. I remember the last day Dad and I spoke about DJ, how he asked me to try to get along. He couldn't comprehend our sibling battles, either.

"DJ," I say.

"Yeah?"

"What do you think about Dad's will?"

He shakes his head. "It's ridiculous. Some wartime fling and we have to pay for it."

"Aren't you the least bit curious? I mean, why he never mentioned anything about her?" I ask for me, if not to DJ.

"Why would he? Would you tell your kids about your sex life?"

The mention of "sex life" throws me off. Of course, Dad wouldn't discuss a love affair, but I can't see beyond his obsession.

"Anyway, I'm taking care of things. I talked to Lloyd again and called Peter." Peter Rieger is DJ's personal attorney and has always set my teeth on edge. He is competent in a slippery sort of way. "I'm not sending a quarter of a million dollars to somebody we don't even know."

"Has Lloyd heard anything from her yet?" I ask.

"No."

"It's only been two weeks." I run my finger along the edge of a silver frame and absently wipe the dust on my jeans. "I was thinking Uncle Bert would know something."

I hold my breath waiting for DJ's reaction. Bert is Dad's younger brother who lives in a tenement somewhere in Atlantic City.

"What?" DJ looks up.

"He and Dad were in Europe together during the war," I add.

DJ shoves the sofa to one side of the room. "Leave well enough alone and forget about that woman and Uncle Bert." He stacks the end tables in a corner.

"I'd still like to know what there was between them." I swaddle a picture in bubble wrap and secure it with a length of packing tape.

"I'd say that was pretty obvious." DJ could be snarky where Dad was concerned.

"What if it was more than a fling?" I say.

He sits down on the easy chair and fixes his gaze on me. "So, you think he never got over her?"

"I'm not saying that. I'd just like to know more." The gift to Emilie Renault hints at a passion that disturbs me. A side of him I never saw. Dad was generous and thoughtful. But passionate? He and Mother had a caring but polite relationship. I don't ever remember them sneaking a kiss or hugging with enthusiasm when they were younger. And since she died over twenty years ago, there hasn't been another woman in his life. That I'm aware of. It seemed to me to be a well-bred, civil marriage, a peck on his cheek, an arm under her elbow. "I remember seeing pictures of Dad and Bert in uniforms."

"I don't even know Bert's address," he says.

"Lloyd probably does."

"He's a derelict and a boozer. Every cent Dad gave him he drank or gambled away."

The tension spreads thickly throughout the room. Uncle Bert is the family pariah; there is no calm way to discuss him. We had all been devastated by the news of the automobile crash on Christmas Eve of 1994. A college student had been hit by a drunk driver on an icy road as he made his way home from a job selling Christmas trees. He died on impact at the scene. The drunk driver was Uncle Bert, speeding and zigzagging all over the place on his way to the house to play Santa Claus.

The incident had turned Bert into an outcast. For the last ten years, he had more or less disappeared from our lives. Involuntary manslaughter had earned him five years of probation and loss of driving privileges indefinitely. At the time, he was still working at Whitman Textiles, but after the accident, he retired. Dad had made arrangements to send him a monthly check.

"Between this woman in France and now Bert...leave it all alone." DJ gathers up the putter and irons and jams them into the golf bag.

I have to say it aloud. "Maybe they were in love." My statement hangs in the air.

DJ releases a deep sigh. His voice is firm but low. "Kate, you dumped on Mom while she was living and now you're doing it again on her memory." DJ slings the bag over his shoulder and bangs the door as he leaves the carriage house.

His words sting. Mother and I had a hard relationship. I was "Daddy's little girl." I looked like him with the same brown eyes, dark wavy hair, and high cheekbones, the same smile. We watched sports together on television and even liked the same foods. DJ was Mother's favorite. I felt slighted by Mother, and DJ felt overlooked by Dad. Poor Billy was the middle child. Easy to live with and easily dismissed. That's possibly why he had a fascination with faraway places.

This Emilie Renault business triggers resentment in DJ. As though she and Mother were competitors. Were they? And I "dumped" on Mother? Where did that come from? I collapse into the easy chair and gaze at the photo I am about to wrap. Dad standing in the garden behind the main house, holding clipping shears in his hands. I thrust my jaw out, thinking it might prevent me from crying. It might stop the tears, but nothing can prevent the pain in my chest or the unbidden recollections that pop up, like bubbles on the surface of water. *Mother*.

I was sixteen. She and I had been battling for years about everything: clothes, boyfriends, school, and politics. I campaigned for local Democrats by passing out flyers around town; Mother, a staunch Republican, took a conservative approach to everything from child-rearing to her book club. Dad was often caught in the middle and remained studiously apolitical.

Sometimes I kept my distance by leaving the house before she and Dad appeared at the breakfast table and staying away from home at dinner time by doing homework with a girlfriend. One Friday afternoon, I went straight home from my last class and unexpectedly caught Mother as she got back from an all-day trip to the city. Her arms full of shopping bags and a hatbox, she paused by the side entrance to the house and waited until I parked my dirty, ancient VW in the space next to her immaculate Cadillac.

"That car needs washing."

"Okay," I mumbled and made a beeline for the door.

"So, we've decided to honor the family with our presence." Mother glared at me.

"Huh?" I feigned ignorance.

When Mother was particularly pissed at me, she resorted to first-person plural.

"I need to get some clothes and stuff. I'm staying at Jane's tonight." I put my hand on the doorknob.

"Wait a minute, young lady."

"What?" I was running late as it was.

"This isn't a hotel." Mother nodded to the door, and I opened it, holding it wide enough for her to enter sideways and avoid banging the hatbox against the jamb.

I wondered what kind of headgear Mother had bought in New York. Before I could comment, she plunked her purchases down on the table in the breakfast nook.

"You cannot drop in and out of here whenever you feel like it. You are either a part of this household, or you are not," she said and waited.

I stared at a spot on the wall above the stainless-steel oven. Was that dirt? Could there possibly be a speck of dirt in Mother's perfect kitchen?

"Well?" she asked.

"Well, what?"

"Are you a member of this family?"

"Of course, I'm a member of this family." My exasperation was no match for her glacial composure.

"Good. Hannah is off tonight so you can help prepare dinner and clean up afterward." Mother picked up her bags.

I opened the refrigerator door, pulling out the makings of a peanut butter and jelly sandwich. "I can't. I'm eating at Jane's."

"Did you hear what I said?" Her voice went up a notch.

"I promised Jane I'd be over by four," I said as I spread peanut butter on white bread.

"Katherine!"

I snapped my head up and dropped the knife on the floor.

"You march upstairs right now, change your clothes, and come down here and help me." Mother's eyes blazed, and twin spots of red colored her cheeks.

"I can't." I scraped peanut butter off the floor.

"Don't you defy me." She took a step toward me. "Upstairs. Now."

For a brief moment, I thought Mother was so mad she had lost all self-control. "I can't," I said again and slammed the refrigerator door. "If Dad was home, he'd let me go."

"Just because your father spoils you doesn't mean that you are going to get your own way now."

She seized my upper arm, and I yanked myself away in a fury, tears about to run down my cheeks. My childish, tyrannical impulses assumed control, and I spewed out the worst thing I could think of. "You don't care about me. You love Billy and DJ. Dad loves me! He understands me."

Mother froze, her arm extended in my direction. "Don't you say that; don't you ever say that," she gasped.

"It's true, and you know it. If it wasn't for Dad, I'd leave here forever."

She slumped into the chair and placed her hands on the table. Then she lowered her head, and, by the subtle twitch of her shoulders, I could tell that Mother was crying. I wanted to go to her and apologize, but my pride won out. I picked up my books and stole from the room.

We didn't speak for days afterward. When I finally had to ask her about school business, Mother was cool and polite, her smile a thin crease across her mouth as if the confrontation had never taken place.

21

4

Lloyd had been cautious but helpful when I approached him about visiting Uncle Bert. He had encouraged me to let the past go, and that included both Bert and Emilie. No, he had not heard from Emilie Renault, and yes, he would continue to send Uncle Bert checks "as per your father's wishes." And, most recently, he had written to tell Bert about Dad's death.

When I requested Bert's address, Lloyd hesitated. "I don't think it's a good idea for you to contact him."

"Why not?" I had two good reasons to visit my uncle: it had been a while since I'd made the trek to Atlantic City, and he might be a missing link in the Emilie Renault story.

"He's not in good shape. I received a call from a clinic in Atlantic City several months ago. The police found him passed out on the boardwalk again and the hospital got him into a detox program," Lloyd said.

"What happened?"

"What always happens. He checked himself out and probably ended up back on the boardwalk somewhere," he said.

"I'd still like to see him. It's been a long time," I said.

Lloyd pulled his Rolodex closer, flipping through a few cards and writing on a Post-It note. He paused. "Give him my regards."

"I will. Thanks, Lloyd." I stuff the piece of paper into my coat pocket.

Now, two days later, with no classes to teach, the sun on the windshield ushering in the first spring day since an unseasonable hot spell in February, I head down the Garden State Parkway. I replay my memory of the last time I'd seen Uncle Bert—six, seven years ago?— when I'd accompanied Dad to visit him. Bert had, once again, collapsed in the casino at Caesars and was rushed to the hospital. Basically, he was suffering from alcohol poisoning, and his internal organs were slowly deteriorating.

Bert had always been the chubby, jolly uncle. Until the crash, he played Santa Claus every year with charming ease. (Though I realized later, his jovial mood was the result of his steadily increasing drinking.) When we saw him, Bert was thin, except for bloating around his middle. His face had sagged, partly from his dissipated lifestyle, partly from shame and remorse at having to see his brother in this condition. The IV in his arm had beeped whenever he rolled from side to side, trying not to look at either of us.

It had been a tense, awkward visit. Periodically I stepped into the hall to give them some privacy and to exhale the smell of decay. Bert's state had been alarming but witnessing Dad's tears as he stared at Bert was heart-wrenching.

I veer off the Garden State Parkway at exit 38 and ease onto the Atlantic City Expressway. I drive past the Convention Center and check off street names: Pennsylvania, Ohio, Michigan, and New Jersey. As a teenager, I had wondered which came first—Atlantic City or Monopoly. Caesars, Bally's, Tropicana, and Resorts rose before me. Uncle Bert had been drunk in most of them.

As suddenly as the casinos appear, they disappear, and I find myself on the edge of the city in the midst of squalor. I turn onto Bert's street. Two rows of dilapidated tenements, some abandoned, line the avenue. Even in the bright sun, everything is dingy. People regard me with a kind of dull despair as I drive by. The contrast between the two Atlantic Cities is startling and never fails to depress me.

I pull up in front of 525 Serenity and study the building. I hit the automatic door lock and pray that the car will be here in one piece when I get back.

Three flights up, I pause in front of 3C and knock tentatively, noticing the smell of urine that permeates the hallway. When there is no answer, I knock louder.

"Whad'ya want?" The voice from inside is unmistakably Bert's, though rougher and raspier than I remember.

"Uncle Bert? It's Kate," I say.

"Who?"

"Kate." And then, because I'm not sure how badly the alcohol has clouded his mind, I add, "Daniel's daughter. Your niece."

I hear scuffling noises from the apartment and the clank of a lock rotating. The door opens a crack, the chain still in place. I see his unshaven cheeks, watery eyes, and red nose that he wipes with his hand.

"Whad'ya want?" he repeats.

"To see you."

"Why?" he asks.

At a loss, I finally say, "I'm family, Uncle Bert."

Bert slowly unhooks the chain, releasing the door. It swings open, and the two of us face each other. I am alarmed at the sight of the frail old man; his stomach distended from the years of hard-drinking, deep wells under his eyes, wisps of straggly hair sticking out in all

24

directions. His plaid flannel shirt is worn; khaki pants hug his waist and bag at the knees. The sweet-sour odor of yesterday's alcohol clings to his breath.

"Well, come in," he says grudgingly, his hands shaking as he reaches to shut the door.

I step over the threshold. The air in the living room is stale. A faded sofa that was once a bright yellow has stuffing poking out from an end cushion. Pillows, an army blanket, and a couple of grayish shirts cover much of it. Two straight-backed chairs sit near a coffee table piled with unopened mail, Chinese take-out cartons, and a half-empty bottle of whiskey.

Bert sees me spy the Jim Beam, and he hurriedly removes it, along with the food containers which he dumps in the kitchen sink. I see dirty dishes stacked on the counter. The apartment reeks of dead air and generally unsanitary living.

"I brought you a cake," I say.

"Put it down there." Bert points to the coffee table. The cake box sticks to the surface of the table on contact.

He turns on the faucet in the kitchen sink and rummages around in cabinets. Is he attempting to wash dishes? Fortunately, he reappears with paper plates and plastic tableware, still in take-out wrappers. And a mug.

"You want coffee?" he asks.

"No, no thanks," I say, assuming his "coffee" had more than caffeine in it. I open the box and cut two slices of crumb cake and place them on the paper plates. "Lloyd said to say 'hello'."

Bert weighs my comment. "He's a good man," he says, draining his cup.

We sit on the sofa, Bert pushing clothes and pillows to one side while I avoid contact with a dark stain. Now that I'm here, I'm a little at a loss. "How have you been?"

"My feet hurt."

"Arthritis?"

"Gout." Bert eats the cake as though it is his first meal today.

I study his swollen feet, crammed into broken-down bedroom slippers. Had someone diagnosed gout, or did he make it up?

"Have you seen a doctor?"

"Can't. Medicare won't pay for it." Bert helps himself to another slice of the cake.

I doubt his excuse. Is he giving a wide berth to doctors and clinics? "You should talk to Lloyd."

Bert explodes, spitting crumbs out of his mouth. "That bastard stole everything my brother wanted me to have."

I am so startled by the outburst that I juggle my pastry, knocking a chunk on the floor. I pick it up and deposit it on the edge of my plate.

"I'm calling Dan tomorrow and I'm taking Lloyd to court," Bert announces with a kind of triumph.

I feel my throat tighten. Is it possible he hadn't read Lloyd's letter yet? I glance at the stack of unopened mail.

"Uncle Bert, Lloyd wrote to you about Dad," I say slowly.

I stop as he swivels his head in my direction. "What about him?"

I hesitate. "He died last month."

Bert's face crumples. His thin shoulders shake as he weeps, and moans softly and then wails from a place of pain so deep that I'm embarrassed to witness it. I feel so anguished over Bert that I ignore the odor and the stain and edge closer until our shoulders touch and pat his hand.

After a half-hour of coaxing and another "cup of coffee," I convince Bert to drive with me over to the boardwalk for a stroll in the sun. He changes his shirt and even shaves, sort of. Shops, with signs advertising taffy, hot dogs and hamburgers, t-shirts, and fortune-tellers, are mostly closed now in mid-April, not yet ready for the summer season and the onslaught of tourists. By Memorial Day, the place will be packed.

We don't talk much at first. I'm not sure what to say about Dad, and Bert seems mortified about breaking down. He views his feet as if concentrating on the weathered, uneven planks of the boardwalk. But the day is pleasant and warm, and, before long, Bert shifts his attention to the sea gulls nibbling on bits of French fries and to the few visitors sauntering by. The air has a calming effect on him.

When I ask a few gentle questions about him and Dad, Bert begins to reminisce: growing up in the Whitman home, summers in the Catskills and winters away at boarding school; his anger at losing his mother as a teenager; his three marriages. The first, to a high school sweetheart in 1945 after he arrived home from the war, lasted five years. The second was a six-month affair after a drunken weekend in Las Vegas. The third, to Josie, the woman I remembered, lasted until she died in 1975.

"She was a hell of a woman," he says. "Knew how to keep me in line." Bert laughs ruefully.

"I was a teenager when she died. I remember vases of white flowers."

"Roses." He sighs.

"She always had peppermints in her pocket for us kids." Memory is a strange thing, like pulling on a loose thread. Events start to unravel, and pretty soon, the past stands naked before you. "I

27

remember laughing so hard one day at a story about a dog. What was his name?"

"Her. Bitsy." Bert sniffs. "Nobody could tell a story like Josie."

Bert's drinking escalated after Josie passed away.

The Three Brothers Diner is open, and when Bert begins to shiver, we go in and sit in a red vinyl booth, away from the restaurant's few other patrons. I order real coffee for both of us, and when it comes, we sip in silence.

After a few minutes, Bert withdraws a shabby leather wallet. He fingers a few items—an expired New Jersey driver's license, a VISA card, a dog-eared Whitman Textiles business card—and then flips over a plastic casing that holds a picture. He shoves the wallet mid-way across the table. The old photo depicts Bert, Dad, and DJ mugging for the camera as they display hundred-dollar bills outside the entrance to the Tropicana casino.

Bert clears his throat with difficulty. "We all won that day." A stubby finger taps himself and DJ, pausing, finally, on Dad. He exhales a little whimper. I nod and return the wallet.

Silence again as the second hand on the big wall clock sweeps over the numbers. Should I ask him? Would he recall anything? "Uncle Bert, could I ask you something about the war?"

"What about it?" His tone is softer now, and he studies his right palm and the empty space where the last two fingers are missing.

Whenever DJ or Billy or I had commented on Uncle Bert's freakish hand, Dad had told us the story. Bert had been hit by shrapnel from an enemy mine in Germany. Even though he was seriously injured, he had dragged a fellow infantryman to an aid station and earned himself a Silver Star. Bert had joked about the incident when I was a kid, and when he wasn't paying attention, I sneaked peeks at his damaged hand. He could have spent the remainder of his life on disability, Dad had always said, but Uncle Bert refused to give in and took his place in the family business.

"You and Dad were in Europe together, right?"

Bert coughs and wipes a bit of phlegm off his lips with a paper napkin. "Dan was in Italy, then France. Me, I landed in Normandy." He scratches his head. "Month after D-Day, and then Belgium." Bert drinks his coffee. "I stayed there until we crossed the Rhine and clobbered those damn Krauts." He hesitates, a fog seems to lift, and his eyes open wide. "Mauthausen." He rubs the place where his fingers should have been.

Stunned, I sit back in the booth. "You were at the camp?"

"They were sticks. Pieces of a human being wrapped in dirty striped pajamas." His eyes mist over.

"That must have been terrible." My hand inches across the table and touches his good one briefly.

"And then the mine..." Bert caresses the scars on his bad hand and withdraws into himself. He hunches his shoulders forward, his hands cupping the coffee mug.

Maybe he had several reasons to drink. "Did you ever meet Dad in France?"

Bert leans back and allows his head to rest on the top of the booth. "Paris." He frowns. "VE Day."

"The end of the war?" I ask.

"Yeah. Everybody was in Paris."

I bend forward tentatively. "Do you remember Dad mentioning a woman named Emilie?"

Bert fixes his gaze on the wall at the rear of the diner. A light goes on somewhere behind his eyes, and he breaks into a smile. "Emilie. Met her."

My heart does a flip-flop. "You did?"

"She was a looker, all right."

"Dad and Emilie were...friends?" How to ask about your father's affair?

Bert shrugs. "We were lonely. Far away from home."

"What happened?"

"Dan didn't think he'd get out alive. None of us did." Bert rubs his chin. "He thought she might be his last chance."

"Did he think about marrying her?"

"Couldn't. He was engaged to Margaret."

"To Mother," I say. Were Emilie and Mother competitors?

"Uh huh." Bert starts to drum his fingers on the table, his focus shifting toward the door. It has been two hours since we left his apartment.

I have to ask. "Did Mother know about her?"

Bert picks at a yellowed, chipped fingernail. "Yeah," he mumbles, abruptly stands up, and starts for the door.

I grab my handbag, pick up the check, and follow him. Try as I might on the ride back to his apartment, I cannot persuade him to talk about Emilie, the war, or Dad. He slumps down in the passenger seat and stares sullenly out the window.

At his door, I kiss his scratchy cheek good-bye. "I'll come and see you again, Uncle Bert."

"Okay."

"Take care of yourself and let Lloyd know if you need anything."

He grunts a good-bye.

I climb into the car, my head throbbing. Mother knew about Dad's wartime lover. When did she find out? What did she think? Yet they managed to stay married for thirty-seven years. That was more than I did.

Trauth

Lloyd has yet to hear from Emilie Renault, but even so, I have to find answers.

5

I haven't been back to the family home since the day of Dad's funeral. When Dad was alive, DJ regularly reminded me that I never came to visit his family, though I was in the carriage house at least once a week, more frequently during the final year of Dad's life. The main house, yards from the cottage, doesn't bring back particularly happy memories: long-ago adolescent battles with Mother, her illness and death, and Dad's funeral. Altogether the house has been the site of too much grief. The atmosphere feels thick with unhappiness, like walking into a wet sheet. It's impossible to breathe easily in the house.

I would have preferred not to be here this evening either, sitting in the same window seat I had on the day of the funeral, sidestepping the crowd of friends and extended family.

"Hello Kate." Lloyd settles himself beside me and offers his plate of cheese and olives.

I decline. "Nancy and DJ should have postponed the party. It's too soon."

"Maybe they needed this."

DJ's fifty-sixth birthday party had been planned for months, and Nancy had said the celebration would help lighten their spirits. DJ's fifty-fifth birthday had been a disaster—preparations for a party last year were canceled when Dad had a heart attack days before; who would have known a year later Dad would again cast a shadow over DJ's big night. He deserved a celebration, but it was difficult to forget the gathering weeks ago.

I'm not sure the party will lighten my spirits. Too many complications cloud the horizon: Dad's will, Emilie, the disturbing afternoon with Uncle Bert, Mother's awareness of Emilie in Dad's life, and, most painfully, the loss of Dad. The discussion in the carriage house with DJ left no room for doubt about his opinions on the will and Emilie. But how would he feel about Mother knowing? I elect not to share my visit to Uncle Bert with my brother.

"Hey, you two, let's party." DJ's twin son Drew—the fun-loving, charming one— snaps his fingers in front of us to the sounds of music wafting in from the deck. He will be twenty-two next month and graduate from college at the end of the summer, two feats DJ and Nancy will be relieved to see. Drew was the less studious of their twins.

"I'll pass," I say.

Lloyd stands up and holds out his hand. "Good idea."

"All right!" Drew smiles with approval.

I gawk at the two of them. "I haven't danced in a while."

"Then you're overdue," Lloyd says.

We thread our way through guests to the patio outside. Nancy had hired a disc jockey who was able to bridge generations; some Motown and Beatles mixed in with ABBA and swing. Fortunately, they'd lucked out with the weather since late April could be unpredictable in New Jersey. Tonight, the air is agreeably mild and dry.

The disc jockey is playing Smokey Robinson, and couples are wiggling, bumping, and shaking, with and without the beat. I marvel at the courage of some people; they have no sense of rhythm, but that doesn't stop them from taking the dance floor and whooping it up.

"Here we go." Lloyd leads me into the middle of the crowd. He keeps one arm around my waist as we twirl and spin.

Lloyd is a terrific partner and dances like a man half his age. Though he's been a widower for many years, he moves like someone who is accustomed to having a woman in his arms. I find myself relaxing and actually beginning to enjoy keeping up with him.

By midnight, everyone is slowing down. DJ and Nancy have enjoyed their own dance, and DJ's sons have delivered toasts to their father, one serious, one silly, including trick candles that refused to be extinguished.

Lloyd was right. It was a nice evening, and we did need to blow off some steam. I can tell I'm having a good time because my feet are killing me. A tap on my shoulder sends me whirling away from Drew into DJ's arms.

"Whoa. Hold on there," he says and steadies me, though it's DJ who's a little shaky on his pins.

We haven't really spoken all evening. "Congratulations." I kiss him on the cheek.

"Well, fifty-six, ya' know?" He slurs his words a bit.

I'm not accustomed to seeing DJ so loose. The music swirls around us, and we gaze at each other. I look over his head at Lloyd, who is chatting with a couple near a row of planters that border the patio. DJ squints at me and backs off a step to get a better glimpse of his little sister.

"Wanna' dance?" he says and swivels his head in both directions as if he needs to locate someone to ask for permission.

I am dumbfounded. He never even asked me to dance at my wedding or his.

"Sure," I say as he self-consciously holds out his hands.

I slip one palm into his and place the other on his damp shoulder. DJ takes a step, and I follow stiffly, robotically we erupt from one spot and then settle into another. It is a jerky affair, and I am uncomfortable but dare not suggest we sit and talk instead. I know DJ is capable on the dance floor—I've observed him and Nancy over the years. This moment's clumsiness could be attributed to our shared discomfort at being so intimate. I am hit with the scents of Scotch on his breath and sweat mingled with cologne.

"It's a great party," I say.

"Yeah. Nancy likes this stuff."

Our hands are clammy.

"You don't?" I try to tease him.

He shrugs. "I coulda' done without. Dad, ya' know..." Voice and thought trail off.

I nod and spontaneously squeeze his hand. "Lloyd said we needed this. The music, the people—"

"I talked with Lloyd," he says.

I feel warm all over from the dancing and a few glasses of wine, and my thinking is a little wooly, but the hurt in his voice sharpens my senses.

"He told me you went to see Bert."

I shift my head to catch his face.

He drops his arms to his sides, and we stand still in the midst of the crowd of couples swaying to the sound of Paul McCartney crooning "Yesterday." DJ looks betrayed. His eyes are shiny, his nose reddens.

"Can we talk about this later?" I ask quietly.

A waiter appears at DJ's elbow and hands him a Scotch and water, and Drew approaches with Nancy, impeccably dressed in pale blue silk, as the music switches to "Tuxedo Junction."

"Hey, Dad. Let's party." Drew bobs in place and gently urges his mother into DJ's arms.

Partiers near us turn and smile, applauding the couple.

Lloyd is suddenly at my side, solicitous as ever. He must have been watching DJ and me.

"You told him about Bert?" I ask.

"I'm sorry, Kate. It came out in a conversation about Emilie Renault."

My buoyant mood deflates. I'm so tired I might collapse in a puddle on the patio cement. The lump in my throat is frustration and sadness. "Don't worry about it, Lloyd. DJ will get over it."

"I don't know about that," he says.

We sit in two chairs in a corner of the patio, away from the crush of guests.

"I never saw Daniel happier than the night you were born. We drank brandy until the sun rose. I was in the hospital the next day and I saw him hold you." Lloyd stops. "You are so much like him."

I nod.

"I've known you and DJ since you were kids. I hate to see this conflict, Kate," he says carefully. "But I am bound by my promise to your father."

"The bequest to Emilie Renault? I don't mind. I think Dad did what he felt he needed to do and DJ and I will live with it," I say. Even though it kills me that Dad kept this secret.

"It's too late."

"What are you talking about?"

36

"DJ filed a legal brief to stop the execution of the will." Lloyd pauses.

I was afraid of this. My voice is low and hard. "This is Dad's life. We can't just pretend it never happened and ignore his last wishes." Was this about the money, about greed? Or was it about DJ's complicated feelings about Dad? Lloyd and I are silent for a moment. "I wish we'd hear from her. I have this need to find out about her. It's hard to explain."

"She was a part of your father's life and you were so close to him. Kate, I think it would be best if you'd let this go, but I can appreciate your desire to know more."

"Thank you, Lloyd." Suddenly the party is smothering me, and I have to get out of here. I rise abruptly and kiss Lloyd's cheek. "I'm going to find out who she is."

6

I stand at my parents' gravesite under an ancient elm tree in Woodside Cemetery. Dad's side of the stone is blank—the engraving is not yet completed—but the other side reads "Beloved Wife and Mother." When she died, Dad had chosen the location, the marker, and the inscription, so his children had little to do but fill in the missing information when he passed away.

I set a red azalea plant on the ground and sink to my knees. Some twigs and leaves have blown around the cemetery during the past week and now cover his grave like a protective shield. The grass seed hasn't taken root yet, so the dirt is still exposed in patches and changes into mud when it rains, as it has the four previous days.

I clear the area around the headstone and push the plant into the wet soil. I water it with a jug I've carried from the car and pick tiny, dead bits off the branches of the plant. I push back on my heels and regard the marker, thinking of my father's secrets.

I glance to the right at Mother's side of the marker. I hadn't been to her gravesite more than once or twice a year since her death. Now I visit Dad at least once a week. I'd like to know what she thought about Emilie. Without warning, my throat constricts, and my eyes start to sting, but today the roiling emotion that surfaces is not the sadness I have become accustomed to. I'm angry at what I don't know and what I don't understand.

I sit beside the marker for a while, then I drag myself to my feet and run my hand over the marble one last time. I turn my back on my parents and step between the graves as I walk to my car.

7

My antidote to emotional turmoil is work. I throw myself into writing an article or grading papers, and once, I painted the living room and dining room in a single weekend to avoid thinking about my crumbling marriage. Terry was a wonderful guy, but we were doomed from the beginning.

We met and fell into a comfortable relationship in graduate school—back-to-back carrels in the library and late-night study sessions that ended either with sex or cheese omelets. Sundays in bed with the *New York Times*, Monday through Thursday teaching and taking classes, Friday night at Benny's, two-for-one with the rest of the department, drinking until the alcohol made you think you could drive between the headlights of the oncoming car on the ride home. Saturday nursing a bear of a hangover and Sunday back to the *New York Times* and Terry's cooking. That was the highlight of the week: beef Wellington, fettuccine alfredo, tasty salads, and soups. Terry would have made a superb chef.

Having lived his whole life on the west coast north of San Francisco, Terry decided to take a job in New York after graduation, and I accompanied him back home. Marriage was a second thought, but I knew Dad would be happy to see me settle down. Returning home and pleasing him felt like the right thing to do, especially since I had left four years earlier on such a painful note. It was my way of reconciling our relationship.

Dad thought Terry was "a hell of a good guy" and dragged him to the golf course when he was hard up for a partner. DJ was always a little standoffish; Terry was too bookish for him, but Billy, whenever he took a break from wandering and popped into New Jersey, clasped Terry's hand and wrapped him in a warm hug. Mother would have approved of the lavish wedding Dad insisted we have. When we took to the floor for the "father of the bride" dance, he smiled so warmly I cried.

I spent a year doing a postdoc at Columbia, happy to be on the campus a second time, and then landed at Dunham University. It's not the academic haven that I had imagined myself inhabiting, but the position was tenure track and in New Jersey, so we could live near Dad. Now I'm committed to teaching undergraduates French I, II, III, IV, and, occasionally, the odd French literature or history class.

While I was slowly but steadily becoming a fixture on the Dunham campus and moving up the academic ladder, Terry became a star at City University. The commute into and out of the city annoyed him, but when he published his dissertation as a book, the administration rewarded him with early tenure and promotion.

We had the picture-perfect marriage, friends said. Yet I wasn't happy. The romance we had kindled in graduate school had extinguished itself. Our lovemaking went up in a puff of smoke. I knew he was seeing—sleeping with—a colleague. I saw the furtive glances and touches and eye contact at faculty parties. But who was I to complain? On Friday nights, when I shared happy hour with a group of friends at Levino's, I sometimes hung around after everyone else left and chatted up this traveling salesman. Once, we ended up in bed.

No explosive fights or tantrums with Terry and me. We woke up on opposite sides of the bed one morning and knew the marriage was over. So the end was a non-event. Terry made a pot of his famous chili, freezing extra portions for my future dinners, packed his shirts, underwear and socks, placed his suits in a hanging travel bag, and disappeared. I cried, then dried my eyes, changed the sheets, sat down at the dining room table, and graded papers. Dad's disappointment in the break-up of our marriage was, however, more difficult to bear than losing my husband.

I received a sympathy card the week Dad passed away. The return address was San Francisco. Terry went home, too.

So, now, I find myself on a beautiful Saturday afternoon in late April in the carriage house surrounded by a vacuum cleaner, mop, and bucket. I have more than enough to fret over; most troubling is the new picture that is forming of Dad, and I need to burn off the frustration.

A deep, rich base cuts through the whir of the vacuum. "Hey."

I flip the switch, and the room is silent.

"I'm the electrician." He pauses in the doorway and brushes a stray strand of salt-and-pepper colored hair from his forehead, and smiles. "Joe."

"Hi. Come on in." I remember then that Nancy had mentioned having some work done in the carriage house. Drew planned to move in here later this summer, after graduation.

"Nancy wants more electrical outlets for Drew's computer and whatnot," he says.

"That's right," I say.

"And track lighting," he adds.

"I tried to talk my father into track lighting. He just laughed and said track lighting would make him feel like he was living in a museum."

Joe places a toolbox on the floor. "I'm sorry about Daniel."

"You knew him?"

"I've done a few jobs here. Spent an afternoon once with him rewiring a lamp and watching the Yankees slaughter..." He stops to think. "Somebody. He was a great guy."

Though a complete stranger to me, Joe made things seem simple, an unfamiliar feeling these days. "I'll get out of your way."

"Thanks." He lays out tools, wire, metal tracks, and ceiling spotlights and quietly goes to work as if he *was* in a museum. For a big man, Joe is graceful, almost dancer-like, as he sprints up and down a ladder. He measures meticulously and marks locations for the row of tracks, and as he attaches a metal strip with the drill, a thin stream of dust from the sheetrock drifts onto the floor. "I'll get that later."

"I'll do it. It's fine." I proceed to sweep the shavings off the carpet. Even though Nancy is having the entire place cleaned and painted, I have a proprietary interest in the carriage house. It had been Dad's home, and I had spent many hours here these last years. I study a stain on the carpet where Dad spilled a cup of coffee the last night we were here together.

"Would you hand me that spotlight, please?" Joe says, atop the ladder. "I never knew Mrs. Whitman, but your Dad spoke warmly about her."

I swallow hard and pick up the round metal lamp.

As if he can read my mind, Joe says, "They say a year and a half, two years is the normal grieving period."

There it was again. The simple, honest, unfussy truth. I try to smile gratefully, but my mouth is crooked as if it's struggling to keep words inside. I look up at Joe, and he is staring at me. "I went into a tailspin when my wife died."

"I'm sorry. Was she...?"

"Ill? Yeah. Five years ago. Sometimes it feels like yesterday." Joe rubs the surface of the spotlight, then inserts it into the socket and twists the bulb.

I nod sympathetically.

Joe points to my broom and dustpan. "Sorry about the mess."

Sorry about the mess. The words trigger a rush of images—Dad, Mother, DJ, Billy. Lately, my past rises to meet me without warning.

I was thirteen in February of 1973, and the house was in an uproar. Billy was due home from his tour in Vietnam the next day. Despite the Paris Peace Accords, the fighting continued. Many in his outfit never came back. Billy was fortunate that he had put in his time and was part of the move to draw down ground forces. Mother was ecstatic and relieved. She never understood why he enlisted in the first place. It wasn't as though he had been drafted; Billy was a sophomore at Princeton—the real brain of the family—studying molecular biology. The anti-war movement didn't seem to affect him. But Billy operated on a different plane, in his own insular world. A bookworm, DJ said, who wouldn't know enough to come in out of the rain even if he was drowning.

During Christmas break of his second year, Billy announced he was dropping out of school and joining the army. His declaration generated an outburst of reactions. Mother said, "Absolutely not," Dad asked, "Why?" and DJ kept saying, "What are you, an idiot?" DJ had managed to avoid the draft through planning: he immediately entered an M.B.A. program upon graduation from Columbia. Though he never completed the degree.

Billy was adamant in a way that impressed me, even as a kid. He defied them all and claimed that he had made up his mind and Vietnam was his next stop. Besides, he said, Dad had served in the war, too. I remember Billy winking at me as though it was all no big deal.

For two years, we were glued to news broadcasts, and Mother kept tabs on the progress of the war through newspapers and news magazines. I listened to Dan Rather and watched his stiff, puppet-like head stare into the camera and describe the atrocities, often with South Vietnamese villagers wandering aimlessly in the background. Dad refused to listen to the news and would get up from the table or leave the room when Vietnam was mentioned. For two years, we actually said grace before eating and prayed for Billy's safe return. That ended when he arrived home.

It was the middle of February when Billy came home in time to be DJ's best man for the wedding. Chaos reigned, and Mother tried to focus on everything she could: visiting relatives, the rehearsal dinner, even the bachelor party. I heard afterward DJ drew the line on her interference there. As a junior bridesmaid, I was caught up in the swirl of activity with my red velvet dress, matching shoes, and the picture of what my hair would look like after Mr. Dino was done with it. The excitement was palpable with Billy coming home and DJ and Nancy getting married in the same week.

At thirteen, I hadn't thought much about the state of matrimony or what impact marriage had on a relationship. DJ and Nancy had been together for six years—it seemed like she had always been at the house for holidays and birthdays. Occasionally, I caught them kissing and cuddling in one room or another; once I popped into the living room unannounced, and DJ shifted away from her while Nancy pulled

45

down her dress and straightened her hair. They were always hand-in-hand walking into the house, sitting on the sofa, watching television.

Would they become Mother and Dad?

So on that evening in February when Mother was haranguing Dad about the snow in the driveway from the recent storm and "people getting their shoes soaked," and DJ was yelling that he'd pick up Billy from the airport, and Dad was ignoring them both and reading the newspaper (now that Billy was safe), I catapulted the conversations to a new level.

"So I guess you and Nancy can have sex now," I said. Sex had been the heated topic of discussion with my girlfriends at Friday night pajama parties: who did it, how you did it, even why you did it. What we didn't know we imagined and giggled ourselves silly.

Mother sputtered and dropped a dish of apple sauce that bounced once and flopped upside down, creating a yellow circle of runny fruit. DJ frowned and grabbed my shoulders, and told me to "shut up," Dad lowered his paper and observed me.

"What?" I said. "That's what married people do, right?"

DJ shook his head and muttered, "somebody should talk with you," and left the house. Dad, obviously uncomfortable, said quietly, "Honey, you are too young to be asking those kinds of questions." Mother's look sliced right through me.

I felt the wall of formality between my parents. It wasn't only the word "sex." It was all that it implied: body heat and passion. I suppose it was at that moment that I decided Mother and Dad were beyond sex. They were sexless beings who were content to share a bed and a peck on the forehead now and then. I felt sorry for them and figured they were too old or disinterested. Of course, by this time, I knew that DJ and Billy and I hadn't come by way of the stork. I never played that game where you imagine your parents locked in a sexual embrace. I couldn't do it.

That's what I was thinking when I saw the apple sauce splattered on the linoleum and said, "Sorry about the mess."

I am standing by the ladder, dustpan in one hand, a broom in the other. How much time has passed? I have no idea, but Joe is looking at me oddly. "Are you okay? Do you need something?"

Yes, I do need something. I need to get my mind off Dad, off his relationship with Mother, off Emilie Renault. My head begins to pound.

Instead, I say, "I need some air." I jam the broom and dustpan into the kitchen pantry and pick up my jacket.

"I'll lock up." Joe is still staring at me. I nod and escape.

8

I observe Lloyd's secretary, Miss Krausseine, her silver hair wound tightly in a knot at the nape of her neck, efficiently sorting papers at her desk.

"Can I get you some coffee? Tea?" Her slight German accent emerges as she pauses to slide a batch of letters into a manila envelope.

"No thanks." I tap my fingers on the wooden armrest of the sofa, the lone sound in the otherwise serene setting. Not for the first time, I wonder about the receptionist. Probably past retirement age herself, Miss Krausseine sits ramrod straight, guarding the door to Lloyd's inner sanctum. She has smooth skin for a woman her age, whatever that is, and a long, graceful neck. Her light gray eyes match her hair as well as her elegant dress.

My mind wanders—gathering wool again—and I begin to imagine her as a young woman.

Miss Krausseine's voice wrenches me out of my daydream. "He's ready for you now." She ushers me into the office, and I see Lloyd's back as he gazes out the window facing Park Avenue. He abruptly turns when I enter.

"I'm sorry." Lloyd crosses the space between us and hugs me warmly. "A conference call."

"I was running late myself. The Lincoln Tunnel was backed up. A car overheated." I can hear my chattering hang nervously in the air. What is happening? Why has Lloyd summoned me here? Has he convinced DJ to drop the legal challenge to the will?

"Thanks for coming, Kate," Lloyd says, escorting me to one of the two plush chairs that face his desk. "I have news that I felt needed to be delivered in person."

"What?" I ask.

"Have a seat." Lloyd moves to his desk and shifts his attention to a black and white print of snowdrifts piled against a log cabin deep in the Catskills. Dad's work.

He clears his throat as though he is uncertain how to proceed. "I heard from France."

"From Emilie Renault? What did she have to say?" I ease myself forward to the edge of the seat.

"Well, I'm sorry to tell you, Kate, but...Emilie Renault has passed away."

The words land with a thud. I'm prepared for battle with DJ and sort of prepared for learning the truth about Dad. I'm not prepared for this. "She's dead?"

"I'm afraid so."

"How? When?" I stutter.

Lloyd picks up a cream-colored envelope and taps it on his thumbnail. "This came yesterday."

"Who?"

"From her daughter. Emilie Renault died last year of heart failure."

Dad and Emilie. Two broken hearts.

"Does DJ know yet?" I ask.

"I called him an hour ago. I also left a message for Billy. But I thought it best for us to talk in person."

He was right. I couldn't have tolerated DJ celebrating a victory.

"Then it's over."

"Yes. I'm sorry. I know you wanted to…understand more about your father and Emilie," he says.

The clock ticks, and I lightly rap my foot against the wood of the armchair.

"I'll do the necessary paperwork and move forward with probate."

I can hear DJ's voice telling me, "You don't appreciate this now, but in time you will, Kate."

"At least DJ's happy."

Lloyd sighs. "I honored Daniel's request. It just wasn't meant to be."

My disappointment is a weight on my shoulders. What was I expecting? What could Emilie Renault have told me that would clarify my view of Dad? Because that is what I crave—clarity.

"Could I see the letter?"

"Of course." Lloyd slips a single sheet of paper out of the envelope and hands it to me.

I read it. "Dear Mr. Davis, I regret to inform you that my mother, Madame Emilie Renault, is no longer alive. She died last year of a heart condition. I thank you for this notification of Daniel Whitman's will. Though I understand the bequest could pass on to me, since I had no relationship with Mr. Whitman, I cannot accept this gift. Please give my sympathy to his family."

It is short and to the point. The English is clear and careful. "Yvette Merint. She doesn't want the money?" I ask, surprised.

"Apparently not."

"So what does this mean?"

Lloyd speaks slowly. "It means the gift reverts back to the estate. To you and DJ. And Billy."

The ride back to New Jersey is frustrating. The will is resolved, and I am left feeling empty. Resentful? Angry? Toward a woman I don't know. When I get home, I wander around the house. From the living room to the kitchen to the bedroom back to the kitchen. I root around in the refrigerator for a snack. I haven't cooked for a couple of weeks, so there are odds and ends: two pieces of fried chicken, some wilted romaine, gently spoiling cherry tomatoes, and a slice of pizza from last week that looks like cardboard.

Fortunately, I made dinner plans with Cheryl a week ago for a Friday girls-night-out to avoid being alone with the shroud of sadness, now combined with frustration, that descended on me without warning. It's usually difficult for Cheryl to get away evenings during the week, what with the kids' athletics, study dates, and Paul working late. Her architect husband travels around the country and occasionally overseas, supervising various commercial designs. So I was grateful for her company. We hadn't really spoken in days.

Two hours later, we sit by a window in Mexicali Mama's. We polished off orders of fajitas and chicken enchiladas and were well into our pitcher of margaritas.

"This beats leftover pot roast," Cheryl says.

"I haven't cooked in weeks."

"Weeks?" Cheryl's eyebrows lift half an inch.

"You got me." I mainly survive on simple fare and take out.

I relax and laugh and let my hair down. Cheryl and I gossip about work. Which colleagues were in hot water with the Dean, who would serve on the Personnel Committee, a new course we want to team-teach next year, our research projects, etc.

I tip my glass and let the slushy end of the margarita roll onto my tongue.

"How is everything?" Cheryl asks.

"Been meaning to tell you. Emilie Renault is dead."

"Oh, Kate, I'm sorry. When?"

"About a year ago. Her daughter wrote back with the news." I refill our glasses. "I'm thinking of writing to her. To ask about Emilie and Dad and the war."

Cheryl wipes her mouth. "Have you mentioned this to DJ?"

"He's not interested in Dad's past. And that includes Emilie Renault."

"You should do what feels right to you."

"Would you?" I ask.

She hesitates. "I don't know. My relationship with my parents is so different from yours." Cheryl cocks her head and studies me. "But it's clear you want some answers. Need some answers. So I say, go for it. What's the worst that could happen?"

I shred the edges of the white paper napkin under the margarita glass. "She won't answer."

"Okay. What else?"

"DJ has a coronary." I feel guilty the moment the words leave my mouth. Given the family history, heart trouble is one topic I shouldn't tease about.

"Don't tell him. Write and wait to see what happens. If anything materializes, you can always fill him in later. By then he might not even care," Cheryl says.

I consider the conversation last month in the carriage house. There is no way that DJ will not care.

"Maybe I will," I say.

Cheryl puts a hand on mine. "Do it. For your own sanity."

"I needed to hear that," I say, and she smiles.

"I have to get home. Before the kids drive Paul crazy." Cheryl pulls out her wallet, but I grab the check.

"I think I'll do a little letter-writing tonight."

9

The New York Times is scattered around the living room of my condo. Reading the newspaper cover to cover is how I ignore the pounding in my head from a slight margarita hangover. I glance at the dining room table and crumpled balls of stationary. Last night after dinner, I made a few feeble attempts to write to Yvette Merint. Then I gave up. What to say? I'm not even certain I know what I want to know. I sit down and pick up a fresh sheet of paper, write the date and Yvette's address, which Lloyd had reluctantly given me. I reject "Dear Madame Merint" in favor of "Dear Madame Yvette." Neither seems right, both too formal.

"Dear Yvette," I say out loud to hear the sound of the name. I imagine Dad and Emilie, hand-in-hand, walking down a winding street in Nice... I stop and sit forward. Something shifts inside me and releases—it is no longer difficult to write her name. "Dear Yvette." The words uncoil slowly.

"I am Kate Whitman, Daniel's daughter. I received your address from Lloyd Davis, the attorney who wrote to you about my father's will. Thank you for your letter telling us of your mother's passing. Please accept my sympathy on behalf of the Whitman family."

54

I read what I wrote. The Whitman family? I hesitate and then decide to leave the sentence alone. Someone has to represent the Whitmans.

"You can imagine our surprise in discovering that your mother, Emilie, was an important part of my father's life during the war. He never mentioned her name, but it is clear that he cared for her. My father was ill for the last year. He had congestive heart failure and he gradually found it more and more difficult to move around. We shared many wonderful hours during his last months, and I am grateful to have had that time with him. I am sure you feel the same way about your mother."

Is this true? I have no idea what kind of relationship Emilie and Yvette had. Does Yvette realize that Dad and Emilie were lovers during the war? Was she as astounded to find out about the will as we were? She said so little in her note and trying to read between the cryptic lines is impossible.

I tackle the letter again. What I'm eager to ask, boldly and clearly, I don't have the courage to write: what do you know about my father's relationship with your mother? Are there pictures? Letters? Evidence? Would she mind corresponding? These questions are too abrupt, too invasive. Now that the bequest is out of the picture, I am depending on Yvette's goodwill and, possibly, curiosity to answer my letter. If I wrote a little about Dad, she might be inclined to share some of Emilie's life.

I tell her that I live in Bennington, New Jersey, not far from Dad's home, about his illness this past winter, how we spent evenings together talking about my work, my classes. I mention DJ's twin sons, the family business, and Dad's photographs.

I pause.

"I know that your mother was an artist. My father had become quite a good photographer and I have inherited his collection of nature prints."

I pull Dad's old brown sweater tightly around my middle. I've taken to wearing it most evenings at home.

"I loved him dearly and will miss his warm smile that would always cheer me up."

I can get sidetracked thinking about Dad, so I resist the urge to wander off. Now is the moment to frame the focus of the letter.

"If it would not be an imposition, would you mind writing to me about your mother? I would like to know more about Dad's life during the war."

I close the letter wishing her the best and extending my sympathy again. There is nothing more to say.

It is early evening by the time I finish. I seal it quickly, without rereading, afraid I might want to change something. The sun is setting, and I adjust the window blinds so that the room is bathed in a yellow-orange glow. I lie down on the sofa, burrow into the soft folds of a blanket, and close my eyes.

10

I open the door to my condo after a long day spent grading exams, attending a department meeting, and holding an office hour to conference with students desperately trying to graduate next year. Dunham University got its money's worth today. Thank God the semester is ending.

I throw my suit jacket and briefcase on a chair and kick off my shoes, tossing a stack of mail on the sofa. I brew a cup of chamomile tea and sit down, wondering what I might do for dinner. I grab the pile of mail: a phone bill, a notice from the cemetery about the engraving of Dad's marker, several requests from charities for money, and a letter.

The return address is L'Avigne, France. I examine the cream-colored envelope — similar to the one Lloyd had received—and flip the letter over to see "Mme. Yvette Merint" printed on the return label. Adrenaline courses through my body, my pulse racing, as I release the flap and withdraw a single sheet of paper folded in half, the same cream color as the envelope. The watermark gives a fluttery sheen to the stationary that makes it seem old and foreign. I unfold the letter and read:

"Dear Ms. Whitman,

Thank you for your expression of sympathy. I do understand how it is to lose a parent. Even though my mother died over a year ago, the memories are fresh, and the pain is always present. I am sure your own memories of your father will help you at this difficult time."

She's right. The pain is always present.

"I can appreciate your interest in knowing about my mother and her time with your father during the war. Unfortunately, I can tell you nothing. My mother said very little about those years. Even my father, who worked with the resistance in 1944 and 1945 and died in 1980, had many distressing experiences that he could never bring himself to discuss.

I sincerely wish that you and your family will remember the joyful times with your father and that this will help to ease your anguish.

Yvette Merint"

I drop the letter into my lap. I can taste my regret. Without actually acknowledging it, I hoped that Yvette would provide a backstory for Emilie and Dad during the war that would explain the money in the will.

Now I'm left to speculate. DJ and Lloyd would say this is all for the best; let the past alone and move on. The will is settled, and everyone can forget about the war and Emilie Renault.

Except that I can't let it go. Something happened in France and, I feel certain, there is so much more to the story than we know. I sip my tea and reread the note: "My mother said very little about those years." Dad said virtually nothing, too. But after the war, he must have been corresponding with her. How else would Lloyd have an envelope with her address? The distance between the image I had of him all my life and the picture that is now emerging is growing. In the middle of that gap is my inexhaustible grief.

Five days later, the mailman rings my doorbell holding a package. I accept it, thank him for taking the trouble to deliver it in person, and shut the door. *L'Avigne, France.* Six inches square, three inches deep, it is wrapped neatly in brown paper and taped securely on all sides. I remove the packing tape to reveal a cardboard box, worn around the edges, with an improvised lid securely fastened to it. On the top, in block letters, is written: *SOUVENIRS*, D. Whitman.

Attached to the lid is a note. "Ms. Whitman, I found this three months ago among my mother's things. Until I received your letter, I intended to throw it away. Now I think you should have it. I do not understand what they mean, but your father must have known. Sincerely, Yvette."

I pull out a sheet of newspaper stuffed in the box to keep the contents from shifting about. Inside is a lumpy brown paper bag. I take the box to the dining room table and cautiously reach inside the bag. I stare in amazement at the kinds of mementos a young girl might keep as remembrances of important events: a dried flower whose petals are fragile and dust-like with age, safely tucked between two sheets of paper; two smooth, shiny, black pebbles; a soiled paper napkin with lipstick stains and a heart drawn in the center; a train ticket stamped "Villers-Cotterêts" dated 1945; and a crumpled man's handkerchief. There is also a snapshot: a handsome soldier standing hand-in-hand with a striking woman. Both smiling, staring into the camera. *Dad and Emilie.*

The souvenirs are pieces of a puzzle, and I need a picture of the finished product to know what to do with them. I'm on a scavenger hunt, and the prize is my father. Yvette is not sentimental about her mother's past, and I'm grateful to have the box of tokens. I should be happy with these pieces of Dad's history and willing to put it to rest.

I sit down with a piece of stationery since I don't have an email address for her. This time the words come more easily.

"Dear Yvette,

Thank you for the box of your mother's souvenirs. Like you, I do not understand what everything means, although the dried flower and paper napkin, I suppose, suggest a party? Naturally, I am curious about each object. Especially the photo."

Yvette doesn't seem curious. Maybe she's glad to be rid of debris from her mother's past. Like DJ.

Then I add: "Someday we might meet, if your travel brings you to the U.S. or the next time I am in France." I reread the sentence. It is polite, courteous, not pushy or demanding. I sign it and address the envelope.

I examine the souvenirs again, taking care as I handle them. Emilie Renault, and maybe Dad, touched these. I can't simply place them in the box and tuck them away in a drawer. I leave everything but the photo, which I put in my purse, spread out on the table.

11

"I wanna see his grave," Bert said the last time I spoke with him. "See where he's buried."

I had toyed with the idea of offering to bring him up here before he mentioned it, but I was afraid he might not be able to handle it. "Of course, I'll take you."

"He's a veteran. Did they put that on his tombstone?"

"Yes, and World War II."

Today I rose early, showered, dressed, and picked up a bagel and coffee on my way to the parkway. The day is warm for the first of June but breezy, and I open the windows to let the fresh air swirl around the inside of the car. I don't mind my hair blowing against my face. I am hopeful, though anxious, as I drive to Atlantic City.

Poor Bert. He had lived there, estranged from all of us, for over ten years. There aren't so many Whitmans alive that DJ and I can afford to dispose of one of them. During my visit in April, I had suggested he have a telephone installed in his apartment so that I could reach him. I am gradually bringing him back into my life, though he usually sounds mystified when he picks up the receiver as if he is thinking, "Why in the world would she want to speak with me?"

I cruise down Serenity Street, thankful to find a parking spot directly in front of his building. The sky is clear, the wind having shifted the damp air to the east. Inside, the pungent hallway, grime on the stairs, and chipped walls are just as I remember. When Bert greets me at the door, he is wearing the trousers of a brown suit. One of Dad's? The waist is too big, but with the help of a belt, the pants cling to his midsection. He's doing his best to respect Dad's memory. With a shower and shave, white shirt and tie, Bert is a new man.

I marvel at the condition of the apartment—he's made an extraordinary effort to clean up the place. The dirty dishes that had filled the sink and spilled out onto the kitchen counter are washed and stacked on shelves. The living room has been picked up some, and a stack of laundry is folded in a neat pile on the end of the sofa.

I check my watch. "Should we go, Uncle Bert?"

He hesitates, and for a minute, I think he has changed his mind. But then he nods slowly. "Yeah. I guess so."

I take his suit jacket off a chair and gently but firmly steer him toward the door.

Two and a half hours later, I ease my car along the roadway that winds through Woodside Cemetery. Neat rows of graves dot the landscape as far as the eye can travel, and a green carpet flows in and around the markers. The rainy weather has kept the grass growing and the maintenance crew busy cutting and trimming.

We pass marble headstones in all shapes and sizes. Some, indicating effusive attention, are shrines decorated with pictures, statues, and bouquets of flowers, while others are plain, without much ornamentation. The Whitman gravesite falls into the latter category. Besides coming here once a week to trim the azalea plant, I bring fresh flowers occasionally, but that's all.

I pull up to the curb, opposite the old elm that stands by my parents' headstone and switch off the ignition. On the way up the parkway, Bert dozed on and off since it had been an early morning for him. Now he sits quietly beside me and holds a small American flag that he wants to leave at the grave.

I touch his shoulder. "Are you ready, Uncle Bert?"

He looks out the window as if he will find the answer somewhere out there among the other graves. "Can't believe it," he says.

"Some days I can't believe he's gone either."

I see the rims of his eyes redden and place my hand lightly on his arm. "Would you like to sit here for a while?"

"Yeah."

"I'm going to go up and you can join me when you want."

He shivers and sinks further into his jacket, even though the temperature is in the high seventies.

I open the door and glance back at Uncle Bert. His eyes are closed, and his arms are crossed protectively across his body. It's possible he's sleeping again.

I pick up loose roses tied together with a white ribbon laying on the back seat, and head up the knoll. The lawn is damp, and recently cut grass sticks to my shoes. At Dad's grave, small patches of green are taking hold; soon, they will outnumber the brown, muddy ones. I turn to view the car; maybe Bert is too broken up to actually visit the grave, and this is as far as he's able to go.

To give him a few more minutes, I brush some dirt and debris from the marker as I place the mix of red and white flowers at its base. I have barely positioned the stems and pushed the arrangement into the soft earth when I hear a door slam. Bert stands forlornly by the car.

I wipe my dirty hands on a Kleenex and hurry to his side, taking his thin arm, the skin loose under the jacket. We inhale in unison, his eyes meet mine, and we walk up the rise, pausing halfway for Bert to catch his breath. Under the tree, Bert suddenly shuffles his feet as if eager to be gone. But we're here now, and it's good for him to see Dad's grave.

Slowly we inch forward until we stand opposite the stone.

He breathes through his nose loudly and reads the inscription. "Beloved Husband and Father."

And brother.

Bert seems to be absorbing the scene: the tree, the marker, and the patches of dirt on the grave. One hand twitches at his side.

"Do you want me to place your flag?" I ask.

He shakes his head and lifts the flag to shoulder level. Then, with difficulty, he bends down and allows his weight to rest on one knee. He sticks the miniature flagpole in the ground and blinks rapidly. Two streams move down his face, and he makes no effort to wipe them away.

After the cemetery, I take Uncle Bert to lunch at a Chinese restaurant. I had hoped he would spend the night, but after the emotional breakdown at Dad's grave, he appeared drained and said he wanted to go home. Barely speaking or eating, Bert never mentions a drink once. Within forty-five minutes, he's ready to leave, most of his kung pao chicken still on the plate. Once in the car, he settles into the seat and shuts his eyes. We ride for an hour in silence, and then, around exit 98, Bert sits up straighter and says, "Dan was a war hero."

I slide my eyes sideways. "What do you mean?"

"He rescued guys. Saved their lives. One of 'em..." He glances upward and studies the car ceiling. "...named Jimmy. Still kept in touch."

"Jimmy? How did Dad help him?"

"Don't know," he mumbles.

"What was his last name? Where was he from?" I ask, eager to hear even scraps of information about that time.

"Don't know."

I focus on the road. "Uncle Bert, do you remember when we talked about Dad's friend Emilie?"

"Huh?"

"The woman Dad met in France."

"Oh. Yeah."

I hand him the picture of Dad and Emilie that I'd slipped out of my bag earlier. "I found this." No need to share details of Yvette's box of souvenirs.

Bert studies the photo. "That's her. Emilie."

"I'd like to ask you a question." I wait to see if my request registers. It's difficult to tell. "How did Mother find out about Emilie?"

"I don't know," Bert yawns. "I told Dan people like us...like our family...don't marry war brides."

"What do you mean? 'People like us?'"

Bert spreads his hands helplessly. "We had money. Dad did business with her family."

"Mother's family?" I didn't know that part of the story.

"Couldn't throw her over and marry Emilie," he says.

"I guess not."

"Yeah. It was hard on Dan. He felt real bad," he says. "I told him, Dan, you'll get over her." He stares at the passing countryside, the marshy inlets, and the boats bobbing in brackish water.

"Do you think he did? Get over her?" I ask.

Bert shrugs. "I'm ready for my nap." He lays the photo on the dashboard.

A loud jangling pulls me out of deep sleep. I reach for the alarm clock and push a button. The harsh sound continues. Why won't it stop? I think groggily, my mind a blur of images from the dream I am still half in. Confused, I bring the clock to my face. It's four a.m. Why is the alarm going off at four a.m.? The clouds part for an instant, and it dawns on me that the phone is not the alarm. I pick up.

"Kate? It's DJ. You've got to come to the hospital," Nancy says.

"What...? What happened?"

"It's his heart. Come now." Her voice quivers.

I stare numbly at the receiver. "DJ," I say aloud. Then I race around, grabbing clothes, shoving my feet into shoes, running a brush through my hair. I swear as I search for my car keys—I threw them on the sofa when I got home last night.

I had been asleep for two hours. Yesterday after four trips up and down the Garden State Parkway, at two and a half hours each, I pulled in from my last trip and wanted nothing more than to rip off my sticky clothes and crawl into bed. But my insomnia acted up, and I found myself staring at the wall, with thoughts of DJ, Bert, Dad, and Mother, at midnight, then one a.m. At two, I finally dozed.

I run from the parking garage to reception in the lobby of the hospital, ask for Daniel Whitman's room, and am sent to the fourth floor cardiac care unit. The elevator doors open, and I confront a waiting room: institutional green paint, a television with a CNN talking head droning on and on, and a vending machine with coffee and snacks. Drew and Nate, in shorts and tees, sit hunched over in orange plastic chairs with bad bed hair.

"Aunt Kate." They are on their feet, and we have a group hug. Tall young men, they become vulnerable boys at intimate, emotional times such as birthdays, graduations, their grandfather's funeral, and now this. I become "aunt."

"How's your dad," I ask.

"He's sleeping. Mom's with him," says Nate.

"Room 410," says Drew.

I brush their cheeks and walk down the hallway. I stop outside 410 and peek in. Nancy, in a chair, pulled up to DJ's bed, is holding his hand and rises when she sees me enter.

"Kate," she murmurs.

She looks tired but remarkably calm and collected. We embrace. "How is he?"

"He's going to be fine. There was little damage to his heart." She smiles. "But he'll have to change his ways."

I step to the bed and touch his arm. Asleep, DJ is peaceful and relaxed and missing the web of tension lines that usually covers his face. "What happened?"

"He wasn't feeling well last night. He went to bed early and woke up about midnight. We thought it was heartburn and he took a pill and fell back to sleep. But he woke again at three, gasping for air and clutching his chest. I called 911 and they were there in minutes."

"Was it angina or a heart attack?" Dad had several episodes of angina well before his final attack.

"Heart attack. Not a major 'incident' they said, but enough to scare him."

The IV machine blinks, numbers fluctuating nonstop. "Can I do anything? Coffee?"

"No thanks, I've had a cup and probably won't sleep as it is," she says.

"Nancy, why don't you go home? I'll stay with him."

She shakes her head. "But the boys can leave and come back tomorrow."

"I'll tell them," I say and quietly exit the room. I send Nate and Drew off to get some rest, shove a dollar in the vending machine, and press the black coffee button. The liquid is scalding. Good. It forces me to a level of hyper-awareness, and I walk back to DJ's room.

12

Three cups of coffee have given me a caffeine high. I'm practically asleep standing up while also jumpy. It's eight a.m., and I've finally convinced Nancy to go home for a few hours. DJ is in no danger and will be resting as well, I say. He was awakened to have his vitals checked, and he scans the room, probably for Nancy, eventually alighting on me. He blinks.

"Hi," I whisper.

He drifts off to sleep again. The medication keeps him lightly sedated, so I sit in an armchair and close my eyes. The contours of the chair trigger a muscle memory: the last time I was in this position was three months ago with Dad dying in the bed next to me. The quiet of the room is broken by the beeping of the heart monitor that changes its rate whenever DJ adjusts his position.

I must have slept for a while because when I open my eyes, Nancy is bending over DJ, fiddling with his gown and tucking the sheet around his shoulders. "The doctor said there is no permanent damage, but you need to change your lifestyle."

"My lifestyle?" he asks groggily. "What's that?"

"Don't be smart," she says and glances at me. "Kate's been here most of the night."

DJ looks in my direction and then turns his face away from me in silence. Nancy offers to bring back coffee and pastries from the cafeteria and thanks me for relieving her. She teasingly admonishes DJ to behave himself before closing the door behind her.

"Sounds like you won't be in here too long," I say, hoping to sound encouraging.

"Right."

"How are you feeling?"

He rotates his head, and there is a brief spurt of beeping from the monitor. "How do you think I'm feeling? Lying in bed attached to tubes, can't go to work, this chest pain comes and goes, and nobody is guaranteeing this won't happen again." His eyes fill up.

"You've got to be patient. The healing may take a little time," I say.

"Patient? I don't have time to be patient. I have a business to run." He waves his hand, and the beeping starts again.

I am alarmed at the monitor and wonder if I should call a nurse. "Calm down, DJ. You shouldn't be upsetting yourself."

He glares at me. "What is it about us?"

"What do you mean?"

"Why have we never gotten along?" he asks me.

I intend to say something dispassionate that will keep him tranquil and smooth out the rough edges of the conversation, but his question is laser-like in its honesty. "I don't know." I am light-headed from lack of sleep and lack of food.

"We've been arguing as far back as I can remember. You were Daddy's girl..."

"And Mother favored you," I say. The truth.

Billy got along with both of them. He was mostly neutral where family squabbles were concerned.

"We never had much fun together," DJ says.

"We're ten years apart. Almost different generations."

He looks upward, and I follow his gaze, counting the tiles of the dropped ceiling and studying the water stains.

"We were never kids together," I add. "You were always a grown-up to me."

"Mom didn't understand why we never got along, either."

"She said that?" A wave of sadness catches me unexpectedly.

"When Mom was sick that last summer, we talked a lot..." DJ coughs again, and I pour him a glass of water. He sips a little and passes it back.

I take a paper cup and fill it with water for myself.

"She made me promise to be nice to you," he says.

I nearly choke on the water. Dad had elicited the same pledge from me about DJ before he died. "I didn't know that."

"How could you?" He is weary from talking.

"You should rest now." The room is suddenly stifling, and I unbutton the top of my shirt. I'd kill to wash my face and brush my teeth.

DJ rolls to one side, setting off a series of sharp beeps again.

His eyes follow me as I kiss his forehead.

13

It's been a few days now.

I spend three hours at the hospital visiting DJ in the morning, and when Nancy and the twins appear, I excuse myself and come to the carriage house. I open the door and am hit with the aromas of fresh paint and Lysol. I survey the living room. The old furniture has been carted away except for the easy chair that I am taking to my condo. The little house's genteel charm has been replaced with bright white walls, gleaming glass and metal tables, a black leather sofa, and track lights. I reach for the wall switch.

"They work," says a familiar voice behind me.

I start.

"Sorry to scare you," says Joe. "I saw you go in and I figured I could pick up a few tools I left here."

"Sure."

I hadn't seen Joe since the afternoon he installed the track lights. He goes into the kitchen, and I hear metal clank against metal.

"I love the lighting. It opens up the room."

Joe laughs and calls out, "Yeah, Drew is dying to get his hands on these walls." He returns to the living room with a large toolbox and studies his handiwork. "Not a bad job."

"Are you finished here?"

"I've got a couple of outlets that need repairing in the bedroom. Shouldn't take more than a few hours. I'll be back next week." He studies me as if he could read my mind. "How are you doing?"

Aside from Lloyd and Cheryl, no one asks me how I'm doing these days. His gaze is piercing, and I'm forced to be honest. "Up and down."

"Makes sense. You have to take care of yourself," he says.

I know that, but hearing it come from Joe's mouth makes it sound like comforting advice, the kind a good friend who loves you might offer. "Thanks."

"Sorry about DJ. Nancy says he's coming along."

"He is. Anxious to get out of the hospital."

"Give him my best," he says.

"I will."

"Guess I'll be going. Tell Drew there are extra spotlights in the kitchen pantry." He hangs by the door as if he wants to say more. "So long."

"Bye."

He turns to go, then hesitates. "If you'd ever like to talk…about things. Your Dad…"

I'm caught off-guard. "That's a…lovely offer. I'll keep it in mind." I smile.

"Over coffee or whatever." He shrugs and smiles back.

I watch Joe walk down the pathway to his truck parked by the garage. A nice guy. I wouldn't mind having coffee with him.

There is one last job to finish here. I walk into the bedroom now occupied by a futon and a beanbag chair from the seventies and open the closet door. Nancy transferred a stack of papers and files, which had been tucked away in the safe in the Whitman home, into a box for me to sort through. I pull the cardboard box to the middle of the room and settle myself into the depths of the beanbag and go to work. Dad's will and insurance papers are still in the family safe; what I'm holding here are more personal items, things Nancy thought I might like to see. There are letters from employees at Whitman Textiles thanking Dad for his help with this problem or that issue and a stack of bank statements indicating deposits into an Atlantic City account. Dad had been faithful to his brother over the years.

A bulging manila envelope has "Daniel Whitman" scribbled on the outside. It contains old family pictures—one of Dad, Billy, and DJ sitting in a boat holding fishing poles and smiling broadly. DJ looks about ten, so Billy was nine, and I was a baby at the time. I find Billy's high school graduation photo. He resembles Mother's father with his light blue eyes and blond curls. And there are two passports. I open the first and stare at Dad's picture. The expiration date on the passport is a year earlier, so the picture is about fifteen years old. He is still handsome: deep brown eyes, a youthful smile, and a full head of wavy, gray hair. I open the second. It is Mother's. The face is round and calm and the smile enigmatic, as though she knows a secret she has no intention of sharing with the world. Her hair is light brown and hangs down to the nape of her neck. The photo was taken before the chemo had caused it all to fall out.

It's simple curiosity that makes me flip through the pages to see what story they tell. Mother and Dad hadn't traveled much, but occasionally they visited her cousins in Canada or stayed in a time-share in Cancun. I stop at the Customs stamps for March 1981. I was spending a semester abroad in Paris at the Sorbonne the spring of my junior year at Columbia, and Mother had come to visit. Dad had wanted to accompany her, but Mother insisted on traveling alone to see how I was managing. I study the stamps: JFK airport and…Marseille, France. She came to the home where I was staying in Paris. I never bothered to ask her via what route. Did I know that she'd flown into Marseille instead of directly into Paris? She never mentioned Marseille to me. I feel a chill on my neck though the carriage house is warm and stuffy. France was the last trip she ever took; by the fall of my senior year, she was too sick to travel. My memories of that time are painful, guilt-laden, and I keep them locked away in my own safe.

By the summer of 1982, I had completed the French program at Columbia University, on the Dean's list every semester, though I still managed to have a pretty active social life. Dad was proud of my academic success. DJ had been an average student at Columbia, and Billy, who returned to Princeton after Vietnam, struggled to find himself and dropped out a second time for good.

Dad had promised me a year earlier that when I graduated, I could travel around Europe and then go back to Paris and visit the friends I had made during my semester abroad studying at the Sorbonne. But in November, Mother's cancer, which had been in remission, reappeared, and the whole family was in a state of constant upset. By May, after another round of chemotherapy, she had stabilized. There was much discussion on whether or not I should go to Europe, but Mother was unyielding. The trip had been planned for months, and all preparations were made. Dad wasn't sure my leaving was a good idea, but Mother convinced him that I had earned the trip. On graduation day, with both of them beaming at me, I unwrapped a three-piece set of luggage. I was torn. A part of me wanted to stay home, knew that I should stay home. But another part was so excited to be traveling again that my darker angels won.

"I know how much this means to you," Dad had said.

"Mother told me to go and have a good time."

Dad was silent.

"I'll be home by the Fourth of July." I threw my arms around his neck.

"Okay. I'll tell your mother that we'll have a big blowout for the Fourth. Billy and DJ. The entire family."

"That'll be fun," I said.

I packed and repacked my suitcases, comparing notes with two friends who were traveling with me, cramming in much more than I would possibly need for the four weeks of travel through Germany, France, Spain, and England. In the days before I departed, Mother was tired much of the time and stayed in the bedroom reading with the television on mute. On the day Dad took me to the airport, I stood outside her room and knocked softly on the door.

I heard a muffled sound. "Come in."

I opened the door cautiously. Even though the late afternoon sun streamed into every other window facing west along the back of the house, the drawn shades had made the room dark. Normally cheerful floral patterns on the curtains and bedspread were transformed into shadowy, grim shapes. Mother had pulled the sheet up to her chin, her face barely visible from the depths of several pillows.

"You need some light."

"No, please," Mother protested, waving an arm that had materialized from beneath the bedcovers.

I fiddled with the embroidered loop on the bottom of the blind.

Mother thrust her right elbow into the pillows and pushed herself a few inches higher. "Come here."

I crossed the room. She took a moment to fill the glass she kept on the nightstand with water. Sipping slowly, she observed me above the rim of the tumbler, then patted the bed, and I perched on the edge.

"Have you packed your raincoat?" she asked.

"I have an umbrella."

"No, that's not enough. England can be very damp."

"We're only going to be there for a few days at the end." The old resistance rising, an instinctive reaction whenever Mother tried to exercise some authority. "Most of the time we'll be in France and Spain. I want to see the south of France and of course the Chivals in Paris." The family I stayed with the year before. We were all ready for the sunny beaches of the Riviera and guys in skimpy bathing suits.

"...a heavy sweater, too."

I'd drifted off and missed the last few minutes of Mother's lecture on the weather in Europe. "Fine. I'll pack one."

"And don't forget to let us know if you change the itinerary." She coughed into one of Dad's large linen handkerchiefs. The chemotherapy had left her susceptible to a respiratory infection that reared its ugly head every few weeks. Antibiotics helped, but the symptoms had to run their course. She inhaled deeply. "We want to know where you are at all times."

In the silence, I heard Dad saying, "...your mother may need you," but I pushed his voice out of my head, stood up, and bent down to kiss Mother's cheek.

Her affection with me usually consisted of brushing my bangs out of my face or delivering a kiss on my forehead. But today was different. My lips had barely touched her cheek when I felt her arms clasp my back and pull me against her frail body in a crushing hug. I hadn't remembered Mother embracing me so thoroughly since I was in middle school. She released me after a moment, and her eyes were misty.

"Now you have a good time." It was an order.

Something caught in my throat, and I stuttered. "Mother...what...do you...?" I don't know what I was going to say, but my hesitation gave her enough time to pull herself together.

"Don't forget your raincoat."

"Maybe I should stay home," I said.

She shook her head vigorously. "You are going to Europe and that's final."

I nodded dumbly, and Dad appeared at the door.

"Are we ready?" he asked.

I glanced at Mother enveloped by the cover, bobbing her head up and down. "She's ready," she said.

14

DJ is released from the hospital after seven days in the cardiac unit. According to him, it is well past time to go home. He will still need to monitor his medications and diet and rest, which includes a few more weeks puttering around the house before going back to work. I step into his room and see him dressed and sitting in a wheelchair, clearly anxious to leave.

"Hi." I sit on the edge of the bed

He taps the armrests of the chair impatiently. "I don't know why I need this thing. I've been walking up and down the corridor several times every day."

"Hospital protocol," I say. "Where's Nancy?"

"Signing release forms." He squints as he studies me. "I am so bored."

"Boredom's been good for you," I say.

He scowls. "Yeah, right."

"I went to the carriage house yesterday to sort through some things Nancy took out of the safe. It looked great. Fresh paint. New furniture. Drew will enjoy his new home."

DJ grimaces. "Yeah, and give our house a break." We share a laugh, and it feels nice.

79

I pull the photo of Dad and DJ and Billy fishing out of my purse and hand it to him. "I found some old pictures."

He examines the photo then flips it over. There is no date.

"I also found Mother and Dad's passports. Mother was so young," I say.

"Only a few years older than I am now when she passed. Hard to imagine," he says, and we sit silently.

Nancy enters in a bustle, followed by an LPN who will escort us to the hospital entrance. We gather DJ's personal items, a large bouquet of flowers sent from his office, and follow the wheelchair out the door. Nancy is a step ahead of me, and as I pass the threshold of DJ's room, I glance back at the empty bed.

Is it the sudden appearance of Emilie Renault in my life that forces me to confront distressing memories about Mother and Dad? There is no point in resisting any part of them now.

I had promised to stay in touch with Dad and Mother, to stick to the itinerary that they had agreed upon, to call every other day. And I had done that, for the most part. But my girlfriends and I decided to hitchhike from Paris to a little village outside Dijon—off the beaten track and definitely not on my approved program. Telling Dad I'd been hitchhiking would earn a stern lecture since I assured him we would stick to trains. When I finally called after a week, a little high on red wine late at night, the coldness in Dad's voice startled me.

"Where have you been?" he asked angrily.

"We've been staying outside Dijon and there wasn't a phone." My head was swimming, and the sound of his voice reverberated in my ear. I switched the receiver to the other ear. It was no better.

"Kate, your mother..." He broke down.

"Dad?"

"Mom's in the hospital. Intensive care. It's not good." A slight sniffling on the other end. "She went in two days ago. She pleaded with me to reach you."

"Oh Daddy, I'm sorry." I was devastated, both by my mother's state and my father's anguish. "I'll come right home."

It had all happened so quickly. You're not supposed to deteriorate that fast with cancer. At least that's what I thought. I took the first available flight from Dijon to Paris, where I changed planes for New York. I expected to see Billy at the airport, but instead, I saw the driver of a car service holding a placard with the name "Whitman" in bold letters. It was so impersonal I felt afraid of Dad for the first time in my life.

I left my luggage in the corridor as I pushed open the door to Mother's hospital room. Seeing Dad, Uncle Bert, DJ, Nancy, and Billy, all sitting quietly, literally left me speechless. The lines of grief were so harsh on Dad's face that, for a moment, I didn't recognize him. Had I been gone that long? Three weeks. I paused inside the room and waited for someone to say something. No one did. "Dad," I whispered. He held Mother's hand. Her eyes were shut, the breathing machine like a bellows sending puffs of air into her lungs and sucking it out again, keeping her alive though she was unconscious.

His back stiffened.

"Daddy, I—"

As if his head was frozen to his shoulders, his whole body swiveled in my direction, and his glare bored through me. The force of his stare hit me with an impact I wasn't prepared for and compelled me to step backward. Dad said something to Billy, whose eyes were red and puffy, and he abruptly rose.

"Come on," Billy whispered, pulling me into the hallway. "You can leave your luggage in here."

I followed him to a waiting room and threw myself into his arms, and wept, clinging to his neck.

He hugged me tentatively. "Katie, why would you want to hurt Dad like this?"

Billy was the least judgmental person I knew but arriving home too late was too much even for him. I was confused. "Hurt Dad? I don't want to hurt him."

"But that's what you've done. This isn't just about Mom."

My heart dropped into my stomach. I realized that my selfishness might cost me the one thing I didn't think I could live without—Dad's love. He was so disappointed he might never forgive me.

Though I toyed with a salad from the cafeteria, the tight knot in my stomach wasn't going to allow any of it to digest; but eating, or at least pretending to eat, kept me away from the rest of my family. It had been an hour since I'd arrived, and no one but Billy had said a word to me.

And then DJ, furious, opened the door of the cafeteria and stood above me. "You are a total fuck-up, do you know that?" His face reddened, and his pitch rose so that other patrons began to take an interest as the words poured out of his mouth.

"DJ, I couldn't help it. We were in this little town and—"

"You didn't try to call, right? You were supposed to call every other day. Dad didn't hear from you for a week. He was frantic."

"I told you. We got into the village on Tuesday and…"

DJ glowered at me in silence. "If Dad was sick, you'd have called every day. In fact, you probably wouldn't have gone to Europe." His voice cracked.

I swallowed, lowering my gaze to mask my guilt.

"I hope you can live with yourself." DJ spun away.

"How is Dad doing?" I asked desperately.

"How do you think? He's losing the most important person in his life."

Eventually, I entered the hospital room that night and joined the family in a vigil that ended twelve hours later. Uncle Bert gave me a stern look as he hugged me and then smiled encouragingly; DJ ignored me; Dad was silent. I sat next to Mother, memorizing the lines on her face, staring at the blue tubing that connected her to the life support machine. I gingerly touched her hand and brushed a strand of hair off her forehead. I remembered her last hug, and I blinked to hold back the tears and swallowed the hard lump in my throat.

After the funeral, I apologized again, but Dad cut me off. "We won't talk about this anymore."

And we didn't.

The weeks that followed were torturous. The two of us avoided each other—life was more tolerable that way—so I spent my time packing clothes for the fall. I'd been accepted into the graduate program of the French department at the University of Illinois, but on the way home from Europe, while the plane bounced across the Atlantic and I couldn't sleep, I changed my mind. I'd forget about graduate school and stay in New Jersey to take care of Dad. However, with the atmosphere in the house, I reconsidered. Leaving would be best. Whenever thoughts about Mother encroached on my consciousness, I firmly tamped them down. In my mind, I had done my best to return in time to see her before she died.

The afternoon before I was to leave for Illinois, I found myself once more outside my parents' bedroom. I rapped on the door.

Dad had gotten into the habit of taking naps whenever he was home late in the day. He had lost interest in Whitman Textiles and had ceded virtually all authority for day-to-day decision-making to DJ and Uncle Bert. Some mornings Dad took the train into the city and, according to DJ, sat at his desk as if lost in thought. But most days, he worked in the garden or tinkered with his cameras or reclined in his easy chair in the den, staring straight ahead. It was unnerving to watch him withdraw into a cocoon, but instinct told me to leave him alone, and so I did until the afternoon I was leaving.

"Dad?" I whispered, my face resting on the cool surface of the door.

Silence from the other side.

I twisted the knob and slowly opened the door. He was lying on his back, his arms folded across his stomach. With his pale complexion and composed expression, I could have sworn I was gazing at a dead man. I shook his arm.

"Huh?" Dad snorted, and his eyes darted around the room, coming to rest, finally, on me. "Oh." He rubbed his face and rolled over onto one elbow.

"I'm going now."

He lay back down.

"I didn't stay away deliberately," I said, twisting my car keys into a metal knot.

He sighed. "I know. But this is about more than not calling and arriving after your mother was in a coma."

Dad turned toward me; his expression unreadable in the shadows of the late afternoon sun. I waited while he took a deep breath, his exhalation audible like a soft moan. "You never gave her a break."

My heart sank. "I tried to get along…"

He shook his head emphatically. "You were hard on her, Kate."

"I'm sorry. But she was hard on me, too." It tumbled out before I could stop myself.

"It's too late, don't you see that? It's just too late." He swung his legs over the side of the bed. "There were...people and things in her life that were very...difficult."

"What do you mean?" I asked.

"Never mind."

"What do you want me to do?" My chest tightened at the finality of his words.

He stared at me a long time before answering. "You should go to Illinois and sort this all out. Sort out your feelings about your mother."

He wanted me to leave. Somewhere in the back of my mind, I'd expected him to ask me to stay, and I'd happily agree to give up graduate school plans.

I approached him uneasily and gave him a quick kiss on the cheek, and silently stole away. I heard him settling once more into the recesses of the mattress as I left the bedroom.

A month later, I received a call from Billy. Dad had had a mild heart attack; he was fine and resting comfortably in the hospital.

"I'll be on the first flight home."

"Wait a minute." There was a long pause on the line. "I don't think that's a good idea."

The impact of his words dawned on me.

"DJ thinks—we all think—it might be easier on Dad if..."

"If I stay away." I finished his sentence. "Sorry. I'm coming home."

"Katie, it's not a good idea."

"Why not? I need to see him, Billy," I said.

"He needs to avoid excitement and...upset."

"You all think I would upset him?" No response on the line. I bit my lip. "If that's what you think is best."

"For now. I'll call you tomorrow and keep you up-to-date."

"Sure," I said dully.

True to his promise, Billy called frequently and gave me detailed health reports. Dad's heart would beat for another twenty-three years, it turned out, but mine had a tear in it that would never mend.

15

Sunday is sunny and warm, and I drive to DJ's to check-in. My mind skips over the events and recollections of the past few months, and I realize that Dad was a private man who expressed his feelings carefully, as though he could not quite bring himself to completely open up to any of us. I can see that, now that he's gone, I didn't know him as well as I assumed I did. Dad had boundaries and emotional armor; he had secrets. His relationship with Mother had to be complicated.

When I arrive at the house, both twins are there, joking, trying to get a rise out of their father. It's good for DJ to fool around with his sons, teasing and laughing.

We chat for a while, eat lunch on the patio, then Drew and Nate take off, and Nancy reminds DJ that it's time for his afternoon nap, and so I leave. I head my car in the direction of home, but I'm restless, and when I approach the entrance to the highway, I impulsively turn the steering wheel to the right and follow the flow of traffic into the city. The skyline of New York stretches across my windshield, and I'm at the Lincoln Tunnel in fifteen minutes. The crawl across 57th Street to Park Avenue is maddeningly slow, with taxis zipping in and out of lanes, pedestrians taking their time at intersections, and the occasional horn blaring.

I park in my usual lot and walk the half block to Dad's apartment. Mine, now. It's been months since we first heard about Emilie Renault and my ordered world became a little unglued. Whatever they had, whatever their relationship, it is now buried along with them. I am still curious but am gradually surrendering to the past. My path will not cross Yvette's. At least not in this lifetime.

Today I need to be where Dad had been. I open the door to the apartment and inhale the mustiness, the still lingering aroma of cigar smoke. I drop my purse in the foyer and walk around the place—the living room, kitchen, guest room, and finally Dad's office. Everything is just as I'd left it, including the indentation in the pillow where I had placed the bag containing Dad's clothing that I carried out of the apartment.

Gingerly I sit on the daybed. I swing my legs off the floor and settle them on the spread. I have never lain in this bed. I'm like a kid taking liberties by sneaking into my parents' domain and eavesdropping on their private lives, finding my father's stash of condoms in the nightstand and my mother's red silk negligee carefully folded at the bottom of a drawer.

My eyes roam around the room, and it occurs to me I hadn't gone through Dad's desk weeks ago when I cleaned out his closet. I approach the "holy of holies," as Billy called it. None of us had ever touched a single piece of paper on this desk. That was the rule. I imagine Dad positioned here. I open the top drawer and find pens, pencils, paper clips, and staples neatly organized. Another drawer holds Whitman Textiles letterhead and legal pads of various sizes. An envelope contained ticket stubs from Broadway shows over the past decades.

I pull the handle of the bottom left-hand drawer, and nothing happens. Opening the drawer feels like an invasion of his privacy, but I'm curious. Why is it locked? Technically the contents of the drawers are mine. I scan the top of the desk and choose the letter opener to pry the drawer open. When it refuses to budge, I insert the tip of a penknife into the keyhole, rotating it back and forth until the lock pops.

In the drawer, there is a red, dog-eared French-English dictionary, military issue, whose publication date is 1940. I page through it. My students would laugh at the little, well-thumbed, red book. Their hi-tech vocabulary CDs and online resources are so much more sophisticated.

I reach for the top drawer on the right side of the desk and find more office supplies, a flashlight, and more boxes of staples. Dad bought them by the gross. The second drawer is empty. Then I tug on the third. Like the drawer on the other side of the desk, it too is locked. I don't hesitate to use the penknife this time.

From inside, I withdraw a hard, square object and confront a book with a thick, brown cardboard cover worn on the edges. My heart thumps. I lift the cover. On the top page, I read:

Emilie Caronne Renault
Nice, France

I flip through the pages, in French, of course. The paper is parchment-like and brittle, the ink clear in most places, blurred in a few others. My head spins. How did it get here? Dad couldn't have read it in French. Has anyone else seen it? I flick on the overhead light in the kitchen and settle myself at the table. It will take time and some effort to interpret the handwriting. I turn the first page and read slowly.

16

May 1946.

I am writing to tell my story. Someday someone will read this. Or perhaps not. It does not matter. But it cannot die within me.

It has been nearly two years since my life turned upside down. I think about these months, and I need to remember everything, every detail, every moment of that time. I want to remember the joy and the pain. I must do this while my memories are still sharp and clear. So many feelings and thoughts crowd my mind and my heart as I pick up my pen.

In January 1944, I arrived in Nice. After graduating from the Art and Design School in Monaco, I could not live at home anymore. There was no work for an artist or photographer in the city. I used to sketch tourists in the square. But the tourists were gone. I would need to find work in Nice. I missed Maman and worried about her constant cough, and Papa was angry with me for leaving. On my first night in the city, I cried myself to sleep. I was so grateful for Victoire's offer to share her apartment for a few weeks. She graduated from the Art and Design School with me and then moved to Nice and painted buttons at the factory.

In the spring of 1944, Nice was a city under siege in a country ripped apart by hate and despair. I found a temporary job taking newspaper photographs for *Le Petit Niçoise* since their photographer had been arrested by the Gestapo. I tried to save money so that I would have my own place to live. Victoire's apartment on Rue Saint François de Paule was a few blocks from Vieux Nice and Le Cours Saleya. The best location! But with three rooms there was only space for two of us and when her lover Jean spent the night I slept on the sofa. Victoire had known Jean for six months, and she hinted about marriage to me though Jean never mentioned it.

I was fortunate to have a job with *Le Petit Niçoise*, if just for two months. If I could not paint or sketch for a living, I would take photographs. Every day I took my most prized Leica camera that I received from Professor Tourdon as a graduation gift and traveled around Nice, taking pictures of officials, both French and German, and daily events. Then one day, the editor of the paper hired an older man with many years of experience and friends in the German military. I lost my job.

I searched up and down Nice for work. Staying with Victoire was impossible now. Jean appeared every night, and I was tired of sleeping on the sofa. Sometimes when Jean came in the door, I was embarrassed to be seen in my nightgown, so I pretended to be asleep. One night he walked to the sofa and stooped down, so his face was near mine. I smelled wine and body odor and felt his hot breath as he stared at me.

I was lonely and frightened. It was a cold March, and my teeth chattered as I walked the Promenade des Anglais and down every side street, into every shop asking if there was a room available. The biting wind and rain made me happy to be indoors. But with every "No," I walked outside and into the frigid air. Finally, I found a room above a bakery on Rue de Rivoli.

"How much?" I asked.

"Fifty francs a week," the baker said.

Fifty francs was nearly all I had. If I took the room, I would not eat again that day, or I would have to trade something for food coupons. I was hungry and cold, and my feet were wet. I needed a place to stay. The baker wiped the flour off his hands and handed me a key.

I turned away from him, and he clamped a sticky hand on my arm. "You pay now." The baker had puffy cheeks, like the dough that he pounded, but his wife was kind and gave me a warm roll behind his back.

I had a few francs left, enough for a visit to a café if I drank ersatz coffee. My tiny room had no heat, ashes in the cold fireplace, a layer of dust, and a wobbly nightstand. The mattress on the single bed was stained yellow, and the metal springs creaked when I rolled from side to side, but I was out of the cold and wind.

I awoke to the fragrance of baking bread. I was always hungry at that time, and I still needed to find a job. I was afraid that if I was not working, I would be picked up and sent north to a labor camp. Victoire's cousin Gracielle had been deported to a camp in February.

Those first mornings when I went downstairs to the bakery, there were always German soldiers sitting at café tables eating rolls and drinking coffee. They had gleaming belt buckles, polished boots, and acted important and confident. They were my age, but they looked healthy. I felt older, and the mirror told me I was too thin. The early years of the war were easier, and some vegetables and meats arrived from farms in the countryside. You could find food in the markets. When the Germans occupied the south of France in 1942, things changed. Travel was difficult and food disappeared since the German army took crops for themselves. Stories of arrests and torture at Gestapo headquarters in Nice were everywhere. *Les boches* marched along the Promenade des Anglais and filled the cafés and brasseries. They were smart enough to defeat France but not smart enough to understand the whispers, turned heads, and sudden need to spit on the sidewalk as they went by. We all mocked them if it was safe. Otherwise, it was *verboten*. We obeyed the curfew.

I walked long hours down the Promenade, past the Negresco Hotel where German officers lived, searching for work and to avoid my room and the aromas of the bakery. I saw drunk German soldiers and French women arriving and leaving. The women had painted lips and cheeks, and they adjusted their hats and checked the seams in their silk stockings. Before they walked into the hotel, they looked around to see if anyone was watching. I thought they seemed disappointed to have no audience. I promised myself one day I would walk into the Negresco, sit on a velvet banquette, and order champagne!

One night I walked along the Baie des Anges for a few kilometers until my legs were too heavy to go further. I went in search of my sister Marie. I hadn't seen her in a year, but I knew she sang in Vieux Nice at Le Café Figaro most evenings. Marie entertained those Niçoises who still had a little money to spend on cheap wine or real coffee. I passed Le Cours Saleya and the Place Rossetti. Le Café Figaro was so deep in the back streets of the old town the Germans had not yet found it.

I remember I stepped over a puddle of rainwater and caught the heel of my wooden shoe on a paving stone. When I fell and scraped my knee, I ruined my one pair of stockings. I wanted to sit down on the sidewalk and cry, but I was too cold and hungry.

Le Café Figaro was warm and steamy, full of smoke and noise and the strong smells of bodies, wet wood, and spilled wine. People argued freely, and whispering lovers made me wish for someone to touch me. Old men snored, and prostitutes smoked at a corner table. I recognized Marie's voice above the noise, loud and deep in her throat, singing a song about better days. I admired her long blond hair and curvy figure, but Marie also looked older than thirty-one. No one listened to her. Who could ignore food shortages, Germans on every corner, and no work?

I sat at a table near the piano next to a young man and a pale little girl, maybe sixteen.

I almost regretted coming, but I had no one else to turn to. I hardly knew her; she'd left home when I was seven, and I was always a little nervous around Marie. She made me feel like a child, even at twenty-one. When she left home, *ma père* was angry with her. They did not speak very much in those years.

The singing stopped, and Marie eyed me as she walked to the table.

"So, *ma petite*," she said.

"*Bonsoir*."

Marie waved to a waiter. "You must be desperate to come here." She pulled a *Gauloise* from a gold case and bent forward to accept a light from the young man at the next table. She placed her hand under my chin and lifted my face. "*Regarde-moi*." Her voice was low and raspy.

Her lips were bright red, and her violet eyes darkened by make-up. Her tight black dress was frayed. I did not know then how Marie managed to survive. She was surprised to see me in Nice, she said. She asked me about Maman and Papa. She rarely went to Monaco.

"When did you eat?" she asked.

"This morning." Marie knew I was lying.

The waiter set two glasses, a small bottle of wine, and half a loaf of bread on the table. I stuffed the bread in my mouth.

"*Tiens.*" Marie reached into the front of her dress and withdrew some francs and a ration book. She laid them on the table and took a sip of her wine.

I stopped eating.

"Buy some food and then find a job."

"I had a job taking photographs for *Le Petit Niçoise*," I said, my mouth full.

"And?"

"They don't need me anymore."

Marie borrowed a pencil from an old man scribbling in a notebook and wrote an address on a scrap of newspaper. "He will hire you to clean his house."

I stared at the paper. "Cleaning houses? No! I am an artist."

"Do you want to eat?" Marie threw the words at me, and I took the address.

It was the end of March, and I searched for work in art studios or photography shops in every neighborhood. I came back to the bakery each night and collapsed on my bed. I had arranged my easel by the one window in the room, but I was too tired to paint or even sketch. I finished Marie's coupon book and spent her francs and then knocked on the door of 14 Avenue Félix Faure. I asked for Monsieur Boudreaux and said Marie had told me to come. MB, as I called him, was a wealthy businessman who manufactured turbines. For the month of April, I cleaned his house.

17

Holy shit! I spent so much time trying to establish contact with Emilie's daughter, only to be told Emilie had died and that she, Yvette, basically had no interest in learning about the past relationship between her mother and my father. And meanwhile, here, hidden in almost-plain-sight is Emilie's record of that time. I recognize the streets and squares she mentions. Paris has always been my default city in France, but I spent enough time in Nice to remember the places Emilie referred to. *Le Cours Saleya...Baie des Anges...Place Rossetti...Vieux Nice...and the Promenade des Anglais.* I walked most of these streets and squares during my visits to Nice in the past. The most recent being five years ago. The memoir paints vivid images of her life in 1944 but no mention of Dad. Early spring of 1944. Before D-Day. I know from family lore that he served in Italy before landing in the south of France. He must have been in Europe during the period she wrote about, but they hadn't met yet.

I can feel my skin crawl, recalling a conversation with Dad last fall before he went downhill so rapidly. We sat in the carriage house playing cards, and he suddenly stopped.

"I have to give you something," he said.

"Sure. What?"

He waved away my question and rose from the recliner with difficulty.

"Let me," I said.

Dad ignored my offer of help and shuffled to a cabinet in the kitchen, where he withdrew a leather pouch. I knew it held a spare set of keys to this apartment. He handed them to me. "You'll need these." He sat and gave me a sly smile.

I took them and eyed my father. Then, gently, "Dad, I already have the keys." Did he forget that I spent a good amount of time there over the years? Had his mental ability deteriorated that badly? DJ had questioned, that day in Lloyd's office, if Dad was in his "right mind" when he changed his will. He never gave me the slightest hint that his memory was slipping away.

Dad had stared at me as if puzzled, then his face cleared. "That's right. But you might need a spare set. Well...I just want to make sure you can get into the apartment."

"No problem, Dad. All good."

"Now you remember, the apartment is yours when I die. And everything in it."

"Dad—"

"DJ will have the house but you...you always liked the apartment best. And I'm not going to be around forever, you know." He chuckled.

My eyes stung. I wasn't ready yet to face the inevitable.

He retrieved his cards. "Who's winning?" He peered at me over his reading glasses.

"You are."

"Ha. As usual," he teased.

Everything in it. At the time, I thought he meant the furniture. He knew the memoir was locked away in the drawer.

That night, months ago, we played a while longer, then he removed his glasses and studied me thoughtfully. "I'm glad you decided to teach French."

Was he telling me something? Was he telling me to read the memoir? And then what?

I glance at my watch. Light in the kitchen is dimming, the sun shifting lower in the sky. I weigh my options. Leave the city now, go home, and eat dinner. Or I could read a few more pages. My eyes are tired, but I'm wide awake, the most alert I've been since Dad passed.

18

My artist's hands were rough and red from lye soap. I cleaned the foyer, four rooms on the first floor, and three bedrooms on the second floor. I spent my time dusting furniture, polishing silverware, scrubbing floors, and washing the dishes from parties MB gave. Renée, the housekeeper, very bossy and nearly deaf, made me scour the hallway tile until "one of MB's fine lady friends could eat off it." In 1944, in Nice, people were starving, and here there was champagne, caviar, fruits, and cheeses. I could have gotten fat just breathing in the house. I ate whatever food was left over for dinner—bread and cheese, foie gras or roast potatoes, or a cutlet. Sometimes there was a stew.

Renée would not raise the heat in the rooms I cleaned because she did not want to "waste MB's fuel." I listened to her dreadful stories about past lovers, and I was amazed at the amount of time *she* wasted.

Every day MB stopped in whatever room I was cleaning.

"Emilie, eh?" Monsieur Boudreaux was very fat, and his huge, bald head seemed to pop up out of his collar. His body would have made two normal size humans.

"Monsieur?"

"I must go out." He wore calfskin gloves that caught on the diamond ring on his little finger.

"*Oui*, monsieur."

"*Au revoir*, eh?" Halfway out the door, Monsieur Boudreaux stopped. "Have you seen Marie this week, eh?"

"*Non*, monsieur."

"Ah. When you do, tell her I asked for her. She is a very special friend, eh?"

"*Oui*, monsieur." I wondered what he meant by 'special friend.' His smile when he said this made me fear for her. But I knew Marie always managed to take care of herself, and I was grateful to her for this job.

So, my days were spent working at 14 Avenue Félix Faure, and in the evening, I went to my cold room above the bakery. Sometimes I sketched the beaches along the Mediterranean I visited with Maman and Papa as a child. It kept me warm.

But at the end of April, I was in trouble. MB organized a party for his important business friends, and Renée gave me extra francs to work. I had never served company or waited on customers, and I felt self-conscious in the black dress I had to wear. I rolled the waistband to shorten it and tied a white apron around me. My job was to carry trays with caviar on bread into the drawing-room from the kitchen.

My mind was distracted by Philippe, who was hired to serve champagne, and I tipped the platter and dropped one piece of bread. I wished to scrape the caviar off the floor and eat it. Who could blame me? Caviar in 1944 was unheard of. He laughed at me. "You should serve with your eyes open." He had already taken advantage of some "spilled" champagne.

I ignored him and lifted my tray higher. In the drawing-room, German officers in their gray-green uniforms, with black boots shining, drank and chatted with French women in bold make-up and expensive dresses. If everyone froze, I could have painted this scene.

Light from the chandelier threw a rosy glow over the room. Except for the German uniforms, the colors were bright, and the people animated. Outside there was a war. Inside, time stood still, and men and women laughed as though the party could go on forever.

Music floated around the room. A man in a tuxedo played a grand piano, and next to him, a woman sang. My sister Marie. I was surprised to find her here and decided to move around the room until I stood near the piano. I needed to say "thank you" for this job.

I approached the guests. *"Voulez-vous…?"* and held out the platter of bread and caviar.

"Emilie, eh?" Monsieur Boudreaux pushed me toward some German officers. His face was bright red, and the odor of his perspiration strong. I found myself next to a massive man who stood well above MB. My hands trembled.

"Herr Gunter. Please try my caviar. It is the best there is in France," MB said.

Without a word, the German grasped the bread and popped it into his mouth. He nodded approval, scooped several more off the tray, and turned his focus back to his lady friend.

"Smile, Emilie, eh?" Monsieur Boudreaux whispered to me.

I crossed the room and approached another group of German soldiers. *"Pardonnez-moi, messieurs."* Two of the officers twisted their necks around.

"Caviar?" I smiled and held out the tray.

A blond boy smiled back and helped himself to the food. *"Danke."* His companion leaned into me and said something in German, making his friends laugh. He reached for the caviar closest to me and allowed his hand to grasp my breast for a moment. I jumped and juggled the tray as the remaining pieces of bread fell to the floor. In horror, I backed up, right into Philippe and his tray of full glasses.

A huge crash sent the wine everywhere, splashing onto Philippe and me and the German soldiers. Monsieur Boudreaux stepped forward to calm his irritated guests. They were no longer laughing. Embarrassed, I started to cry and stumbled out of the room. I hid in the bathroom, trying to wipe the champagne from my soaking dress and apron. When I finally opened the door, I found Marie standing outside, smoking.

"So, you don't like my singing?" she asked.

"Stop, Marie." I was afraid to face MB.

"*Ma petite*, there are easier ways to bring a party to a quick end."

"I feel so stupid."

"You shouldn't. They are boors, these friends of Monsieur Boudreaux," said Marie.

"And the women?"

My sister shrugged. "There are many *Niçoises* who will do anything for money."

I did not want to say what I was thinking. "You must be careful."

Marie smiled. "I am always careful." She took a small comb from a handbag and ran it through my hair, pinning and adjusting limp strands. "Emilie, why don't you go home to Monaco?"

"I like my room above the bakery." I was grateful for her kindness. It was the second time that month she had come to my rescue.

"It may be difficult to keep it after tonight," Marie said.

She was right. I had to leave MB's service after the dreadful episode. Besides, Renée had a niece who needed work. I accepted the week's wages, plus the few extra francs I'd been promised for the party. That night in my room above the bakery, I counted my little bundle of francs. Not only would I have to forget about buying the paintbrushes I'd seen in an art shop on Boulevard Victor Hugo, I could not pay the next week's rent. Soon I would be walking through the city and begging for work again. I cried myself to sleep. When I lost my job at MB's, I was heartsick and scared. But then Victoire invited Guy and me for dinner. Guy was the most talented artist in our class at Art and Design School, and when he moved back to Nice, I saw him from time to time at Victoire's.

That night so much changed for me. The brutality of the war and the arrival of the Allies became real. On my way to Victoire's, I ran into the Place Masséna, the square across from MB's house. German soldiers were on patrol and Gestapo agents, in their Citroëns, cruised the streets.

Victoire and Jean had gotten a bottle of wine, a cheap piece of beef, and some fresh fruit from Victoire's mother—she had a farm in La Turbie—and they wanted to celebrate. By the middle of the evening, Jean was drunk.

He pulled Victoire onto his lap. "Give me a kiss."

"Jean, *arretez*," said Victoire. She was embarrassed and pushed him away.

"Have some fruit," she said to me as Jean emptied the last drop of wine into his glass.

"Guy, when the Germans are gone, we can be men again. And get the respect we deserve." Jean's politics were mostly self-serving since he often attacked both Vichy and the resistance equally. Jean sided with Jean.

"We are men now," said Guy.

"*Les batards!* They take our food, our women, our jobs. What kind of a man stands for that?" Jean pounded the table, and Victoire rescued the dishes.

Jean had worked on and off since the occupation delivering goods from the Port Lympia in Nice to businesses in the city proper in an old *camionette* that he owned with his brother. When the truck was running, and petrol was available, and not too watered down, they managed to make ends meet. At other times, Jean and his brother spent their days in a café. He was a short man, barely inches taller than Victoire, but still a bully.

"It's just a matter of time," said Guy with confidence. "Patience, Jean."

This was strange, coming from a man who was famous for his impatience at Art School or when he passionately attacked the Vichy government. I wondered then if he knew something the rest of us did not.

"*Je suis un français*. I have no patience." Jean rose from the table and grabbed Victoire.

"We should go," I said.

"I'll walk with you," Guy said.

"It was a wonderful meal. *Merci*." I forced myself to kiss Jean goodbye; it was difficult to avoid his wet lips on my cheeks.

On the street, I took Guy's arm; it was reassuring to feel his firm muscles. He could have been a farm laborer like his brothers but chose to become an artist.

"Poor Victoire," I said.

"*Oui*, poor Victoire. But poor Jean, too."

"How can you say that? Victoire has to live with his moods and his drunkenness."

"Jean is a fool, yes. But like many other *Niçoises* now. He is blind. He can't see what is happening."

"What *is* happening?" I asked.

He scanned the street. "The Allies are going to land in the north soon," he said quietly.

"We've heard that rumor for months."

"I have friends. They know." We continued along the Promenade des Anglais and stood for a moment with the Mediterranean below us. The water rolling off the smooth pebbles on the beach made a clattering noise.

"Tell no one," he said. A black Citroën, anticipating the approaching curfew, cruised down the boulevard.

"*Je comprends.*"

"Emilie, many people are losing their lives every day because of secrets like this."

The bitterness in his voice stunned me. "Guy?"

"L'Hermitage."

We had all heard reports about Nazi atrocities at the Gestapo interrogation center in Nice. But something else was bothering Guy. That he was thin and pale could not be blamed on his diet. Everyone in Nice was thinner. I had not noticed how hard his face had become. He reminded me of dockworkers in Marseille I saw years ago. They were still youthful, but their features were aged by dangerous work. Guy looked the same, like a hunted animal. When I asked if he was painting much, he shook his head. He began to weep.

"Guy, please tell me."

He blew his nose. "They killed her."

"Who?"

"Bibi."

Bibi had been Guy's girlfriend at art school. Everyone knew he loved her more than she would ever love him. So, for the last two years, they were just friends and worked together at a photography studio retouching prints. She was beautiful, soft, and light as air.

"Nazi bastards."

I was astonished. Who would want to kill such a gentle person? Who could she possibly threaten?

"She was *une résistante.*"

Bibi? Who always seemed bored with talk of the war or politics of any kind?

Guy answered my unspoken question. "Just a few of us knew. She was caught in a raid on a house in Beaulieu. They were printing an underground newspaper."

The words tumbled out of him.

"There were photographs of German military installations along the coast. Bibi and the others tried to destroy them, but it was too late. There was a traitor in the group."

"They were arrested?"

"Five of them were brought to L'Hermitage for interrogation."

"Oh, Guy, I am so sorry." I read about French *résistants* who smuggled a truck full of school children out of the city. They had traveled ten kilometers when the Gestapo found them, shot the driver, and dragged the children back to Nice. I wondered where they found the courage.

"They tortured her for days, but she never gave in. She told them nothing." Guy closed his eyes tightly. "They plunged her hands into boiling water and laughed as strips of her skin melted off the bones."

I breathed deeply to keep from throwing up. "Before you said 'us'."

"*Oui. Je suis un résistant aussi.*" He was one of them. Guy caught my arm. "Are you still looking for work?"

"Why?"

"There is an opening now at the art shop retouching photographs."

I was afraid to sleep for fear of a nightmare about the Nazis. My heart felt broken and my body heavy, and I wanted to do nothing but stay in my bed and cry. That night, the forthcoming arrival of the

Allies became real. I had no idea that when they landed, my life would never be the same.

19

Still no mention of Dad. Poor Emilie. So young. About my age when I graduated from college. My greatest challenge at Columbia had been finding time to study and pass classes while partying; Emilie was trying to stay alive and support herself in war torn Europe with the Nazi presence a constant danger. She mentions the arrival of the Allies. That means Dad.

I flip to the next page of the memoir. There is a bookmark, a small group photo. I hold it up to the light, but it is still difficult to make out the faces. I remember seeing a magnifying glass in Dad's desk.

I return to his room and sit on the bed, carefully scrutinizing the picture. Half a dozen young people, probably in their early twenties, laughing, arms around each other. I recognize Emilie from the photo among the souvenirs. She is wedged between a short, plump woman—Victoire?—and a thin, frowning man. Possibly Guy. On the other side of the man is a tall, blond woman staring off as though she's in another world. It might be Bibi. Two other men hold up papers as if showing them to the photographer. My imagination runs a little wild. Could they be graduation degrees? Their clothing indicates warm weather, the background an outdoor square with columns. People walking behind them appear as tiny figures. I turn the photo over.

Someone, probably Emilie, has written "Monaco, 1943." How carefree they all look. Emilie arrived in Nice in January of 1944. This might have been the previous spring or summer. They could be a group of my students.

It's night now, and I lay back on the pillow and close my eyes, partly to rest them and partly to visualize what life was like for Emilie in Nice. As much as I am yearning to understand Dad's past, I have to admit that I am now equally curious about this woman.

My cell phone rings. I look at the caller ID.

"Hi Drew. What's up?"

"Hey Kate." He paused. "So, like, Nate and I forgot to ask you this afternoon..."

I glance at the memoir, eager to continue reading. "Yes?"

"We're wondering if it's okay for us to...uh...stay at the...uh...your apartment in the city next weekend?"

Neither of the twins had ever asked this of me before. My first instinct is to barricade the door and protect Dad. And, bizarrely, Emilie. As though the two of them only exist in this space that housed the past. Of course, that's ridiculous. Dad would want me to allow his grandsons to enjoy a weekend here. I glimpse the picture of Emilie and her friends. Then I think of Nate and Drew and their girlfriends.

"Sure. Your Dad has a set of keys."

"Thanks."

"And Drew?"

"Yeah?"

"Leave the place in one piece?" I add lightly.

He laughs. "Got it."

"It's nice that you're moving into the carriage house. Grandpa would have liked that," I say.

"Yeah." His voice is shaky. I'm surprised to hear my devil-may-care, easygoing nephew sound emotionally vulnerable when his grandfather is mentioned. After a beat, he says, "Grandpa...we...we talked about stuff."

We talked about stuff. This is news. Somehow, I never pictured Dad and Drew having a heart-to-heart. But why not? It's one more surprising revelation about my father and the ones he loved.

"That's great Drew. I'm happy to hear it," I say.

"Yeah. Photography. My painting. We were gonna take a trip to MOMA. Just the two of us."

In the silence, I can hear a nonverbal shrug.

"But then he...got a lot sicker."

"I'm sorry."

"It's okay. I like to remember him in the carriage house. Living there'll feel like I'm, you know..."

"Close to him."

"Yeah."

This is the most intimate conversation I've ever had with my nephew. It rattles me. Maybe almost as much as finding Emilie's memoir. Nevertheless, there is a warmth rising in my chest from hearing Drew's confidence. Like something is opening there. "Hang on to those beautiful memories, Drew."

"Will do, Aunt Kate. You too, okay?"

"I'm doing my best."

20

On May 1, everything changed again.

Victoire came to my room above the bakery very early. Her eyes sparkled, and her laugh was easy. "I have wonderful news."

"*Oui?*"

"Monsieur Carné is coming back to Nice."

Monsieur Carné is a famous filmmaker who began work on his latest movie, a passionate love story of 19ᵗʰ-century Paris, last year. He filmed crowd scenes and interiors at the Victorine Studio outside Nice in August 1943. Then the Germans closed down the production and ordered Carné back to Paris. Victoire was *une figurante*, an extra, in the street scenes about life on the Parisian Boulevard du Temple. She was ecstatic being in the company of such famous actors as Arletty and Jean-Louis Barrault.

"The Germans have allowed him to come back to Nice. We are going to act," she told me.

"Victoire! I am not an actress. I could photograph the setting, but get up in front of a camera? *Non.*"

Victoire ignored my protests. "You need a job. I am here to rescue you. We are going to the casting call for Monsieur Carné's movie."

"Guy said there was an opening at the art shop. I will ask him about a job there."

Victoire ignored my protest and pulled me to my feet. "We must hurry."

"I don't want to be in his movie."

"Do you want to pay your rent?" Victoire asked.

I did need a new job immediately. "For one day. How much will I earn?"

"Hurry!" she said. "Enough of cleaning houses and painting buttons."

Victoire was an average artist. She had always wanted to perform, and the movie was her chance to play a role. Besides, she had lost her job at the button factory.

We waited in line for hours. Two Gestapo agents stood behind the casting director—hundreds of actors were needed for the street scenes. There were many in Nice out of work, and so the line wound through the entire movie set. Every once in a while, the line stopped while one of the agents handed the casting director a file.

In front of us, a young man said, "They are checking lists. *C'est rien*. The Germans are making sure that a percentage of the actors come from local unions they want to reward."

I understood: reward for collaboration. The casting director motioned to the next person in line, and the column surged forward. A French *gendarme* thrust a baton into the crowd of extras, pushing people back.

"Swine. They act like that to impress *les boches*," the young man said. "The Germans are uneasy whenever a crowd of French people gathers. This *flic* knows he has to keep us in line. Last week the *Maquis* struck outside Tourettes-sur-Loup. The Nazis should be the anxious ones."

I was next in line, my papers ready—identity card, ration book, work permit.

"*Le nom,*" the casting director said.

"Emilie Caronne."

"*L'addresse.*"

"18 Rue de Rivoli."

"*Quel âge avez-vous?*"

"Twenty-one."

"*Les papiers d'identité.*"

I offered my identity card, and she studied me for a moment.

"*Trés jolie.* You will make a lovely *ingénue.*"

"*Merci.*" I took the receipt required to pick up my costume. I enjoyed the atmosphere. I would get paid for having a good time!

Victoire was upset. "What does she know?" She tossed her head at the casting director.

"What are you?" I asked.

"A peasant." She stuffed her receipt in her pocket. "I should be *une prostituée!*"

A thousand extras in costumes from the 1800s filled the streets of the set. I was entranced. In the middle of the crowd, I saw a circus! Jugglers tossed everything from pins to fruit, a weightlifter adjusted his barbells, and the tightrope walker fiddled with a cable. Suddenly a wave of energy moved through the crowd.

"What is it?" I asked.

"Monsieur Carné," said Victoire.

He was short, and I could see the top of his head.

"*Attention, attention,*" he called out. Monsieur Carné climbed onto the platform next to his star, Jean-Louis Barrault, and introduced the assistant director, Miguel. "Welcome to our *little* movie," he said, and we all laughed at his joke. For the next few weeks, he would use the thousand extras for all exterior scenes on the "Boulevard du Temple."

"He doesn't seem unpleasant," I murmured, remembering Victoire's stories from her first experience on Carné's set.

"Wait until someone makes a mistake." Victoire waved her hand dismissively.

Our first day was exciting but tedious. By the middle of May, we had spent days moving up and down the boulevard pretending to have real conversations with other actors. Sometimes we were told to enter one of the fake storefronts that lined the street. I felt foolish at first, but soon I began to enjoy the spirit of the movie. When Miguel blew his whistle, we stopped and stepped aside for a horse-drawn carriage to pass. The extras rehearsed this moment for hours, then on to another event in Carné's story. The days passed slowly, and I began to understand why extras were paid. The sun was hot, and the heavy costumes made us perspire.

At pauses in the filming, Victoire and I ate bread and cheese she brought from home. They sold black-market sandwiches of bread, butter, cheese, and ham, but even one would cost a whole day's work. Then Victoire picked up an apple from a plate of food that was part of the scenery. Carné had warned us not to eat any of the props on the set. It was cruel to tempt us with delicious-looking bread and fruit.

She passed it to me, and I was about to take a bite when a man dressed as a clown struck my hand. "Don't eat that," he said, "It would make you very ill. To keep us from eating the food, Carné injects it with acid."

I dropped the apple.

The days dragged on with Miguel urging us to go from scene to scene quickly before the sun set. Being a photographer, I knew how important it was for Carné to have the correct light to capture the images on film. One day Victoire poked me. "*La! See!*"

Arletty, the fashion model and star of French cinema, was escorted down the Boulevard. She was magnificent! I saw her in other movies, and each time she made me cry. Barrault was a celebrated mime, and together their work was fantastic.

Some days we occupied seats in the upper gallery of a theater and acted like unruly Parisian spectators. The gallery was filled, with some actors jammed so tightly together we sat two to a seat. The novelty of moviemaking wore off after filming the same actions again and again, and I thought about taking pictures of the celebrities on the set. Since the camera would draw too much attention to itself, I decided to sketch caricatures of the actors in the various scenes.

Once, the theater went black. The action and music stopped. At first, there was silence as we sat in the darkness, followed by shouting from the balcony and Carné demanding, "Light!"

"A fuse has blown or the cables on the generator have worn out," someone said. "Everything breaks down these days."

A sudden explosion of light was greeted by cheers from the gallery.

"Miguel? Drop the curtain! Miguel!" Carné screamed.

Miguel entered, trying to calm Carné. Two German soldiers escorted Henri, the production manager, across the stage and out the door of the Victorine Studio.

Someone said, "I heard he is a Jew. It's hard to keep something like that quiet."

I had a new admiration for Carné. He risked the Gestapo interrogation center if he hired or hid Jews. Miguel tried to move forward, pushing the actors back on stage, but it was no use. Everyone had lost heart.

Victoire and I felt rich from our weeks of filming, so we ate at La Ronde. Thin stew, bread, and half a bottle of wine. I remember when the stew was full of meat and vegetables in 1943. By 1944 it was mostly water and potatoes. The door opened, and some men with caps pulled low over their foreheads came inside. I barely gave them notice until I heard my name. The voice was rough. "Emilie." It was Guy. I had not seen him since the night of Victoire's dinner. He was unshaven and looked tired.

"Where have you been?" Victoire asked.

He said, "Working."

Victoire told him about Carné's film.

"Carné stayed in France while other filmmakers left. Monsieur Carné is too friendly with the Vichy government. Maybe the Germans are financing his pictures," he said.

I tried to chew the lump of bread in my mouth, and then I felt angry. It was a movie. There was nothing political about it.

As if he could read my mind, Guy said, "Everything is political these days, even films."

He sounded so bitter.

Nice buzzed with talk of an Allied invasion. It was false gossip, according to the Germans. More troops patrolled the streets and marched down the Promenade every day. There were more of them on the movie set too. A ring of Gestapo agents became a permanent fixture. I still sketched scenes of the actors in costume and sometimes sold them for a franc or two. I would not go back to cleaning houses.

At the end of May, it was time to film the Carnivale scene. Victoire and I were ladies of the night with black half masks and red satin dresses. All of the extras laughed and shouted and threw confetti like a mob of revelers. There were times I could hardly keep my feet on the ground as we were swept along. I felt anxious.

Victoire complained, "There is too much pushing and shoving. Someone will get hurt." The light was fading, and Miguel frantically blew his whistle and directed us this way and that.

We took a break, and I sat on a bench and massaged my feet and began to sketch. I saw Arletty and Barrault rehearse a scene with another actress. I overheard Arletty say, "...every day...and even at night, all the nights I spent with someone else, all those nights I was with him." Even today, as I write this, my eyes fill up. Much later, I came to understand what the words really meant to me.

Miguel blew his whistle. It was time to start again, but two voices were shouting from somewhere down the street. A boy dressed as a clown climbed onto the shoulders of a circus strongman to report to us.

"What's going on?" everyone asked.

"It's a fight," he said. "Two men are hitting each other."

I did not know how it happened, but hundreds of extras turned into a mob. Half of the people ran forward toward the argument, and the rest went in the opposite direction. I pushed against the panicked crowd. Victoire's hair had come undone, and her skirt was ripped. She was clinging to a pole attached to the tent of the fortune teller.

"Victoire!" I yelled.

German soldiers appeared from everywhere and stormed onto the boulevard—beating, shoving, and driving us back up the avenue. I shouted to Victoire again, but the shrieking of the troops and the extras drowned out everything else. The Germans were outnumbered at least twenty to one, but some began to shoot into the crowd while others were slashing at us with batons. A number of actors, protected behind their Carnivale masks, had the courage to grab pieces of timber that held the set together and attacked the soldiers.

I hid behind a café storefront and could see Victoire still in the shadow of the fortune teller's tent. I pushed through the crowd and tore at the fake wall of a restaurant that blocked my way. The flimsy wood of the roof collapsed. A German soldier spun around and swung his baton as Victoire stood up to meet me and struck her face. A line of blood ran from her left cheekbone to her mouth. Her eyes were wide with shock, and she sagged to the ground. I screamed.

I couldn't let Victoire die. I had to save her. Without thinking of my own safety, I threw myself on top of her, my face buried in her stomach, my heart throbbing. I prayed, waiting for the soldier to hit me too.

Then a masked Pierrot picked up a wooden beam and knocked the German to the ground. He bent down to help me lift Victoire as the soldier reached for his gun.

"*Non!*" I shrieked, and the Pierrot lunged at the soldier, slapping his gun to the ground. Then he climbed on top of the German and strangled the soldier until he stopped struggling.

"Is he dead?" I couldn't move, I was dizzy, my vision blurred. Happy the German was dead but sick to my stomach.

Hurry!" The masked Pierrot picked Victoire off the ground and carried her. I looked back at the German soldier. He was still.

I knew Victoire should have been in a hospital, but there was no time to get her back to Nice. The Pierrot carried her to a doctor who had a private clinic in his home a block from the Victorine Studio. He stitched the cut. Thankfully, the German soldier missed her eye, but her beautiful face was badly damaged.

Our Pierrot disappeared as soon as we placed Victoire on the emergency operating table. I had no time to even thank him. We spent the night in the clinic and went back to Victoire's apartment in the early morning in the back seat of the doctor's ancient automobile.

The riot had ended as actors moved into the streets surrounding the studio. Later, word spread that over a hundred people had been seriously hurt from gunshots or from injuries, and no one seemed to know why it started. With the set destroyed, Carné went to Paris to finish filming interiors since he had enough film of the Boulevard scenes to complete his movie.

Jean appeared at the apartment and glared at Victoire's swollen face colored purple and blue. Blood stained her red satin gown.

"What am I supposed to do with her?" Jean had spent a long night unloading cargo at the Nice docks. I wondered if he was working for the German military.

"She needs rest and quiet."

"I told her that film was trouble. You stay with her."

"*Non*, I must find work."

Jean forced himself to look at Victoire. "This should take care of things." He threw two hundred francs on the bed, like a customer paying for a prostitute.

"Where are you going?" I asked.

"I'll stop by later," he said, but I knew he was lying.

I was afraid to be alone with Victoire. She was restless and moaned in her sleep.

The doctor said to expect some fever. He gave me a sedative to keep her quiet and salve for the stitches. I watched her breathing. What if the cut became infected?

"Emilie." Victoire moaned.

"*Ma petite*, I'm here."

Her eyes searched the room. "Jean?"

"He was here before."

She settled into a deep sleep. My stomach was a dull ache, but I was too exhausted to move. There would be time to eat later. Soon Victoire was sipping broth from a spoon I held to her lips. She touched her tongue to the liquid and sucked some into her mouth like a kitten with a dish of milk. It was painful.

"We need money. We have the francs from Jean..." I had already explained his leaving as kindly as I could. Victoire was not fooled. "...and what we have left from the movie." It was not enough.

Victoire asked me to move into her apartment. It meant giving up my room and the rent and also that Victoire was not hoping for Jean's quick return.

21

I awake with a start. It's seven a.m. My body, cramped and clammy, is still in my clothes from yesterday. I scan the room. Dad's apartment. Dad's bedroom, my bedroom last night. I roll over onto something hard, poking me in the back. I retrieve the memoir from where it had gotten tangled in the covers when I fell asleep last night. I read well into the evening, too fascinated to stop until ten o'clock. By then, I was too drained to handle the drive home and opted to spend the night here. I glance at the bookmark—the picture of Emilie and her friends—I'd placed in the memoir, and the last pages come flooding back. Emilie and Victoire at the Victorine Studio on the movie set.

I've studied and taught twentieth-century French history and culture and recognized the movie in the memoir. Carné's *Les Enfants du Paradis: Children of Paradise*. I know its history. Epic romantic drama. Made during the German occupation of France. The story of a beautiful courtesan and the four men who loved her.

I know I have a copy of the film somewhere at home. I dress quickly, hurry to my car, and join the line of traffic to the Lincoln Tunnel, Emilie's memoir tucked safely in my bag.

"Hope I'm not calling too early," I say to Nancy in between bites of toast.

"We've been up for a while. You wouldn't believe it, but DJ and I take a long walk each morning through the neighborhood."

"Really? That's..."

"Surprising?" Nancy chuckles. "DJ has always avoided exercise. That was one of his problems. But now...?" Nancy pauses.

"Well, good for you. DJ's going to get healthy in spite of himself."

We laugh together. It feels good. "So...can I speak to him?"

Nancy hesitates, still wary about my upsetting DJ, about our history. "Is it important?"

"A small matter. I'd like to get the combination to a safe in Dad's apartment. I've been cleaning out some of his things there."

Nancy sighs, apparently relieved. It *was* a small matter.

"Hold on."

I sip my coffee, now lukewarm. I realized on my drive back to New Jersey that the last place I hadn't searched in Dad's apartment was a small safe in his living room. Who knew if it held anything of importance? But given what I'd discovered in the locked drawers of his desk, I have to check it out too. I am a woman on a mission, energized. Focused.

"Hey, sis. What's up?"

DJ hadn't called me "sis" in years. "You're sounding chipper. Must be that early morning walk."

"Yeah," he grumbled. "So what's this about a combination?"

"I'm working my way through the apartment. Going through Dad's things."

"Find anything interesting?" DJ asks.

Do I detect a note of uneasiness? Is DJ anxious about what I might find? Hidden secrets. If only he knew. I wish I could divulge the existence of the memoir because I have an impulse to share my discovery with my brother, but this is a delicate time in our relationship—our hearts are slowly healing, both physically and emotionally. I need to keep Emilie to myself. A part of me is happy and relieved, possessive about my find. The other part is guilty. There will be time later, I tell myself, to share everything. Assuming his heart can take it.

"The usual. Clothes, desk supplies, pairs of magnifiers."

"Sounds like him, all right." DJ laughs. "Predictable. You could always count on Dad. No surprises there."

Except for Emilie, I want to add. DJ doesn't appear to recognize the incongruity in his assertion. "Right. I have the combination to his safe somewhere, but I can't find it," I say.

"Got a pen? Here it is."

DJ gives me the numbers I need. "Let me know what's in it. I'm curious," he adds quickly.

"Have you ever been in the safe?"

DJ hesitates. "Only once. Long ago. I was in the apartment sometime in the late eighties. I had some papers he had to sign, and he told me to meet him there. So, he signed the papers and asked me if I'd seen his will. I figure it's in the safe at the family house but as long as I'm in the apartment, what the hell, I'll check the safe there. He went into the bathroom, and I started to dial the combination. But I didn't even finish before he came out and confronted me."

"What do you mean, he confronted you?"

"He said stuff like, 'What are you doing? That's my private property. Nothing to do with Whitman Textiles.' Etc. Etc."

"Wow. Doesn't sound like Dad." I am more curious than ever to see what he kept in the safe. "Kind of like he had something…"

"Hidden. Yeah." DJ sighs. "Maybe he wasn't as predictable as I thought he was."

We chat for a few more minutes, and I hang up. DJ's memory triggers my own recollection. Dad and I in the apartment, sitting in the kitchen with my ex, Terry, the three of us having a glass of wine before a Broadway show. *Les Misérables*. Dad scanning a letter—at the time, I didn't question his receiving mail at the apartment—Terry telling us a story about some event at the university. Dad smiling and nodding, as though paying attention, though, thinking back, he wasn't. He walked into the living room and said he'd be right back. I heard him at the safe while Terry rambled on. When Dad returned, coat in hand, he glanced at me and smiled. "Just doing a little business," he'd said.

I spend the rest of the morning rummaging through boxes of stuff I'd squirreled away in the guest bedroom closet when I moved into the condo several years ago. I have a copy of *Les Enfants du Paradis* somewhere. I should have thrown away, or given away, most of this. An extra set of dishes that was a gift from Terry's aunt, clothes from the 1990s that I will never wear, boxes of files from classes I taught years ago. In one of them, I find maps of France from trips taken during the past two decades. I flip through them and find one of Nice. I put it aside, but so far, no film.

After a day on campus, I am ready to pick up where I left off. In my eagerness to read the memoir, I pick up a fast-food chicken Caesar salad on the way home from work. It and a glass of wine are tonight's dinner. I drop onto the sofa, surround myself with pillows and my meal, and spread out the map of Nice I found this morning, locating the places Emilie mentioned. I see Le Cours Saleya and the Baie des Anges and trace the warren of alleys that make up Vieux Nice where Emilie's sister Marie sang in a café. Now able to trace Emilie's whereabouts, and maybe even Dad's, I open the memoir.

22

June 6, 1944. My memory of that day is very strong.

Victoire was healing well. She moved around the apartment and ate a little but was depressed. I had to ask Guy if the job was still open at the art shop where he worked. We were almost out of money, and I was worried. Nice was a more dangerous place since arrests were frequent now, and people were thrown into the back of a truck or a Citroën and never heard from again. Though I had nothing to hide and my identity card was in order, I was still nervous when I passed German soldiers on the street.

I walked three kilometers to Zazou's Art Studio. I loved Victoire, but some days I could not tolerate being imprisoned in the apartment. After thirty minutes, I stopped in front of 33 Rue Berlioz. I almost smelled the paints and felt the brushes in the shop window. An old man with thick glasses and wild white hair stared back at me through the window.

"*Allez-vous!* We are leaving early today," he said.

"I would like to see Guy."

"Why?"

"It is personal business."

"He is not here." The old man went to the door and hung the closing sign.

"I need to see him!"

"*Non!*" he yelled and turned off the lights. He pulled a shade down over the glass. It was two o'clock in the afternoon. I panicked because Victoire was depending on me. I had to beg for a job.

"Please!" I knocked on the window.

He took off his glasses, opened the door, and brought his face close to mine. Then he walked to the back of the shop and called out for Guy.

"Emilie!" Guy was as thin as before, but now he was alive, his eyes full of confidence.

"I am so happy to see you," I said.

"I heard about the riot on the film set. I'm glad you escaped unharmed."

I could not help myself. I broke down crying. "Victoire was beaten, and her face is destroyed. We have no money, and I must find a job."

He led me down a steep staircase to the basement, where he had a darkroom set up with developing equipment, pans of chemicals, a vat of water, and a clothesline with pins to clip drying pictures. I inhaled the sharp smell of the chemicals. Guy switched off the white light bulb, and the room glowed red. I was thrilled to be once more in a darkroom. I felt at home.

Seeing Guy was like finding a guardian to take care of us. Someone strong and capable. I had never thought of him that way before.

"How is Victoire?" he asked.

"She is healing but she is not the same Victoire."

He offered to speak with Monsieur Zazou about a job for me. I watched him develop photographs, envious of the time he had to spend with the equipment. I will never forget how he leaned into me.

"Remember this date."

I wasn't sure of the date. "June 5?"

"*Non!* It is June 6. The Allies are in France."

"*Mon Dieu!* How do you know?"

"Word has come through channels." Guy pinned a few prints onto the drying line. "Once the Nazis know that they are in danger, the crackdown will begin."

"When will that happen?"

He shrugged. "In a few days, maybe tonight."

I looked at the drying pictures of the Nice docks with German cargo ships unloading tanks and supplies.

"What are the photographs for?"

"The Allies need to know German military strength and locations of bunkers and mines along the coast. For when they land here in the south."

"Guy, will that really happen?" I clapped my hands in joy, and Guy picked me up, swinging me around as if I were a child.

"Monsieur Zazou, is he...?"

"Yes, he's one of us. We are everywhere."

"You are a brave man, Guy."

"I love my country. I loved Bibi," he said.

Monsieur Zazou had agreed to hire me part-time to take inventory and develop photographs, even though there was very little business. I was employed in the afternoons four days a week. In the mornings, I forced Victoire to walk with me to the Place Masséna and sit on a bench and breathe in the perfume of the azaleas, camellias, and hydrangeas. She would not go out in public unless she wrapped a scarf around her neck and face. She never looked in the mirror. The stitches had left a red ridge that ran across her left cheek, ending at the corner of her mouth.

We saw a few people cross the square. I had my camera, and the weight of it felt good in my hands. Now working at the shop, I bought film cheaply and developed it there. The afternoon light in Nice is white and brightens everything it touches. I snapped pictures of houses and the flowers in the park.

One of the houses was MB's. The front door of No. 14 opened, and MB appeared in the doorway. His neck still bulged, and his head still seemed ready to pop off his shoulders. I took his picture. A second man appeared, and the long, black coat gave him away. A Gestapo agent. I was not shocked to see MB with a German agent, but I was shocked to see the fear on MB's face. They both got into a waiting Citroën and drove off.

I walked Victoire back to the apartment so she would not have to be on the street alone. Sometimes people stared at her and waiting in a queue at the market on Le Cours Saleya might send Victoire to bed weeping for the rest of the afternoon.

Since I was late, I took a shorter route to the Art Studio and stopped at a street corner. There was movement down a passage to my right. Two men ran out of a cellar door dragging a suitcase. A Citroën raced into the alley and came to a halt pinning the men against the back wall of an apartment building. I hid in the entranceway of a closed café, but I could still see the alley. One of the men emptied the suitcase on the ground and tried to burn papers while the other pulled out a gun and fired twice.

I reached for my camera and snapped pictures as four German soldiers got out of the car and rushed to the men kicking and beating them until their bodies flopped about like rag dolls. Then one of the Nazis fired a bullet into the head of each of them.

The Germans picked up the suitcase and the half-burned papers, and I turned my face to the café door and vomited on the window. I did not hear the Citroën drive away. I was no longer a bystander.

"Emilie! What were you thinking?" Monsieur Zazou exclaimed and watched Guy develop my film.

I was still sick, and my hands shook, but I had anger in the pit of my stomach. "I am a photographer. I take pictures."

Guy recognized the two dead men. "They were part of the Nice network gathering intelligence for the Allies."

"What were they carrying?" I asked.

"I don't know. Maps, reports, documents identifying other underground agents. Possibly radio transmitting codes to contact London. At least they died quickly," he said.

Guy attached the last pictures of MB to the drying line. "Who is that?"

"Monsieur Boudreaux. I cleaned his house for a few weeks."

He had heard of Monsieur Boudreaux but had no idea what he looked like. MB was a known collaborator, he said. He studied the Gestapo agent and shouted, "Kroner!" According to Guy, the Gestapo agent in charge of the Lyon region was not dead as the resistance thought but in Nice probably to supervise more arrests and interrogations.

Guy was excited. "You are a resister. Emilie, we need pictures."

"I am not part of the resistance." I was afraid after my experience with the Gestapo agents.

"I would never ask you to do something that was too dangerous," Guy said. "Do what you did today," he said. "Watch the house and see who goes in and who comes out. That will tell us much about Nazi plans."

I decided then that I would help.

For several weeks in June, I did as Guy asked and sat in the Place Masséna and watched number 14 Félix Faure to see who visited MB. Sometimes I went in the mornings and sometimes in the afternoon. I would pretend to read or sketch when German soldiers on patrol appeared. My heart would beat rapidly then. Whenever someone entered or left MB's house, I would become alert. Most days, I would see Renée or MB or delivery men come and go.

I was tired of sitting for hours day after day. Then finally, I saw a black car drive around the square and stop in front of MB's. Two men got out and went inside the house. I did not see their faces, but they were dressed in dark suits. They did not look like Gestapo agents, but I photographed them anyway. I decided to wait for a little while. In half an hour, the door to MB's house opened again, and MB stood in the doorway shaking hands with the men. All of them were smiling. As they walked to the car, the men raised their heads, and I took their picture. I rushed to the Art Studio, exhilarated with my first assignment as *une résistante*.

Guy had no idea who the two men were, but the photo would be passed on. Then he hugged me and poured a little brandy in two glasses.

I sipped the warm liquor. "I was a little afraid today."

"Of course you were. We all are. Fear keeps us careful and alive."

I ran to get home before the curfew. I was exhausted but thrilled, and the brandy wrapped me in a comfortable blanket.

When I got to Victoire's apartment, I saw Jean, drunk, twisting Victoire's arm while she tried to resist. The top half of her dress was torn.

I didn't stop to think. "Victoire!" I rushed at Jean and yanked her away from him.

"Get out of my apartment!" he shouted at me.

I knew he must be broke and homeless and needing a place to stay.

"It's not your apartment anymore." I sat Victoire on the sofa and covered her with a shawl.

I have no idea where my courage came from, but I decided our only choice was to fight back. I picked up an empty iron pot from the stove and threw it at Jean. It grazed his head, and he fell backward. I threatened to scream for the nearest policeman if he didn't leave.

"You are an ugly bitch," he told Victoire. "No one will ever touch you again."

Victoire shrieked and covered her face with her hands.

Jean stumbled out the door. "No man will want you," he yelled.

I cradled her like a baby, and she cried all night.

By the beginning of July, the Allies were slowly making their way across France, but Guy was right. There were more arrests, and people were disappearing from the streets. According to London, the invasion in the south could happen at any time. Life was more uncertain. Shops were closed, and finding food was nearly impossible. We lived on shriveled vegetables, stale bread, and the occasional piece of cheese.

Monsieur Zazou worried in those days because Guy was gone much of the time on assignments. Even with Guy gone, I was not busy in the shop since there were few customers. It was a hot July, and the apartment was uncomfortable. Victoire kept the windows closed, afraid someone might peek in and see her.

Around the first of August, Guy rushed me into the basement at Monsieur Zazou's and said the Allies would land in the south in two weeks. The resistance needed a courier to pass off intelligence to a London contact.

"Emilie! Can you do it?"

I would need to meet the woman at a certain time and place and hand her my sketch pad which would have an envelope glued to the last page. My papers were in order, and my name was not linked to any underground group or incident. I was an ideal courier. Guy told me to notice people around me and, if it felt too dangerous or I sensed a problem, to leave and go home. He kissed me and whispered, *"Vive la France."*

I waited at the dockyard at seven in the morning for a woman to meet me. "Madame Sarah," would be wearing a blue dress and a green scarf. At seven, the crews reported for work, and there would be traffic coming and going. It was a good time to disappear into a crowd if I had to.

I was to sketch on the pad and pass as an artist until my contact arrived. It was not unusual even then when the world was burning to find an early morning artist drawing scenes along the Quai des États-Unis.

A German soldier appeared. *"Nein,"* he said and waved at my drawing.

I did not know what to do. I had to stay until I met my contact. I faced away from the docks and began to draw the row of houses lining the Quai. I showed him the drawing and pointed across the street.

"Nein," he said again and reached for my pad.

My stomach tightened. Before he could grab it, I flipped to a clean sheet and began to sketch him. He stared at the paper and smiled. For ten minutes, he posed, and I drew. It was nearly eight o'clock. Where was the contact?

There was movement in the harbor. A German ship glinting in the sunlight was weighing anchor and preparing to leave. The German soldier looked over his shoulder then asked to see his portrait. I held it up to him, and a whistle blew a sharp blast.

"Mademoiselle Emilie. I have been searching for you. May I see your sketches?" The woman in blue put her hand on my shoulder.

The soldier reached out to take his picture, but a loud explosion drew his attention to the dockyard, and he seized his gun and ran down the Quai. Madame Sarah took the pad and flipped through pages pretending to study several sketches. Then she said softly, "You will want to go home and rest after your busy morning."

More explosions pulled my attention back to the pier. Without warning, the ship that had begun to move out to sea was burning.

One blast after another set the docks on fire. I felt glued to the ground as I stared at the workers panicking and running for safety, like ants scrambling back and forth. A chunk of blazing metal sailed through the air and landed on a truck at the edge of the harbor. I closed my eyes in horror as the truck and the man inside exploded.

I forced myself to cross the street and walk slowly home trying to block out the screams and sirens.

The Nazis responded to the bombing of the docks by arresting dozens of suspected resisters. Stories circulated about torture with electric shocks, crushed bones, and victims beaten senseless. It was horrible and terrifying. I wanted to talk with Guy, but he was gone with another resister. He and his comrades were very vulnerable now. The day before he left, he took a burlap sack from beneath the floorboards in the basement at the art studio. It had a Sten gun and a box of cartridges inside. For protection, he said. He spoke so confidently, but I knew keeping a gun broke German law and was punishable by death.

By the middle of August, we were desperate, hungry, and frightened. Some people ate birds and rats to stay alive. I found a small, shriveled rutabaga at the market, and I cooked it with an onion I had been saving for a special occasion. What occasion was that to be? The Allies arriving?

Victoire had lost all will to keep up her strength. I urged her to eat, but she said she was not hungry.

"I have given up hope of being liberated," she said.

"At any moment word will come that we are free." A soft knock on the door made us jump. I opened it to a man in a dirty jacket and worn pants with a day-old beard.

"Emilie Caronne?"

"Oui."

"Guy has been taken on the road from Toulon. Be careful. They were watching him and might know about you."

I shut the door and tried to breathe deeply. I cried myself to sleep over Guy and woke with swollen eyes. Every time I drifted off, I would see Bibi and then Guy being tortured. I went to visit Monsieur Zazou, and it was a frightening sight. The news about Guy had reached him, and he sat in his robe weeping and shaking his head, saying Guy's name. I put my arms around him.

Reports reached the city and spread like wildfire. Towns and villages were liberated every day. I thought of Guy and prayed for his safe return. Madame Lanvin, from upstairs, passed on rumors she heard from her nephew who worked at the Negresco Hotel. The Germans were gone, and Gestapo headquarters had been emptied. Some prisoners were sent to a transit camp on their way to Germany. Others were shot and buried, dead or alive. When Toulon and Marseille fell to the Allies, I wept and whispered my thanks over and over.

23

I'm in the morning meeting of our annual faculty retreat discussing fall class assignments, summer teaching schedules, and available travel money. I am detaching from the fray, hovering above it all, totally disengaged from my academic duties. Since I started reading the memoir, my mind is in 1944. Hard to plan a schedule for *teaching* French when I am *in* France. Emilie's story is turning my world inside out. I'm desperate to share it with someone. Anyone.

The afternoon session is no more engrossing for me: strategic planning, curricular revision, and visiting faculty. I am jittery inside like I'm having an adrenaline rush, and yet I stifle a yawn. When the department chair glances my way for feedback on his proposal for renovations to the language labs, I nod my approval. I have no idea what he's asking me. The memoir and Emilie's voice are so loud they occupy all available mental space.

When we break at the end of the day, I grab Cheryl. "How about a cup of coffee at the diner?"

She checks her watch and then studies my face.

"I need to talk," I say.

"Fine. I have an hour until I pick up the kids."

Cheryl follows me to the parking lot and says she'll meet me there. I concentrate on driving the half-mile to the restaurant and wait until we are seated and have ordered. Then, I withdraw the memoir and place it with two hands—as though it were a priceless antique, which maybe it is—on the table between us.

"What is that?" Cheryl asks.

"A memoir," I say. "By the French woman Dad left the money to."

"Huh? Where on Earth did you find that?" Cheryl gasps.

The waitress arrives with water and coffee, and I pour milk into my cup until the coffee is a caramel color. Cheryl, who drinks hers black, waits impatiently.

"Dad's New York apartment. In a locked desk drawer," I say.

She takes a sip of her coffee and tentatively reaches for the book. She flips a page. "French. Obviously. Have you read it?" she asks eagerly.

"Started on Sunday. I'm almost halfway through."

"What does she have to say?" Cheryl asks.

I take a deep breath. I've been waiting for this question all day, and a torrent of words pours from my mouth: Victoire, Jean, Guy, Marie, and Monsieur Boudreaux. The lost job, riot on Carné's movie set, the explosions at the dock, the arrival of the Allies. The details of her story are so revealing I'm getting to know Emilie in a very intimate way. I am just grateful that Cheryl is interested.

"My God, her life sounds like the History Channel," Cheryl says. "She was an extra in *Les Enfants du Paradis*? Unbelievable."

"I know, right?"

Cheryl turns a few more pages, and a photo falls out. "Who's this?"

I take the picture. Not the one of Emilie, Guy, and Victoire in Monaco but another, larger, one. A huge man stands beside a black car, flanked by two other men in long, black coats. I shiver, though the diner is warm. "Has to be Monsieur Boudreaux. Next to a Citroën, a favorite automobile for the Nazis. And those other two must be Gestapo agents. Emilie took this." No one in the picture is smiling.

"When she was working for the resistance, I guess," Cheryl says.

"Yes."

We gaze at the photo, imagining all that it implies.

"Her story is fascinating by itself," Cheryl says.

"What do you mean?"

"Even if she had no connection to your father, I'd love to know more about her."

Cheryl is right. I've been reading the memoir as Dad's daughter, looking primarily for pathways into their history. But the memoir was as much about Emilie's history.

"Look at her life. Emilie was more than your father's wartime lover. The resistance…"

"She defended Victoire against Jean's abuse with an iron pot!"

"How old was she?"

"Twenty-one," I say.

"There were a lot of young people in 1944 risking their lives for their country."

"She had nerve; I'll give her that. Scared but determined to challenge her fears."

I'm seeing Emilie in a new light. I wish I had half as much courage to show the memoir to DJ.

"Any talk of your father?"

"Not yet. The Allies have landed and are making their way east. I guess they'll be in Nice any day now."

"Guess I know what you'll be doing this evening," she says.

I finish my coffee and dig into my purse for money.

Cheryl says, "I cannot imagine reading about my father with another woman. I don't think anyone besides my mother could have put up with him."

"You want to know the truth? There's a tiny part of me that doesn't want to read any more."

"What? Why?"

"I'm terrified that he won't feel like the same father after I'm done. That the father I knew will be gone," I say.

Cheryl shakes her head and laughs at me. "Do you really think you can have this book in your possession and not finish it? Impossible."

"All I have of him now are the memories I'm clinging to. What if she's written something that changes how I see him?" I ask. And erases the heroic, glorified image that I've nurtured forever.

"Is that so bad? Maybe you'll see this new, more interesting version of your father," Cheryl says gently. "Someone...human."

"By the way, did I lend you my copy of Les Enfants du Paradis?"

24

August 29, 1944.

We awoke very early to a banging on the door. Madame Lanvin stood in the hallway in her pink bathrobe with hair standing on end. "Emilie and Victoire! *La liberté!*"

I hugged Victoire then Madame Lanvin, but she kept saying, "Come, come. There is an American soldier in the street."

Victoire and I joined the crowd forming on the Promenade des Anglais. *Niçoises* poured out of apartments and shops, cheering and hugging. An American soldier leaned against a jeep that had two more soldiers in it. Women touched and kissed them, and they laughed.

"*Bonjour, bonjour, merci,*" the soldiers said. It was probably the only French they knew.

Victoire said, "Ask about others."

"*Excusez-moi.* More soldiers coming?" English felt funny in my mouth, and I was not sure they would understand.

"American paratroopers." He pointed down the Promenade behind his jeep.

The sounds were harsh to my ears. It had been years since I heard English while sketching British visitors in Monaco. I had set myself on the square by the casino and caught them as they entered and left.

They talked, and I listened and tried to repeat what they said. By the time I began my art classes, I could have a small conversation with Professor Tate, who was British. I tried to speak English often then and studied it when I was at the Art School. But American English was different, flat, and rough like scratchy material.

"*Je ne comprends pas.*" I didn't understand what he was saying.

The soldier jumped from the jeep and flapped his arms and fell to the ground. The other soldiers laughed. This is when I learned they were "paratroopers." He grabbed me and kissed me on the lips. His beard scraped my cheek, and he smelled of cigarette smoke. I was thrilled to be in his arms.

Jeeps and trucks drove down the Promenade from the west and created a parade. Horns honked, and hundreds shouted as the soldiers waved. They were boys, the same age as the German soldiers who occupied Nice for two years. These American paratroopers had dirty uniforms and cigarettes tucked behind their ears, and all of them grinned. They seemed so confident and happy to be in Nice.

Many French girls gripped their hands and were pulled into the laps of the soldiers. I stared into the eyes of the Americans as they passed. I wondered where they had come from. One looked at me and winked! Victoire and I cried. Liberty at last.

For days we sang *La Marseillaise.* Cafés poured free champagne, and we danced and laughed. It was strange to be free and not to worry about a curfew or a black Citroën coming around the corner. Victoire was happy for the first time since the riot. A few shops reopened and passed out whatever food they could afford to give away. It was a time of generosity and kindness.

Ships appeared in the port, and soldiers and sailors poured into the city. Many stayed in Nice while others fought the Germans north and east. There was still a war on French soil. The young men stationed in Nice began to change the city. They had money and spent it on food and wine, and film.

I received a letter from Monaco. Maman was not feeling well. She was often ill from respiratory infections. I had not been home since January. Since Guy had left me his bicycle before he went on the mission to Toulon, I decided to ride to the temporary headquarters of the Free French army on Rue de la Préfecture to see if the road to Monaco was open. I was told it was clear. The day was very hot, and I rode for nearly an hour on the lower coast road through Villefranche-sur-Mer and Beaulieu. I saw many American soldiers in crowded streets and passed villas that were now occupied by the Allies.

One soldier was directing traffic by the gate of a large villa and motioned for me to stop.

"Bonjour, mademoiselle," he said. I had never seen such red hair and freckles.

"Oui?" I asked.

"Parlez-vous English?"

"Yes."

"Where are you going?" He was so friendly.

"To visit my parents in Monaco. My mother is ill."

His name was Sergeant Donelan. He explained that a sniper had been seen an hour earlier, and the army was holding up traffic.

I was not sure what to do.

"You hungry? You can eat with us."

He said I would be able to go to Monaco when he got the "all clear." He took my hand. His was strong, hard, and calloused.

I wiped the sweat off my forehead with the cuff of my blouse, and the sergeant handed me a box and smiled. There were tins and crackers and bright, hard pieces of candy. The sergeant showed me how to open a tin and handed me a spoon. I had never seen anything like the food in the cans. It was gray and brown and packed together into a cake. It wasn't very appetizing, but the men were eating it and seemed to enjoy it. I was very hungry, so I tasted a bit. I could not force much of it down. The crackers were stale, but the candy was sweet. The soldiers spoke so quickly I did not understand much. I learned that they were called "GIs."

After a while, when the road had not reopened, Sergeant Donelan took me to the infirmary, where I would be safe for a few more hours until the sniper was captured. He put my bicycle into the back seat and drove with one hand on the wheel and his left leg hanging outside the jeep. He was casual, yet he wore the expression of a determined warrior. We rode over the coast road until we arrived at a seaside hotel that was now a medical dispensary. It flew a large white flag with a red cross.

Here I would stay until I received word that it was safe to leave for Monaco.

The Sergeant told two soldiers who were "medics" to take care of me. "Give her something to eat." He called dinner "chow." There were so many English words that I did not understand. The medics were not doctors but assistants who cared for the soldiers in battle. They sat on the ground surrounded by cartons of medicines.

One man was a giant with blond curls. He pointed to himself. "Norman." Then in very bad French, he said, "*Comment vous appelez-vous?*"

"Emilie."

The other medic had brown eyes and wavy dark hair. He looked like a movie star. "My name is Daniel."

That was our first meeting. As I write his name, I see his face and smile.

I had nothing to do until the road was safe, so I helped Daniel and Norman unpack boxes. I tried to learn English words, so I repeated the names of equipment after Norman said each word: "Morphine, bandages, tape, scissors."

"What is this?" I held up a bottle.

Norman made a snoring sound. Sleeping tablets! Daniel laughed at Norman. I enjoyed Daniel's big laugh. I felt comfortable with these two men, and when I was busy, I could feel Daniel's eyes. I wanted to stare back, but I was a little unsure.

In the middle of the afternoon, they led me into the lobby of the hotel. The American and Free French soldiers were living here temporarily, each at a different end of the room. The men talked, ate, and played cards. Some were stretched out on the floor wrapped in blankets, and one was getting a haircut. When I entered, several men whistled and called out to me, but Daniel told them "to stop" in words I did not know. He took my arm and led me to a corner.

"Would you like something to eat?" His voice was so calm and his smile so kind I almost forgot how tired I was.

"Oui." I hoped this time the food would be different. The box Daniel handed me had hard biscuits, dried sausages, cheese, and chocolate. It was a feast to me.

From where I sat, I could see Daniel and Norman. While they wrote lists of the medicines, I stayed in my corner and ate the food from the box. I watched the other soldiers. They spoke and laughed loudly. They chewed their words and then spit them out. There were none I understood. I wondered what their future would be. Where would they go to fight? The Germans would not give up easily, and I knew many of these men would die trying to make them surrender.

Daniel gave me several blankets to sit on because the floor was hard and uncomfortable. Sometimes my eyes closed, and once when I

143

reopened them, I saw him staring at me. The sun was lower in the sky, and I was worried. Where would I spend the night? I could not ride to either Monaco or Nice in the dark. Late in the afternoon, Daniel and Norman left to treat French soldiers who had been shot by the sniper.

I decided to return to Nice and visit Maman and Papa later since it would be dark in another hour and the sniper was still in the hills. I wanted to say goodbye to Daniel and Norman, but I had no idea where they were. I saw my bicycle leaning against a tree up the road from the entrance to the hotel. It was dusk, and the trees on the side of the road threw shadows around me. A light breeze caused them to sway, and I imagined there were people watching me. I was afraid for the first time that day. I saw a point of light and heard voices speaking English. I realized the dot of light was a burning cigarette, and I felt safe again.

Two soldiers walked to me, talking loudly. I heard "grab her," and I froze a few meters from the bicycle. Their laugh was an ugly sound. One came close and called me "Frenchie" and said, "kiss me." I forced myself to remain calm. I was certain a jeep or a truck would come by soon, so I pretended to ignore them and put my hands on the bicycle. I did not see their faces clearly. One with sour breath stroked my hair. I yanked my head away and searched for the right English words and yelled as loudly as I could.

"Please help me!"

"She speaks English," one soldier said and backed away. The other soldier put his mouth next to my ear and repeated, "prostitute" and "money." The stink of his body made me gag. He took money out of his pocket and pushed it in my face.

I got on the bicycle.

"No," he said and pulled on my arm, and tried to kiss me. I screamed, and he slapped me. I kicked hard, and he yelled.

In the dark, I heard a pounding sound. "Let her go!" It was Daniel. He pulled the soldier from me and threw him to the ground before the man crawled away. Daniel brushed my hair out of my eyes and lifted me into his arms. "It's all right. I'll take care of you."

I knew my cheeks were wet, and I laid my head against his clean uniform as he carried me to the infirmary. Daniel saved me that night.

I was not badly hurt, just frightened and angry that American soldiers treated me like a prostitute. Daniel gave me his handkerchief to wipe the tears away and said he was sorry the soldier had bothered me. He examined my face and hands and arms to see if I had any wounds.

In the lobby of the hotel, Daniel spoke with an American officer and a Free French officer. The night was black when he led me to a jeep and helped me into the seat. I asked where we were going, and he said there was a villa in the hills above the Mediterranean where I might stay for the night. Tomorrow someone would take me back to Nice. I could not say everything that was in my heart. So I said, "thank you, thank you." I still held his handkerchief.

As the jeep bounced over the winding road that took us into the hills, Daniel turned his head and looked at me. He asked about my trip to Monaco and who I was visiting, and how long I had lived in Nice. I explained, as best I was able, about Maman and Papa, art school, and living with Victoire.

When the jeep hit a large rock in the road, and Daniel jerked the wheel, I grabbed the door. He leaned over and placed his arm against me to stop me from hitting the windshield. "I'm not the best driver in the army."

I laughed, and Daniel smiled.

"I'll take care of your bicycle. Someone will pick you up in the morning." He touched my hand as he opened the door. At that moment, I began to fall in love.

25

Dad and Emilie. Finally. I have a tangle of feelings. I knew it was coming, but the first mention of Dad's name, seeing it written out, hearing his words as Emilie remembered them, stops me cold. She prompts lovely memories of him. His laughter, kindness, chivalry, calmness under pressure. Even the fact that he admitted he wasn't the "best driver" back then. Still wasn't as a much older man. At the same time, Dad feels like a character out of a 1940s wartime movie. This courageous soldier, watching over her, saving her from assault, the two of them driving off in the jeep. Someone I know and yet don't know.

The photo of them that was included in the box of souvenirs showed Dad and Emilie hand-in-hand, smiling into the camera. They looked so happy. Had I ever seen that big of a smile with Mother? She'd been ill much of the last years of their marriage. In their wedding photo that hung on the living room wall in the family home, their expressions were formal and polite. Come to think of it, why aren't there more pictures of the two of them? As a photographer, Dad wasn't big on being the subject of snapshots. As far as I knew, the two I found on his refrigerator, along with the fishing photo of Dad, Billy, and DJ, were rare family moments captured on film.

I remember a relative's wedding when I was eight or nine. My flouncy dress was layers of crinoline, my new shoes white patent leather. Mother tried vigorously to get our family together for a picture. I was running around, Billy was off somewhere with a cousin, and DJ and Nancy held hands at a table. When she'd managed to corral us, Dad took the camera and aimed it our way. Mother insisted he join us and have someone else take the photo. They argued quietly, after all, we were surrounded by a couple hundred guests, and Dad eventually gave in. As he often did with Mother. I never saw that picture in a family album—Dad frowning and Mother looking frosty. What was he avoiding? A record of his life with Mother? With us kids?

"Hi, Dr. Whitman."

A student, backpack slung over one shoulder, in jeans and a Dunham University tee-shirt, smiles at me. Next to her is a young man with a scruffy beard, same clothes, same backpack.

"Hi Tracy."

"This is Brock." She grins at the guy, and he nods at me.

"Hi Brock," I say.

"Hey," he answers.

"Nice out here, isn't it?" Tracy tosses her head, swishing a blond ponytail, and glances right and left.

The day is beautiful, sunny, and breezy. Perfect for an afternoon break on a bench tucked into a corner of the campus, away from my office and the demands of my job. A haven for contemplating the latest chapters of the memoir. I angle my face upward and shade my eyes. "It sure is."

"Did you get my email about changing our meeting tomorrow?" she asks, anxious.

Though the semester is over, Tracy is concerned about the credits needed for graduation and is contemplating summer school. "Yes. No problem. We can reschedule."

"Thanks. Feeling kinda stressed this week."

"I get it. We can talk next week."

She notices the memoir on my lap. "Hope I didn't disturb your reading."

"No. I need to head back to my office."

"Oh. Okay. So…see you later." She strolls off.

As they walk away, arms around each other, they are the embodiment of a couple in love. Tracy and Brock. Emilie and Daniel. All young, growing up in uncertain times, trying to navigate the demands made upon them, though their life and death experiences are worlds apart.

I scan the campus and see no one. I should relinquish Emilie's world and get back to my office. But not yet.

26

Madame Moineau was a large woman, *formidable*, dressed in black. Was she in mourning for someone? The villa had a kitchen, a dining room, a living room, a large bedroom, and a bathroom on the first floor. She said I could bathe and eat something afterward. I saw clean white towels.

I locked the door and switched on the faucet. I left home twelve hours ago, and now I was sweaty and dusty. I took off my clothes, and I began to sob as if something inside me had broken open. Was it the soldier who assaulted me? Was it Daniel? I stayed in the tub for half an hour before drying off and putting my clothes back on.

In the dining room, two places were set with bread, wine, cheese, and fruit. It reminded me of MB's. Madame Moineau told me to eat, and she sat opposite, watching every move I made. I said *merci*, and she nodded. I ate quickly while Madame Moineau sipped wine and took a few bites of bread and cheese. I asked if she had lived in the villa for a long time, before the war. A shadow covered her face, and she placed her hands in her lap. The Nazis had lived in the villa for two years before leaving a month ago. They occupied most of the house, and she lived in the attic bedroom on the third floor. She became their servant. Her husband and son had died in 1941, and her daughter had been taken to a work camp. Her eyes were suddenly bright, and I wanted to hold her hand but was afraid to invade her grief. Madame led me to a room upstairs that was clean and comfortable. I climbed under the covers and slept as though I was dead.

In the morning, I drank coffee on the veranda facing the Mediterranean and the breathtaking view of the sea and the curve of the pebbled beaches. I kissed Madame Moineau good-bye and said thank you again. She hugged me, and I wondered about her daughter.

A soldier with an MP armband picked me up and took me back to the dispensary. I had told Monsieur Zazou that I would be gone one day, and now it was already two. I was going to ride my bicycle back to Nice, but Daniel said no, that he would take me if I could wait a few hours. I did not hesitate to say yes.

On the second floor of the hotel, I helped Daniel and Norman fold bandages. They had created a temporary hospital for the wounded men. Sometimes Daniel or Norman would treat GIs. One had fingers torn off by a mine, and another suffered from dysentery. I saw Daniel speak calmly and encourage them. His eyes were the first thing I noticed yesterday, but today it was his tenderness and caring. Yet, I also saw confusion when he thought no one was watching when he looked at the broken bodies of soldiers in the infirmary. In those moments, a darker emotion seemed to struggle with his usual peacefulness.

Late in the afternoon, Norman gave me a package with coffee, soap, and a can of strawberry jam. So thoughtful! Then, Daniel drove me to Nice with my bicycle in the back seat. He made me laugh when he tried to speak French. *Comment-allez vous, merci bien,* and *comment-vous appelez vous.* It sounded like he was eating the words!

When we reached the bridge separating Eze from Beaulieu, there were French soldiers standing in the road. An ambulance was parked nearby. Daniel stopped the jeep and ran to see if he could help the two soldiers lying on the ground. One had a bloody uniform and cuts on his cheek and forehead. He was leaning up on his elbow, smoking a cigarette. The other man was not as fortunate. Where he should have had two boots, there was one. The right leg was soaked in blood. He jerked violently, and his lips quivered. I said a prayer for him.

Other soldiers placed the stretchers in the ambulance, and Daniel returned to the jeep. I asked if the ambulance was going to his dispensary. He said no that it would go straight to a field hospital in Nice.

We rode in silence, and once or twice Daniel looked at me and smiled. At my apartment, he helped me out of the jeep and walked me to the door. I said good-bye, and he tried to say *au revoir*. We both laughed. He touched my hand, and I nodded, and then he was gone.

It was the first week of September.

The days were a routine for me. I rose, dressed, and ate much better now that the Allies had arrived in Nice, and the port was open for shipping. Sugar, flour, and coffee were available thanks to the liberation. Shipments of film arrived from Paris. Life changed daily.

Victoire and I walked to Monsieur Zazou's Art Studio. There were many more customers since soldiers poured into the city every day. Mostly they wanted pictures developed and were willing to pay whatever Monsieur Zazou charged. Without Guy, I was busier in the developing lab downstairs and had less time to manage the customers upstairs. I suggested to Monsieur Zazou that Victoire might help out. She needed a job now, and he needed a clerk. We settled on Victoire coming four mornings a week. She was grateful but worried at first.

What if her scar disgusted the patrons, and they stared at her? I convinced her that the men she would serve had seen much worse wounds on their friends and enemies. She gave in and began to sell art supplies.

One day I found Daniel's handkerchief in the pocket of my skirt. It had streaks of dirt where I wiped my face the night he rescued me. It was the one souvenir I had of those two days. My memories of meeting Daniel had a soft place in my heart.

27

Oh my God. Dad's handkerchief? I quickly abandon my lunch in the
kitchen of my condo and go to the bedroom to find the bag of
souvenirs I'd received from Emilie's daughter, Yvette, weeks ago. I
pull out the dried flower, pebbles, paper napkin, and train ticket and
set them aside. Then, lastly, I carefully remove Dad's handkerchief
from the bottom of the bag. I spread it out on the dining room table.

The stains on the cloth are her tears. I touch the material with my
fingertips. A pale, olive-green military issue. Faded and worn, as
though someone had repeatedly grasped it, crushed it, folded, and
refolded it. How many times had Emilie clenched this piece of material
and dreamed of her days with Dad? I run my finger around the edges
of the cloth, noticing a spot where the hem has come undone. Dad
touched this. 1944. Sixty years ago...

Pictures and stories are one thing. Handling something they both
held is like a gut punch. So much more real, it takes my breath away. I
think about everyone who would be shocked to see this, a piece of Dad
from all those years ago: Uncle Bert, the twins, maybe even DJ.
Someday soon they will, I tell myself, when I finish reading.

28

In the middle of September, Monsieur Zazou raised my salary ten francs a day. He was happy to have both Victoire and me in the shop. Old patrons returned as life reappeared in Nice and the Allies brought money and hope. Monsieur Zazou relied on Victoire more and more. I often saw the two of them speaking with their heads together. She made him smile, and he gave her some purpose in her life.

A soldier grinned at me in the shop, and I imagined it was Daniel. On the Promenade des Anglais, another one's shoulders and head reminded me of Daniel. I followed him for a few minutes. He took off his cap and brushed the dark hair off his face. But then he crossed the street without even glancing behind him. Everywhere I looked, I thought I saw Daniel. Many soldiers passed through Nice, and Daniel was only one of them. I was grateful to him for saving me, but I did not think I would see him again.

About this time, there was fierce fighting to the north and east, but the Allies were pushing the Germans out of France, and everyone said the war would end by Christmas. What a glorious idea that was. I wondered who Daniel was caring for. I prayed for him and the men who were probably dying around him.

It was still warm at the end of September, and I discovered an American phrase: "R and R." GIs came to Nice for a few days for rest and a break from the war. Soldiers who had been in the north of France since D-Day were in Nice to sit on the beach and breathe the sea air. They stood on the Promenade and watched women sunbathing with bare breasts. Some GIs were scandalized and stared at us like they were in a movie theater. When I saw several laughing and poking each other, it reminded me of the soldiers at the dispensary. Sometimes a soldier and a French girl would walk hand-in-hand down the Promenade, and she would lay her head on his shoulder. I wanted that too.

On the first of October, I arrived home from the Art Studio, and Madame Lanvin said a soldier had been at the door to see me. He told her he would come back later in the day and left a bouquet of flowers. I washed and changed my clothes. I was in a hurry, and I dropped my tiny glass bottle of perfume that Maman gave me for my birthday. The odor of citrus was everywhere! An hour went by, and then I heard a knock on the door. I opened it. Daniel.

We stared at each other, neither of us saying anything. Then at once, I said "hello," and Daniel said, "bonjour." He played with his hat nervously, and I asked him to sit down. He took my hand, and we talked. The Allies had moved the dispensary from Eze to Lantosque directly north of Nice. He had spent his days driving the ambulance north to La Turbie to collect the wounded. The mountains there did an excellent job of hiding the Germans. Then Daniel made trips to Nice with the ambulance to bring the wounded to the hospital.

He asked if I ever visited Monaco to see my parents, and I said no, the trip would have to wait until Christmas. We stopped talking, and Daniel put his arm around me, holding me tightly. I felt the wool of his jacket against my cheek. He stared into my eyes and placed his lips on mine. His breath was sweet and warm, and his lips were soft. When he pulled away from me, his eyes were shining. My arms were weak and not under my control. I felt like I was disappearing into the cushions of the sofa. I had been kissed by men before, but I don't remember ever feeling this light, this excited.

Daniel took me to a café by the beach. Le Marin was full of military men. We sat at a table on the patio where it was cool, where we could hear the sound of the waves rolling over the pebbles. It had been a long time since I sat on the beach and relaxed. We sipped real wine, not watered down like it often was for the past four years.

"Your eyes are as blue as the Mediterranean," he said.

"You have beautiful eyes too."

Daniel laughed and said his brother Bert would love that. When Daniel was a child, he had a "lazy eye" and wore a patch over it. Bert was in the north, fighting his way across France. Daniel said he was a "pistol." I was confused, and he explained about American language called "slang." I kept a list of all of the new words I learned. A "pistol" was someone who was funny.

"Do you have any brothers or sisters?" he asked.

"Only my sister Marie. I have no idea where she is." Still with MB, maybe.

I told him Marie and I were not like him and Bert. We were not close friends. I said I missed Maman and Papa. He missed his father too. His mother died many years ago.

Then Daniel jumped up. "This song is swell."

I could barely hear the music above the talking and laughter. "Edith Piaf."

"Would you like to dance?" He held out his hand and led me to an empty part of the patio.

At first, he held me lightly. I felt the heat from his body, and even with the breeze, my hands were damp.

"Okay?" he asked. I nodded, and he pulled me closer.

I rested my head on his shoulder.

"Emilie," he said in my ear as if he tasted my name for the first time. I had not danced this closely for a long while. When he touched me, I felt electricity pass between us.

We walked to the edge of the water and took off our shoes and stockings. Daniel rolled his pant legs to his knees, and I unpinned my hair.

"I can forget the war on a night like this." He tossed a stone into the Mediterranean. I asked if it was painful being a medic. I remembered the shadows on his face in the dispensary. Daniel pointed to his heart. "Here." Everyone he saw die was in there. I touched his shirt where he pointed and said my friend Guy was also gone. Thinking about Guy made me cry, and Daniel wiped away a tear and kissed me. He pressed me to his chest as though he was afraid I might disappear.

My souvenirs from the evening were two smooth flat pebbles that Daniel picked up from the beach. "One for each of us," he said.

After that night, Victoire teased me. I told her about Daniel and blushed every time I mentioned his name.

"*Ma petite,*" she said. "You have a good time with *l'Americain?*"

"*Oui.*"

"I think you are in love with this Daniel."

"How can I be in love? I've only seen him a few times," I said, hiding my true feelings.

Daniel was a medic in a war zone that was very dangerous. Would I see him again? "We are friends who had a pleasant night together."

But Victoire saw the truth on my face and warned me that I could get hurt. She was right. American soldiers were here for a short time, while Victoire and I were here forever. When I closed my eyes, I felt his arms around me as we danced.

Though many men were wounded and dying, the war news was good. The Allies pushed the Germans east. Monsieur Zazou was happy that there were many customers, but he missed Guy terribly and had given up hope that he might be safe. I saved my salary from the Art Studio for a new dress. Blue to match my eyes which Daniel said he loved. I dared to hope I might see him again.

Then at the end of October, Daniel came to Nice one morning to bring the wounded to the hospital. Victoire and I were eating breakfast, and he appeared on my doorstep.

"*Bonjour, mademoiselle!*" He picked me up and twirled me around.

Victoire ran into the bedroom and wrapped a scarf around her head. When she returned, Daniel introduced himself and kissed her on both cheeks. She was polite, but I could see the doubt on her face.

He waved a piece of paper. "A pass! We have the whole day."

I pleaded with Victoire to make my excuses to Monsieur Zazou. She agreed but frowned when Daniel said *au revoir* and we left hand in hand.

We spent the morning strolling along the Promenade, so different now than during the German occupation. The weather was still warm for October, and the beaches were full of sunbathers. We stopped to listen to the water rolling off the pebbles. Then we walked until we were hungry and had dinner at a restaurant off the Quai des États-Unis. Fish stew and wine. It was heaven. My appetite had grown since the Allies arrived, and my waistband had grown too!

The waiter treated Daniel like a celebrity. Most Niçoises considered Allied soldiers to be heroes. He said some days at the dispensary in Lantosque were busy, and blood-soaked GIs covered the floor of the clinic. Other days there was nothing to do. Some of the young men were very frightened, and he lied to them and told them they would survive. It made him angry that no matter what he did, many died anyway. I saw his shoulders tense and his face become hard.

I told Daniel about the riot on the movie set and Victoire's injury. "I was scared. I had little medicine and didn't know what to do if the wound became infected."

"You sound pretty brave to me," he said.

"*Non*, Guy was brave, the soldiers you take care of are brave. You too."

Daniel took my hand and traced the lines of my palm as if he could read my fortune. "You're easy to talk to," he said.

"I enjoy listening to you. The sound of your voice." My ear was understanding American English more easily.

"You like my New Jersey accent?"

"*Pardon?*"

"Never mind," he said. "I'm going to learn French better. *Je m'appelle* Daniel," he said and pointed to himself.

The afternoon sun was warm on our backs, and we returned along the Quai to the Promenade. My body was loose, and my head light from the wine. We passed a flower shop, and Daniel bought me a bouquet of roses. Even the flowers seemed healthier now that we could breathe freely again.

Daniel asked about my life, and I told him about growing up in Monaco, studying at the Art and Design School, and coming to Nice to live and work. He described his life in New Jersey. His mother died when he was sixteen, and his father had a business in New York called "Whitman Textiles." I had so many questions that I could not find the words for. When I mentioned his time in the army, he said he was very lucky. He had survived Italy and France so far.

Daniel had two more hours, so we walked back to the apartment, and I went to the kitchen to make coffee. Victoire was still at the shop, and I knew she would not be home for a while. I stood by the sink, and I did not see Daniel behind me but felt him there. When he put his arms on my waist, I dropped the coffee pot. I turned around, and he kissed me deeply, full of passion. His lips lingered on mine. I could feel his heart beating and the heat between us. He pulled me against him, and we had no thought of where we were. I was barely able to breathe. We forgot about coffee, and I felt my body saying yes long before he looked at me to see if I agreed.

In the bedroom, we removed our clothes, and his body pressed into mine. I gasped, and I heard him moan. The two of us held each other tightly, and his hands caressed my damp skin. Soon the light began to fade, and Daniel had to return to Lantosque. He kissed me one last time, and then he dressed and left while I still felt his hands on my back and his breath on my neck. I wanted to rise and dress too, but I could not bring myself to move from the bed. I had to hold on to my memory of the past hours. I was in another world called Daniel.

Everything changed that night. Later I pressed a rose between two sheets of paper.

29

Emilie and Dad. In bed.

I nudge the picture of them aside and visualize the two smooth, blackish-green stones that they picked up on the beach in Nice, along with the dried pink rose that Emilie carefully preserved between the pieces of paper. The first time they made love was the day she touched the flower. I feel heat move into my face. I'm a little uncomfortable reading about their intimate moments but desperate to grasp the passion between them.

The noise of the restaurant swirls around me. My coffee is cold. I motion to the waiter for a refill and check my watch. Anxious to dive back into the memoir, I resign myself to meetings and appointments the rest of the afternoon and early evening. When the young man fills my cup, I hand him a couple of bills for the check and take a sip of the hot coffee.

Questions nag me. Did Dad share this kind of passion with Mother? Ever? What kind of relationship *did* they have behind closed doors? I know this question is none of my business and will never be answered, but I'm struck by the discoveries in Emilie's writing and trying diligently to match the man in her life with the father I knew. To my utter amazement, I feel defensive for Mother, something I never have imagined myself feeling. And Dad? I can understand his attraction to Emilie and the desperation of his existence on the front lines of the war. Still, I wonder about his loyalty to the home front.

Now more than ever, I wonder how much Mother knew about Dad's wartime affair. How and when she found out about Emilie. And did any of the conflict between Mother and me originate in France? My love for the country and the language, Dad's enthusiasm for, and encouragement of, my career? The friction between Mother and me escalated when I entered high school and began to study French in earnest, spouting phrases and repeating verb declensions around the house until everybody told me to shut up. Except Dad. He simply smiled at my efforts.

Something pricks at my memory: the last moments with my Mother before I set off for Europe that summer of 1982. The last time I would see her alive, as it turned out.

"Wait for me downstairs," Dad had said to me after I said goodbye to Mother and then directed his attention to her. "Can I get you anything?"

As I stepped into the hall, I stole a last look backward. Dad knelt by the bed and held Mother in his arms. Then he kissed her on the forehead. It was the most tender moment between them that I could ever recall.

Dad was quiet as he drove me to Newark airport. "Be sure to call—"

"Every other day, I know."

"And if you change your—"

"Itinerary. I will."

He pulled the car into a parking space at the underground garage and shifted sideways in his seat. "Katie, you need to understand your mother. What she's gone through."

"I do understand."

"It's not only the cancer…" He paused as if about to say more. Then he shrugged.

"We'll spend time together when I get back," I said.

30

November passed slowly. In the north, the Allies fought their way east to Germany, and I no longer thought the war would end by Christmas. When I dreamed of our afternoon together and remembered Daniel holding me, I was excited and felt loved, but then I became afraid. How would I feel when he was gone forever? What if I never saw him again? I knew I had to keep my head and not lose myself in him.

Monsieur Zazou was ill with a cold and took to his bed. I tried to force him to drink hot tea, but he complained and pushed it away. Victoire and I managed the Art Studio, but we knew something was happening because fewer soldiers arrived in Nice for "R&R."

Then without warning, Daniel was at our door. My heart was light again. The USO in Nice had arranged for a dance at the Ruhl Hotel, and he wanted Victoire and me to come. I had not heard a live orchestra since the war began, and I was eager for a night of dancing. Daniel left us alone to dress, and I agreed to meet him at seven-thirty.

I began to pull dresses out of our closet, but Victoire said she would not come. For three months since I met Daniel, Victoire had been quiet when I mentioned his name. She made me doubt myself and my feelings for him. She told me, "he is going to leave" and, "soldiers are just looking for fun," and, "you are a fool to fall in love." I understood her bitterness. Since Jean had disappeared, Victoire was beginning to believe him—no man would ever touch her again. She never knew how much her words hurt me, and the tension between us was thick. But I was going to the dance and thought a night out would be good for her.

"Victoire, tonight you are joining me."

"*Non!*"

"You are coming to the dance at the Ruhl."

"I am not going!" Victoire yelled at me.

After an hour of trying to convince her to go with me, she finally surrendered when I said I would not go without her. By seven o'clock, we were dressed and staring at ourselves in the mirror.

The lights of the hotel ballroom glittered like diamonds. Soldiers filled tables covered with white paper tablecloths. Some couples danced, and the orchestra played American songs I had never heard. Daniel told me the names: "Don't Sit Under the Apple Tree," and "You'd Be So Nice to Come Home To," and "I'll Be Seeing You." The soldiers sang along with the orchestra, and the war seemed far away.

When we arrived, Victoire and I saw Daniel and three other soldiers at a table. I heard bits of the songs they were singing, "...seeing you..." in "familiar places," "my heart embraces." I wondered who they were thinking about when they sang.

Daniel introduced us to his friends. "This is *Mademoiselle* Victoire."

"Hello," Victoire said shyly. She never spoke English, but I knew she understood some.

Daniel pointed to each one. "Fred, Norman, and Jimmy."

I remembered Norman from the day I met Daniel. Jimmy was short and dark, and Fred was tall and blond. I was thrilled dancing with Daniel again, and he led me around the floor easily. Over his shoulder, I saw Norman and Fred talking to Victoire, who seemed confused. Daniel said he was glad she came. Then Jimmy took Victoire's hand and walked her to the dance floor. He limped a little as he danced, and Daniel told me that he had been badly wounded in Italy. A mortar exploded in front of him, and he nearly died. Daniel carried him a kilometer from the front line to an aid station.

Victoire and Jimmy danced to every song and then disappeared halfway through the evening. Poor Norman and Fred! I danced with both of them. Fred stepped on my feet, and Norman's hands were wet, and he left a spot on my dress.

At eleven o'clock the party ended. On the street, Daniel was a little drunk from the whiskey and started to sing. So many American songs were about lovers back home. He hugged me, and we danced to his singing. When he twirled me on the sidewalk, a sailor and his girl walking by laughed at us. He kissed me in the middle of the street, and I did not care because I felt safe in his arms.

Daniel and I had an hour at the apartment to ourselves. We made love quickly and lay in each other's arms, and Daniel ran his hands down my back, his fingers stroking my spine. Then he said the words I had been waiting to hear.

"I love you Emilie Caronne and I don't want anything to change."

"I love you too." It was true. I had known Daniel for only three months, yet I was in love.

At the time, I was lost in our fierce passion and never knowing from day to day what my fate might be. But even then, I knew that Daniel was different from other men I had known. I was young, yes, but I had boyfriends who were also students at the School of Art and Design in Monaco. They were wild, fun, and eager to make love, but Daniel was special. He was handsome and kind with his patients and tender with me. When he touched me, I felt both secure and aroused as I never had with other men. The night of the dance, Daniel drew a heart with an arrow through it on a paper napkin. It was my souvenir.

Victoire came home the next day. She and Jimmy spent the night in the Ruhl Hotel. She smiled shyly and hugged me, thanking me over and over for forcing her to go to the dance. I had no idea then how that night would change her life. She was so excited to be with a man again. I laughed when she said she did not understand most of what Jimmy said, but when he looked into her eyes, she saw the truth of his feelings. Now it was my chance to tease *her* about *l'Americain*.

I did not believe the change in Victoire. She hummed in the morning and talked about Jimmy all day. He had an R&R before he was sent north, and they spent it together at a hotel. She had known Jimmy for less than a month, but they were serious. Some French people thought the Americans came to Nice for pleasure and then left the women behind. I hoped this would not be true of Jimmy. But what of Daniel? When he was with me, I was confident and strong. When I did not see him for weeks or months, I felt weak, and doubts crowded my mind.

At the end of November, Daniel sent me a long letter. It was the first time he had written to me, and I felt he was trying to tell me something. Some of what he wrote was difficult to understand, but some of it made me sick to my stomach. I had too many emotions. I knew the day would come when he moved north with the troops, but I tried not to think about it. I dreamed that we might spend our lives together, but he never mentioned that. Then I thought, what if he is killed in the north? Maybe it was better that he left. My heart would be safer, and it would be easier to live my life. I remember feeling very tired, as though a heavy weight rested on my shoulders.

Trauth

My list of American "slang" grew: "take a powder" and "blow a
fuse."

31

My breath catches. I stare at a sheet of paper I remove from between the pages of the memoir. This is one letter Emilie kept. The folds are worn and perforated as if someone had opened and closed it numerous times. The pencil lead has smeared in places. There is a small, bright red stain in one corner. My eyes blur as I scan the sheet, and before I can focus on the content, the writing confronts me. Dad's hand, the penmanship neat and cramped. I received similar-looking notes when I was away at graduate school. I read it slowly, savoring each word.

Dearest Emilie,

I miss you. This letter will have to do until I can get another pass. Wasn't the dance swell? If I shut my eyes, I can see us together. Well, we're busy here. Our outfit is fighting Nazis in the countryside between Turini and Peïra-Cava, and right now, I can't leave the dispensary. How is Victoire? Jimmy clammed up when I mentioned her name, but I think he's got it bad for her.

I hate to say this, but I will be heading out soon. It sure looks like the war won't be over by Christmas. The Germans are stronger up north than we thought. We were hoping they'd take a powder, but I guess not. My battalion is being sent to an area called the "Ardennes Forest." Do you know it?

Anyway, Emilie, I have to say some things to you and can't find the right words. I love you. You know that. I'll always love you for the rest of my life. Nothing will ever change that. So don't forget it.

But I've been thinking of Italy lately. In Anzio, men died everywhere. Bodies torn apart by mines and mortars and guys had their legs ripped off right in front of me. The blood was terrible. Then in March, we fought the Germans for five hours to occupy two houses where they had set up headquarters. By dawn, we had the houses, but half of my company died, including the other medics. Men cried and screamed, and all I could do was stop the bleeding, wrap the wound, give them morphine, and call for a litter. I dug my fingers into dark holes and body parts and pulled out a man's intestines.

You see, Emilie, most of the guys had sweethearts and wives writing to them, and at the end of the day, they would crawl into a foxhole or get some shuteye in the basement of a house we captured and read letters. It was lonely, and I was happy to hear from people at home. When I'd write to someone, or they would write to me, it took my mind off the war. I didn't think I'd make it home, and the letters were a comfort.

Then five months later, I met you, and everything changed. I've never met anyone like you, Emilie. You are so beautiful. When I think of you, I want to cry. I am a lucky guy.

Please keep praying for us. Even though I'm not a Catholic like you, I guess your God is pretty much the same as mine. Though sometimes I feel like God abandoned us in Italy. But all the same, we could use the help.

By the way, I have learned a few new words: "ici," "les assiettes," "la salle de bain." That last one is pretty important. I'm sure my French still sounds like a truck's gears grinding. My red dictionary does the trick.

Well, Emilie, I need to go back to work before Doc Pinelli blows a fuse. Some days it's hard to believe just over the mountains there's a war going on.

Love to my girl,

Daniel

He had to be talking about Mother here. '*...I was happy to hear from people at home...I didn't think I'd make it home, and the letters were a comfort.*' Dad was trying to tell Emilie he was engaged but couldn't bring himself to say it outright.

Italy was horrendous for him, and meeting Emilie had, in a way, saved his life. Certainly his heart.

I lay my head against the sofa cushions. I see Dad in the infirmary writing a letter with a stub of a pencil and Emilie reading it in the basement developing lab of Monsieur Zazou's Art Studio. His words finding their way into her heart, two young people negotiating their love amidst the constraints of the war. It seems so romantic now, but in reality, it had to be an unbearable, painful time. I ache for them but feel a twinge of jealousy. What would I give to receive a letter from a lover so passionate about me? It had never happened with Terry or with the other men I'd known before my marriage and after my divorce.

If Emilie was Dad's girl, where did that leave Mother?

32

Winter was in the air. The Allies were fighting a war against a desperate enemy, and I was fighting a war to put Daniel out of my mind. Nice prepared for the first Christmas since the liberation. The shop was busy, and some days I was so tired when I returned to the apartment, I would eat very little and fall into bed. Victoire had a letter from Jimmy, and she read it many times and then folded it and placed it inside her dress next to her heart.

I hardened *my* heart and forced myself to accept the loss of my lover. Daniel said he would try to come to Nice once more before he left, but I was not counting the days.

Victoire found me weeping one day in the bedroom. She rocked me in her arms. I had done this for her many times since the riot, but this was the first time she had to comfort me.

"I cannot live without him," I cried.

"*Sh, ma petite*. You are strong. You will survive." She pulled me upright to face her. "You should let him go."

"*Oui*, I am."

"*Maintenant*. Let him go now."

I started to cry again. "*Non, non*, not yet."

I dreamed that Daniel and I had a picnic in the forest as the sun set. We lay on a blanket together, and Daniel told me, "If I die in battle I will die a very happy man," and I said, "I have a feeling you will live a long time." I woke and found my pillow damp. Then I closed my eyes again, but he was gone.

Jimmy mentioned marriage in his letter, and Victoire was ecstatic. She was afraid to tell her mother she wanted to marry an American soldier. I wondered what Maman and Papa would say if Daniel proposed to me? I was happy for Victoire but also jealous. Would that ever be Daniel and me?

At noon on December 8, Daniel appeared at the shop. I introduced him to Monsieur Zazou, who shook Daniel's hand vigorously as he did all customers who were Allies. They had saved his beloved country. Daniel's company had moved to Saint-Jeannet, twenty minutes from Nice. It was the last place they would stay before being sent north. Victoire knew we needed to be alone and told me she would be busy and away from the apartment that evening.

Daniel and I spent the afternoon in bed. I rubbed his back, and he took my hand and held it to his chest and kissed it. After these past months, my body knew his, the curves where we fitted together and the places where we were different. His mouth and hands were eager but gentle. Daniel talked quickly and said many things. I have never forgotten them.

"I'd like to show you New York City. Walk down Broadway and see a show, then have dinner and go dancing. I'd take you to Coney Island and we'd get on the roller coaster and eat hot dogs."

"Oui."

"We'd drive down the Jersey shore and spend a day on the beach, eating lobsters and corn on the cob." Daniel stared into the distance.

"And Bert would come and bring whoever he's dating at the time. He has a lot of girlfriends, you know."

"*Oui.*"

Then he suddenly threw back the covers and slammed his feet on the floor, pulling on his trousers.

"Daniel?"

"I'm allowed to die in this war, but I'm not allowed to be with the woman I love," he said, so angry.

"*Je ne comprends pas.*" What did he mean? Daniel held his head in his hands for a long time, and when he looked up, he had tears in his eyes.

"I'm sorry. So sorry."

What was I going to say? He never mentioned a life together after the war like Jimmy and Victoire.

Before I rose from the bed, Daniel kissed a spot behind my ear and asked me to pose for him. I faced the camera with a paintbrush in my hand. I was too modest to model completely nude, so I stood behind the easel that held a painting I had started. Daniel took my picture and teased me, and I laughed at him. Then I asked him to sit by the window so the sun would fall on him just so and his head would fill the entire frame. His cheekbones were prominent and absorbed the light. Shadows fell in the valleys of his face. I tilted his head, and he smiled up at me, and I took his picture. Then I bent down and kissed him.

We ate supper at a café and drank wine and walked down the Promenade des Anglais. Daniel paid a photographer to take our picture on the beach. We stopped in front of the Hotel Negresco.

"Want to go in?" Daniel said. "We have time."

"It is *très cher*," I said.

"What's a little money when it comes to my girl?"

I liked the sound of "my girl."

The lobby was as I remembered. The furniture and artwork still elegant as though the Germans had come and gone and the hotel had not been affected. I imagined romantic rendezvous between German officers and their French lovers. But there were already acts of revenge in Nice and other towns against collaborators who had given help and comfort to the enemy. People were denounced every day. Women who had relationships with Nazis were often most at risk. I thought about Marie.

Later we stood on the Promenade by the railing and watched the sun set over the Mediterranean. Couples strolled past us. Nice had become a city of lovers. Daniel seemed unhappy, took my hand, and said he would ship out the next day. Hearing the words crushed me even though I expected them.

Daniel pulled me close to him. "If I don't survive the campaign, don't forget me." I blinked hard to stop my tears. I could never forget him.

We had an hour before the truck would take him back to Saint-Jeannet, so we returned to the apartment and our bed for the last time.

"If I do survive and you ever need anything, I'll make sure you'll always know where to reach me." Daniel kissed me again, dressed quickly, and left. I felt desperately alone in the warm bed where his body had lain next to mine.

For the rest of December, I served customers, developed photographs in the darkroom, and went home in the late afternoon to eat my supper alone. Victoire had gone to visit her mother in La Turbie and give her the news about Jimmy. They planned to marry as soon as the war ended.

I wanted Daniel beside me. I wanted to hear his voice, but I had to stop thinking of him. I comforted myself with the thought that even though our affair was brief, I had passion and kindness in the midst of all the terror I had known these last years. That should have been enough. Some days it was, and some days it was not. Many nights when I could not bear to sleep alone in the bed, I wrapped myself in a blanket on the sofa rolling the two stones from the beach between my fingers.

I tried to paint and pushed myself to pick up my brushes. I worked on watercolors of the flowers in the Place Masséna, I painted the houses that lined the Quai. I painted beach scenes of the Mediterranean. Then I thought of Daniel and walking down the Promenade, and I could paint no longer.

On Christmas Eve, I offered to close the shop, but Monsieur Zazou said no, he would stay and that I should go home. He was afraid I would forget to lock the door as I had once before. My mind was not on my work, and he could see that. I asked about Christmas and if he was seeing his nephew in Paris. He said no that he was tired and glad the shop was closed the next day.

"Joyeux noël," I said and walked out the door and into the traffic on the sidewalks. It was not a good time of the year to be alone, and I planned to go to Monaco on Christmas Day to see Maman and Papa. It had been almost a year since I had been home.

When I got off the train in Monaco and walked down the boulevard, my heart beat fast. I brought gifts of coffee, cigarettes, and a can of strawberry jam that Daniel gave me. Maman threw her arms around me, and Papa kissed me silently. His hair was grayer and his body thinner. Business in the butcher shop was light in recent years, but people still needed to eat, Papa said. Yet without tourists, the city was not as healthy as it had been before the war. Maman's face was pale. She had worked hard making dinner. We ate our stew and listened to Papa complain that I had not come sooner and that the war should have ended by now. Papa disliked all foreigners and refused to credit the Allies with freeing France. I said he should be grateful the Americans did not hate foreigners as much as he did.

They asked about Marie. They had not heard from her since last winter. What could I say? I told them I had not seen her for months and reassured them that Marie would write when she was less busy. Papa wanted me to stay in Monaco to work in the shop. I told him my life was in Nice now. I was sad on the train ride home.

The week after Christmas, I was shocked when I collected my mail. There were five pieces from Villers-Cotterêts. Daniel had written on the back of each card: *Nous sont ici*. Each one showed a different view of the village. I had never been there, but I knew it was northeast of Paris. He did not reveal anything about his work or the war. I was glad to receive the postcards, but each one hurt. Would it be better not hearing from him? I prayed every day that he was safe and well.

January 1945

After the New Year, Daniel wrote another brief card saying he was at the general hospital in Villers-Cotterêts. The village was far away from the front lines where he was spending his days safely as a medic.

Monsieur Zazou had decided to take a trip to Paris to deliver prints to Madame Harieu, an old friend and customer from before the war. He had received no word from her in years. Now she wrote, and he was so happy. Monsieur Zazou wanted to visit his nephew also. I had an idea. Paris was a short way from Villers-Cotterêts, and I could travel with Monsieur Zazou. Now with towns liberated and businesses thriving, travel was possible.

Victoire agreed to keep the art shop open though she was against my leaving.

"You are going to be hurt again," she said. "It would be better to forget about Daniel."

"I want to see him one last time."

"Does he know you are coming?"

"*Non*." I shut my ears to her advice.

I would stay overnight at a hotel near the train station in Paris and go to Villers-Cotterêts the next day. I had saved every centime to have a little extra for my trip. We boarded the coach early in the morning and sat opposite each other in a compartment. The train swayed from side to side and stopped suddenly now and then. Military transports had priority, and the tracks had been damaged by artillery, so the trip was roundabout from Cannes to Toulon to Marseille to Paris.

The compartment was crowded with passengers, many of them soldiers. I was wedged between an old man stinking of garlic and cigars who fell asleep against my shoulder and a mother with a baby who cried for half an hour. At every stop, the passengers shifted, and soon I sat between a Free French army officer whose hand brushed my leg and a nun who murmured prayers. Monsieur Zazou slept throughout the day. It was very cold, and I saw my breath in puffs of chill air. I bundled my coat around me over my wool sweater. My fingers were numb even with my gloves.

We had packed crackers, sugar, coffee, and some bread. Whenever we sat in a station longer than a few minutes, I found hot water to make coffee for Monsieur Zazou and myself. I was beginning to wonder if my plan was wise. Since Daniel didn't know I was coming, what would I find in Villers-Cotterêts?

We arrived in Paris at nine o'clock and were very tired. It was too late to visit Madame Harieu, and the hotel by the train station had tiny rooms on the top floor, so we took them. That night I dreamed of

Daniel running toward me. Then some loud sound stopped us, and I awoke frightened.

It was dark when we arrived, but in the light of the next day, I saw Paris for the first time. There was damage to the city, and the electricity did not always work, so lights were on and off. The streets were crowded with many men in uniform, as in Nice. But here, no one relaxed in the sun. The newspaper described the war in Belgium; the news was not good.

It was freezing as we walked the kilometer to Madame Harieu's house by the Seine. I did not remember ever being this cold and had to wrap my scarf around my head as I carried the prints. Madame Harieu was a small, shriveled woman with thin gray hair and green eyes but had the sweetest smile. I was moved when I saw the two old friends greet each other. Monsieur Zazou kissed her warmly, and she cried.

We had coffee and pastries, and she told us about the German occupation during the past four years. Her house was magnificent, and I saw the foyer and parlor, but I imagined it had many rooms on its several floors. I wondered if she had Germans staying there as Madame Moineau had. After an hour, I stood to leave. I needed to take the noon train to Villers-Cotterêts, and I knew these two had much to talk about.

The train to Villers-Cotterêts jolted to a stop, and sadness greeted me. The station was bombed, and snow lay on crumbled walls. Buildings without roofs sat next to houses where no more than one wall remained. A sharp wind blew through the station, so I tucked my chin into my scarf and walked to the Hôtel de la Gare. I asked the clerk for hot water since my hands were stiff and nearly purple. He called to Claire, his little girl, to bring the water, and I made myself a cup of coffee.

The door opened, and a GI walked in and thumbed a little red book.

"*Bonjour, monsieur,*" he tried to say and stared at a page.

I recognized the army dictionary and the shoulder patch that he wore on his sleeve. He was in Daniel's company. When he finished his business with the clerk, I approached him.

"Can you tell me where the aid station is?" He was surprised to hear English.

"Come on. I'll take you." He picked up my suitcase.

I felt the clerk's disapproval as I left with the American soldier. Was I just another French woman in love with the American army? Despite the fact that the Allies had liberated France, including the owner of the hotel, I was a French woman and, to some, being with an American GI was as disloyal as being with a German.

An old French army barracks had become military headquarters. We entered a gate onto a large square surrounded by buildings. The soldier pointed to a Red Cross flag and handed me my suitcase. I ran across the square and opened the door to the dispensary and walked into Norman! He looked exhausted and much thinner.

After he hugged me, I asked, "Where is Daniel?"

"Daniel was sent to the front two weeks ago. He's due back any day now."

What was I thinking at that time? I do not know. Did I expect Daniel to be here waiting for me? Could I have come all this way for nothing?

Norman walked back to the hotel with me.

The clerk, Monsieur Cachet, was writing in a ledger.

"I need a room," I said.

"*Pas de chambres.*"

"What did he say?" Norman asked.

"The hotel is full." Was it because I was a French woman with an American soldier? I noticed the empty lobby and told Norman I would have to find another hotel. Norman placed a handful of francs on the counter and stared at the clerk and asked politely if he could please find a room. The francs made a difference because I had a place to stay that night. After a meal at the hotel café with Norman, I walked up the three flights of stairs to my tiny room. It was the same size as my room above the bakery in Nice but much more welcoming. Even though drafts of cold air blew in the window and made the lace curtains flutter, a quilt with patches of green, yellow, and blue covered the bed and reminded me of wildflowers.

I spent the next morning at the dispensary. Daniel had not yet arrived from the front, and I had nothing to do. The doctors were happy to have another pair of hands, so I helped maintain a large pan of boiling snow on the stove for washing patients and medical instruments. I rolled strips of cotton into bandages and wrote letters for GIs who could not hold a pen. Most of them were in good spirits despite their injuries. They wanted to go home.

One GI's hands were bandaged because a grenade exploded a few meters from where he stood. He was shy and didn't know what to say to his girlfriend.

"Could you say that I miss her?"

"*Oui.*"

"Say I'm coming home in French. That will impress her."

"*Je viens à la maison.*" He tried to repeat the words.

In the afternoon, a truck arrived from the front line with wounded soldiers. I looked in vain for Daniel. The sight of the men was agonizing; bloody bandages covered holes in their bodies and places where legs or arms had been amputated. Heads were wrapped to cover holes where eyes should have been. Stomach wounds were so deep the centers of soldiers' bodies were empty. The dispensary became red with blood, and I did not want to interfere. I returned to the hotel. I thought about leaving, but since I had come this far, I hoped one more night would be enough.

Claire knocked on my door. "The soldiers are here," she said. I ran downstairs and saw Norman and a few others.

"*Bonjour*, Emilie," said Sergeant Donelan.

I hugged the Sergeant. He was thin like everyone else, his bright red hair as striking as before. Norman unpacked a duffel bag of wine, cheese, bread, ham, coffee, and chocolate bars.

"What are we celebrating?" I asked.

"Seeing a good friend," Norman said.

I asked who that was, and he laughed and pointed to me.

Norman invited Monsieur Cachet to join us, and when he offered Claire a bar of chocolate, the clerk disappeared into the back of the hotel. He reappeared in a minute with wine glasses. I ate enough to last several days, and Norman gave me the leftover food before the soldiers departed. I asked about Daniel, but no one knew why he was late returning from the front. One more night, I promised myself, and then I would go back to Nice.

At the dispensary, a medic asked me to copy the list of those killed in action. I was terrified. What if Daniel's name was on the list? I prayed as I wrote names beginning with T and U and V. Once I passed the W's and wrote the names beginning with Y, I released my breath.

In the afternoon, it felt like hell arrived. The line of jeeps and trucks stretched across the square in front of the clinic. Litters of half-frozen men were carried into the dispensary. Dying soldiers lined the walls, and doctors shouted for nurses and medics. I watched as they stitched wounds, amputated limbs, and covered the soldiers who could not be saved. A surgeon yelled at me to grab some gauze and pointed to rolls of cotton. Blood was flowing from a soldier's chest and running onto the floor. I pushed the cotton into the doctor's hands. "Give me your hand!" he said. He pressed both my hands and an inch of bandage over the wound. The white cotton turned red, and I felt dizzy as the soldier's chest caved in with each breath. Someone yelled that a foot had to come off.

My fingers were sticky with blood. I prayed, *please God, don't let him die.* I started to cry. Tears ran down my cheeks and dropped onto the bandage mixing with the blood. The surgeon told someone to leave the foot alone and come here. A medic replaced me, putting fresh white cotton on the soldier's chest. My hands were red and caked in dried blood. I heard a scream, and the room whirled around, and I ran outside gasping for air.

After a while, Norman came out and asked how I was. I could not see his face, but his big shape was comforting. How could they do it? How could they stand the pain and the blood and the confusion and the death? Norman said they got used to it, sixteen to eighteen hours a day, to keep men alive. Once a surgeon stood so long at the operating table, his feet were swollen, and they had to cut his boots off.

He asked if I was worried about Daniel and said he did not think it was Daniel's time. Daniel had close calls before and survived. Norman touched my shoulder. "When it was your time to go, it was your time to go." I prayed it was not Daniel's time. But maybe it was time for me to go. Monsieur Zazou expected me to be home by now, and I missed Nice. Coming to Villers-Cotterêts had been a mistake, so I went back to the hotel and packed my few things. I would leave the next day.

January 22, 1945. I remember the date.

I was asleep when I heard a knock on my door.

"*Mademoiselle* Emilie." It was the owner's daughter Claire.

I thought, is it morning already?

"*Monsieur Daniel est ici!*"

I ran down the stairs in my nightgown and tripped and landed on top of Daniel's frozen boots. He lifted me up, and I threw myself into his arms. Snow covered his army coat, and his helmet had a layer of ice. His eyes were bloodshot, and his beard rough. Daniel looked like he had not slept or eaten well for weeks.

We climbed the stairs to my room. Riding for nine hours from Belgium to France in the bitter cold had turned his hands blue. I removed his gloves and rubbed his stiff fingers. He said he could feel nothing. I unlaced his boots and stripped off his wet socks and massaged his damp feet. I learned Daniel had eaten no hot food for weeks. There had been three feet of snow and frostbite. With his pants and shirt off, I saw how thin he was. Daniel mumbled about tanks in the woods and snipers and frozen bodies with open eyes. I pulled the blanket over us and pressed his trembling back to my chest. Snow blew in through cracks in the walls.

I had fallen asleep with my head resting on his shoulder when he stirred. I thought he was talking in his sleep, but then I saw he was awake.

"Ran out of morphine...tanks rolling over dead bodies...a truck full of wounded men on litters...we had to leave it behind...and somebody's shouting 'Stay with us'."

"*Sh, mon cher,*" I whispered.

"Two days ago, the fighting was so bad...medics had to pick up rifles. I killed a man. A kid. I shot a German boy. His head exploded."

Daniel sobbed into his hands. His mouth moved, but no sound came out. Then, "Freddie." I remembered Freddie from the USO dance at the Ruhl Hotel. I could not understand all of what Daniel said, but somewhere in St. Vith, the Germans attacked. Freddie volunteered to go with a small group of men to strike back. All of the men were blown up by a mine.

"I found Freddie. He was still alive. Blood coming out of his chest every time he took a breath. Red streaks on the snow. His hair was all red and frozen, standing up on end like he was electrocuted."

I held Daniel closely.

"There was nothing I could do. I kept talking to him. He smiled."

Daniel cried himself to sleep, but I stayed awake until the sun rose. Then we dressed in silence. Was he angry with me for coming to Villers-Cotterêts? We had breakfast at the restaurant next to the train station, and Daniel ate ham and eggs like a starved man. Norman stopped by, and they spoke of the war, but neither one mentioned Freddie. Daniel said he was so weary one night he fell asleep giving a soldier a shot of morphine. Then he took my hand and said he was going back to the front the next day. He kissed me and stared as if he needed to memorize my face. "I love you," he said. He spent the day at the dispensary and promised to come to the hotel that evening.

We huddled in bed as the wind whistled through the slits in the walls. Daniel was excited and teased me about calling Monsieur Cachet for more heat. I was happy to see him lighter and smiling, but it was a strange lightness.

"Are you cold?" I asked.

"This room is like the beach compared to a foxhole in the Ardennes." He ran his fingers around my cheekbones and down to my chin.

"Meeting you has been the best thing that ever happened to me. You gave me something to live for these last months. I was lucky in Italy and France and now Belgium. Maybe my time has come."

I was silent.

"If I die, maybe we'll meet again someday, somewhere."

We awoke at dawn. Daniel said he would come again to Nice if he could. I was not sure I believed him. At the station, we said our good-byes, and I sat on the train waiting for it to leave. Daniel stood on the platform. He raised his hand in a final good-bye, and I smiled then turned my head away. As the train moved away from Villers-Cotterêts, Daniel became smaller and smaller. When I looked back at the station, he had disappeared.

I held my ticket. My last souvenir.

33

I drop my head onto the open memoir. Drained. Exhausted. My eyes burn from interpreting Emilie's handwriting. I had no idea what Dad went through. I shiver at the thought of the freezing cold Dad suffered at the front while Emilie worked at the dispensary, blood pouring out of bodies.

I gaze at the train ticket from Villers-Cotterêts to Paris. It was possibly the final time they saw each other and the last of the souvenirs that Emilie saved in the box Yvette sent to me. I set the ticket aside. No wonder they clung to each other so desperately. They weren't only lovers; they were survivors.

"Don't forget me," and "I'll make sure you'll always know where to reach me," not to mention, "I'll always love you," are not the words of a wartime fling, no matter what DJ thinks. I'm more conflicted than ever about Emilie and Dad and Mother.

My cell rings. I check the caller ID.

As if my thoughts caused my brother to materialize. "Hi, DJ. How are you?"

"Fine. Nancy has me—"

"—on a short leash," I finish for him.

"You got that right." He paused. "You?" he asks tentatively.

This is a first. "Me? All good here. With the semester over, meetings and more meetings."

"I don't miss meetings," he says, and we laugh. "I got a text from Billy."

"You did? Billy texts now?"

"Apparently."

"I was sorry he had to leave so soon after the funeral. I didn't get much of a chance to talk."

"You can make up for it this summer."

"Yeah?"

"He's coming home, well to New Jersey, in July."

"That's great. You think he'll stay for a while?"

"It's Billy so who knows. I thought we'd have a...I don't know. Some kind of party or whatever. Fourth of July."

"That sounds like a nice idea," I say softly. "A gathering of the Whitman siblings."

"Dad always liked the Fourth."

"Yes, he did."

The silence on the line is companionable, not uncomfortable as it might have been in the past. So I take a chance. "Speaking of Dad..."

I sense a bit of tension on the other end.

"What about him," DJ asks, guarded.

"I was thinking about the war this morning. What he went through." Before DJ's imagination can head straight for Emilie, I hurry to shift his line of thinking. "Did he ever talk to you about Italy? What it was like there before he landed in France?"

I hear DJ draw a breath. Then release it. "Not really."

"Some things I've been reading lately...about the war. How bad it was in the winter of 1945."

"Reading this stuff for fun?" he says with an edge that reminds me of the pre-heart-attack brother.

"DJ, I teach French history as well as the language."

He softens. "Yeah. Right." He pauses. "The only time I ever heard him say anything about the war was one time when he and Bert..." DJ coughed.

I resist my impulse to dive in and cover up the awkwardness. If we are going to have a new and improved relationship, I have to allow DJ to be DJ.

"We were having a few drinks at a family picnic. Must have been sometime in the nineties. Before Bert was..."

Banished to Atlantic City, I think.

"Anyway, one of the twins, probably Drew, asked about Bert's hand and the missing fingers. I sort of gave him a poke to shut him up but Bert didn't mind. He went on to explain about the mine that exploded, tearing off part of his hand. And Dad chimed in on what a hero Bert was...and Bert said the same about Dad."

"I remember a similar thing years before when Billy raised the same question."

"Yeah, well, once they were done patting each other on the back, Drew asked Dad if he ever had to kill anyone in the war. I put a hand over his mouth and tried to shush him." DJ stops.

Is that the end of his story?

"But Dad looked at Drew. He nodded. Said it was almost the worst day of his life. Said it was a German boy. I was shocked. Never heard Dad say anything like this before. Even Bert looked surprised."

Almost the worst day? What was the worst?

"The war was hell, he said. For everybody."

Did that "hell" include the loss of Emilie?

DJ sighs. "I'm remembering things about Dad I thought I forgot."

Trauth

Thanks to the memoir, so am I, DJ. So am I.

34

February was gray and depressing. Monsieur Zazou was happy because he had a wonderful time with Madame Harieu in Paris, and now business was strong. I developed pictures and helped Victoire organize the inventory. I forced myself to smile when she talked about wedding plans. I sympathized when she said her mother was afraid she would never see her daughter or grandchildren after the marriage. Victoire and Jimmy planned to move to Toledo, Ohio, after the war to live with Jimmy's parents.

In March, Victoire made me a birthday cake, and she and Monsieur Zazou sang to me. Later we had dinner in a café, and I felt old at twenty-two. Spring was trying to come, and more shops were open, and the shipyard was busy. There was hope everywhere but in my heart. I picked up my brushes and tilted my easel to catch the light, and painted. The work was not always good, but at least I felt like an artist again. My art gave me consolation.

Then after two months, Daniel was back in my life. I received a short letter from Germany that said he was safe and well. He would be going to the general hospital at the military camp sixty-five kilometers north of Reims. There would probably be little work for him there, and it might be his last assignment. He signed the letter: Love, Daniel.

I felt bitter and full of turmoil. I should be joyful reading his words, but I was resigned to his leaving, and I needed to keep my heart in check. I would question Daniel's behavior again and again. Yes, it was wartime, but Jimmy had proposed marriage. Why had Daniel never mentioned marriage to me? I knew the war would end soon, and he would leave Europe. Why did he not talk about our future? I decided not to write to him at the address he gave me.

By April, Victoire had chosen a wedding dress and modeled it for me even though they had no definite date for the ceremony.

She said, "Someday you will come to America with Daniel and we will all have fun together."

"Daniel and I are not Jimmy and you," I said again.

She was sad for me. During the fall and winter, my wish was to see him survive. But now, he was safe. What did he feel for me? Did he really love me?

Then the news came. Germany was near defeat. I was so busy in the shop I had no time to wonder what Daniel was doing. But at night, my imagination ran wild. I saw us together even though he had made no mention of our future. During the first week of May, we heard that Hitler had died. Madame Lanvin and Victoire and I sat together on the sofa and wept happy tears. French prisoners returned from Germany by the thousands.

On May 8, 1945, the war was finally over. Madame Lanvin ran downstairs with a bottle of champagne she managed to save from 1942. We cried again. Everyone ran into the streets and wept and hugged strangers. I ran to the Promenade. The avenue was so full it reminded me of Carné's film. We had waited to celebrate like this for four years, and now it burst out of our hearts and mouths. People sang *La Marseillaise* again, and soldiers kissed young girls like the day the Allies arrived in Nice. Cafés poured free wine, and horns honked.

Victoire was thrilled. The end of the war meant that she and Jimmy would marry. Not only was I losing my lover, I was also losing my best friend. It was a euphoric time but also a mournful one. I needed to be strong and accept that I would never see Daniel again.

Within a day, I received a note from him. He had a three-day pass for Paris and begged me to meet him there. I was torn. I desperately wanted to see him, but I was afraid of leaving him again. At first, I decided not to go because of the shop, but Monsieur Zazou was closing the shop for a few days to celebrate the end of the war. So, I went to Paris.

Daniel had written he would be at the Madeleine metro station at two o'clock on May 11. If I came, he would see me there, and if not, he would understand my decision. My imagination was very active, and I thought Daniel might propose to me in Paris as Jimmy proposed to Victoire, and I felt good even though my heart knew better.

At the station, the crowd was overwhelming. Every GI in Europe had a pass to Paris! I saw a poster of Arletty and Jean-Louis Barrault clinging to each other in the middle of the Carnivale crowd and flowing confetti. Carné had finished *Les Enfants du Paradis*. It felt like a lifetime ago instead of a year.

"Are you alone?"

I turned to see Daniel holding a red rose between his teeth. "Welcome to Paris, *ma cherie*," he said and kissed my hand.

"*Merci!*"

"We are going to have a wonderful time."

I agreed. I was determined to be happy.

We walked along the Left Bank until Notre Dame appeared in our view.

When I knelt inside the cathedral, I prayed for us. I prayed that somehow we could have a life together. I looked at Daniel, and he stared at me as my lips moved.

We crossed the Seine and wandered past artists and vendors who had set up their goods against the concrete walls that followed the river.

Daniel talked about the Louvre like a tour guide. "Did you know it covers forty-eight acres?"

I remembered my French history. "Marie Antoinette lived here during the French Revolution, *oui*? She was a prisoner." We were stunned at the emptiness of the museum. A woman told us thousands of pieces had been removed by the staff and hidden in the south of France to keep them safe from the Nazis.

Daniel pointed to an Egyptian sarcophagus. "Guess this was too heavy to steal."

In the Tuileries Gardens, we watched children sail boats on the pond, and fathers and mothers read newspapers and chat in the shade of the trees. Then a little girl leaped into the water and cried, "Papa, my boat!" It was sinking to the bottom. A man jumped in and grabbed the little girl with one arm and saved the toy ship with the other. The two of them were dripping wet and laughing when they got out. Children would never become a part of our lives.

As though he could read my mind, Daniel jumped to his feet. "Let's go find a place to stay."

We found a room at L'Hôtel des Artistes in the 8th arrondissement. It was small but with clean sheets and a washbowl. We were grateful to have a place at all with Paris full of visitors. We washed and changed for dinner and then a surprise. At a restaurant on Île de la Cité a man joined us. He had Daniel's brown eyes and dark hair but was shorter and heavier. It was his younger brother Bert who also had a three-day pass to Paris. Bert was a sergeant.

I was disappointed at first. I did not want to share this precious time with someone else, but then I became fascinated seeing both of them. They teased and slapped each other on the back. We sat in the café for hours while Bert told stories about the war in the north. I did not understand everything he said, but some words stayed in my mind.

Daniel said, "Here's a real war hero. He landed on Normandy a week after D-Day. He took out a German patrol all by himself." Daniel lifted his glass and saluted his brother.

"Dan's the real hero. Patching up guys, making sure they live." Bert poured more wine. "We couldn't have won this war without medics. Anyway, those Krauts didn't stand a chance. We don't go home 'til we win. Simple as that. They didn't stand a chance."

Such boldness. I never heard any soldiers speak so strongly about the war. His men were exhausted and shaved with ice water and slept in foxholes standing up. When they were called to attack the Germans, the soldiers ignored the Luftwaffe and two feet of snow. They drove the enemy out of the next village.

"Got a letter from Dad last week," said Bert. "Been a while since he heard from you."

"Busy fighting a war." Daniel frowned.

"He wondered if you've been getting any letters from…friends?" Bert asked.

"A few." Daniel put his arm around my shoulders.

Bert stared at me, and I noticed an unspoken conversation pass between them. I excused myself. At the door of the toilet, I turned around, and I saw Bert speaking, shaking his head. He threw his hands in the air, and Daniel slumped in his seat. Bert looked in my direction, and I knew they were talking about me.

The next day we were like tourists and pretended to be happy. We walked and walked through every corner of the city and saw L'Opéra and the Eiffel Tower, a thousand feet of lacework silhouetted against the sky.

Later, we found a restaurant on the Champs-Élysées and ate roast beef and potatoes and sipped champagne.

"Let's have another bottle of champagne," Daniel said.

"We don't want to be late for the show." We had waited in line for an hour to buy tickets to the Folies Bergère.

"We have plenty of time." He knocked over my glass. "Sorry. Think I'm getting a little drunk."

The champagne had gone to his head, but Daniel insisted on finishing the last drop.

The theater was full of GIs, and we had to push our way to the seats. The soldiers whistled and clapped when a line of women floated down a set of stairs and posed in a tableau. They lifted their bare arms and waved large, feathered fans. The dancers were nude from the waist up, and their breasts and torsos were decorated with colorful jewelry.

I wanted to go back to the hotel after the show, but Daniel said there was a nightclub set up by the Red Cross. So we went, and Daniel and I sat at a table by a large dance floor watching the show of tumblers, jugglers, and singers. Champagne bottles covered tables, and soldiers had contests to see who could drink the most. A heavy cloud of smoke hung in the air, and my feet ached. It was hard to breathe.

"Daniel," I said. "Can't we leave?" The nightclub was so crowded when I turned to speak to him, my mouth was close to two GIs at the table beside us.

"Okay." Daniel emptied the champagne bottle.

Counting the two at dinner, he had drunk almost four bottles by himself. I had never seen him like this. He stood up, accidentally kicking over his chair. Then a scream pierced the noise, and everything was quiet. A woman swung a champagne bottle at the head of a GI who held her in his arms and shouted, "you are an animal." The soldier ducked and punched the woman in the mouth. As she howled and clawed at him, everyone around her stood frozen. In seconds two men jumped on the GI and freed the woman.

As the orchestra played, men climbed on tables, shoving and hitting anyone who got in their way. Bottles flew through the air, sending up cries of pain and anger. I tugged at Daniel. He was paralyzed, too drunk to move. The fight swept across the room, and the military police moved into the crowd. It was the riot on the movie set again. I dragged Daniel to a side door and pushed him outside.

I found a taxi, and Daniel fell asleep in the back seat with his head on my shoulder. The hotel proprietor was annoyed at being awakened at two a.m. but helped me carry Daniel to the third floor. I removed his shoes, tie, and belt and pulled a cover over him. I crawled under the sheet. He snored all night, and I did not sleep.

In the morning, we were quiet. My feet were sore from the long night, and Daniel had a headache. We lay awake in bed, his hand on my back.

"You don't think I'm an animal, do you? Like the guy last night?"

"*Non*. But some men are animals. Some French women have been hurt," I said.

"I don't want to hurt you. I never meant to hurt you."

I held my breath. It was the moment for him to talk about our future. But before he could say anything, my frustration and pain burst out. "We love each other. We can stay together. I will live in the U.S. if that is what you want."

He brushed my cheek. "Emilie. I can't take you to America."

Then I heard the words that were a punch to my stomach.

"I am engaged to another woman. I'm so sorry. I should have told you sooner, but I was afraid to lose you."

There was a rushing in my ears that drowned out everything else he said. I could only hear "engaged to another woman." He cried, and I cried, and I said that we loved each other and that he could end the engagement.

He sat on the edge of the bed and hung his head. "I can't." He spoke slowly as if he was searching for words in some deep place inside. "Her name is Margaret. She's been a family friend since I was a kid." Before he left for Europe, he asked her to write, and she agreed. Then when he was in Italy, and the fighting was so bad, Daniel was afraid and lonely. "I asked her to marry me when I got back. She said yes and promised to marry me no matter what happened to me in the war."

She had made a commitment, and he had too. Daniel wanted me to understand that he was an honorable man. Not a bad man, just a man who had fallen in love.

Now I can see him more clearly. He wanted to honor his promise to Margaret. But back then, I was angry and hurt and felt betrayed.

"Why didn't you tell me sooner?" Daniel moaned and I said again, "Why? Why? Don't you have a commitment to me? How am I to live without you? Don't I deserve your honor?"

He put his arm around me, and I pushed him away. I cried because I did not understand. He tried to kiss me and placed his mouth next to mine, and I tasted the salt of his tears. I could not bear to feel his lips on mine, and I covered my face in my hands.

Daniel said he wanted to see me again before he left for home, and I exploded.

"What difference would it make now? Was I your wartime lover who could be used and thrown away?" I jumped from the bed and flung open the door and told Daniel to leave. "I don't want to see you again."

He opened his mouth to argue, then said nothing. As he packed his clothes, I stood by the door and closed my eyes, and held my arms close to my body. I needed to hold myself together. I would not surrender to him again.

I left for Nice later that day. On the train, I tried to sleep, but I was furious with myself and Daniel that fate brought us together only to tear us apart forever. I was sinking into a black hole. My souvenir from Paris was a broken heart.

At the end of May, Jimmy received a twenty-four-hour pass, and he and Victoire married in a civil ceremony. A soldier and I served as witnesses, and Victoire's mother frowned the entire time. Afterward, they had supper at the Ruhl Hotel. Jimmy said it was his favorite place since that was where they met. During the wedding ceremony, I thought of Daniel. I regretted sending him away in Paris. I loved Daniel so much I would have agreed to see him again, even knowing that he was leaving me forever.

On June 6, I waited while a customer in the Art Studio studied the prints I had developed. The bell above the door jingled. My heart dropped. Daniel stood in the doorway with his hat in his hands. On the sidewalk, in front of the shop, Daniel spoke in a rush. He was afraid to write since I might tell him not to come, and he pleaded with me to talk to him. I must have said something, but I cannot remember what it was.

He was leaving France in two days and had only that afternoon to see me. He was determined that we should speak before he left. I was anxious. What was there to say to each other? Daniel waved for a taxi to take us to the Cimiez Monastery. We had gone there in the fall. It was peaceful, and the birds sang, and the trees were full and green.

As we walked up the path to the monastery, I looked at Daniel from time to time. I needed to remember how his boots were shined, his pants neatly pressed, and his dark hair brushed off his forehead. We sat on the ground under a lime tree and said nothing for a time.

"Of all the thousands of men in Europe I'm the happiest because of you. I'll never forget you as long as I live."

He made me promise to tell him if I ever needed anything at any time. I promised. What would I need after he was gone, I wondered?

Daniel held my hand. "We must each marry and build our lives."

I wiped my eyes. He put his arms around me slowly, and I laid my head on his shoulder. His lips were near my ear, and he whispered, "Emilie." It was the last time he said my name.

We sat for a while, and then he kissed me. I tried to memorize the feel of his lips on mine. I knew this souvenir must last a lifetime. He studied his watch and stood and pulled me to my feet. "We will go now without turning around. It will be easier that way."

We started to walk away from each other, but I was desperate and ran to him. Then he backed away, and I watched him, one arm stretched above his head waving good-bye and tears running down his cheeks. Daniel walked to the top of a hill and slowly descended the other side. Soon I could not see his legs, then his shoulders disappeared, and then his face was gone. All that remained was the hand of his upraised arm. It, too, vanished. The blue sky swallowed my beloved.

35

Tears cascade down my face. I haven't cried like this since Dad passed. As the early morning light trickles through my bedroom windows, I weep for my father and for Emilie, for what they had together, for what they lost. Questions instantly emerge: How long had they corresponded? How could Dad have left Emilie after the passion they shared? He may never have seen Emilie after the war, but I feel certain Dad remained emotionally attached to her.

I find myself a few feet away from Mother's side of the headstone. I read the engraving. Beloved Wife and Mother. I kneel at the foot of the marker and trace the dates of her life carved into the marble: 1922–1982.

I hear her voice.

It was another of our disagreements. I wanted to go to a party at a friend's house whose parents were out of town. Somehow Mother found out we wouldn't be chaperoned and put her foot down. Absolutely not. We argued in her bedroom, where she was watching television. Just as soon as our voices surpassed the volume, Mother's demeanor shifted. I saw her eyes shining too brightly.

"I don't know where we went wrong."

"'We' didn't go wrong. Dad didn't do anything wrong." I choked on my own tears. "Dad's the only one who loves me around here."

Mother shot upright, blazing. "What do you know about love? About your father's love?"

Taken aback, I stammered. "Dad would do anything for me."

"You don't know everything about your father," she said vehemently.

I had no response in that moment. What did I not know about Dad?

In an instant, Mother grabbed my wrist, her grip tight.

"You don't know what real love is, what kind of sacrifice real love demands."

I marveled at the strength of her grasp. I tried to pry her fingers loose. "Mother, please," I said.

"Kate, love is not just about doing. It's also about doing without."

I had no idea what she meant that day, and I ran from the room and refused to come to the table for dinner. For days I scrutinized my father's behavior, searching for something he said or did that would shock me. Of course, nothing did.

When I was little and crying because I'd scraped a knee, it was Dad who kissed me and held me until the tears stopped. As a child, I was never really sure my mother even liked me.

Now, as I gaze at her side of the headstone, I wonder what she had done without. If flying into Marseille that summer I was in Paris meant that she visited Emilie, I yearn to know why she went and what was said.

I touch his side of the headstone and then rock back on my heels. This is the first time I am specifically visiting my mother's grave. I yank a few stray weeds from the base of the stone. I wish desperately that now, after years of incessant fighting due in part to my ignorance, I could speak with her in person.

I dig a shallow hole by the edge of the marker and place an arrangement of pale cream calla lilies, Mother's favorite, an inch or two into the earth. I rub some dirt from my hands, brush off my pants, and rise to walk away from the gravesite, but something stops me. The setting sun that breaks over the back of the marker blinds me for a moment, and when I glance once more at Mother's side of the stone, the marble seems brighter and clearer. I drop to my knees and rest my head against its chill surface.

Traffic is light into the Lincoln Tunnel, and I arrive at Dad's apartment in record time. In the foyer, I notice the smells that were present the last time I was here—cigar smoke and dust and aftershave—have been replaced by a floral air freshener and lemon furniture polish. No sign of the twins' weekend in the apartment, either. The cleaning service I hired had left the place shiny and spotless and smelling like new. Not like Dad.

I flick on the air conditioning, drop my bag on the desk chair in the guest room, and open the safe in the living room. Though he kept important family papers in the safe in New Jersey, there had to be a reason Dad berated DJ for going into this one all those years ago. In the interest of being thorough, I want to excavate all dark corners. I twist the tumbler right and left to match the combination DJ gave me.

I'm not sure what I expected to find but am amazed at the contents. A rubber-banded packet of letters, a handful of eight-by-ten manila envelopes, another smaller, business-sized, white envelope, and a couple of file folders. I spread everything out on the kitchen table. Before me is a treasure trove of history, the record of a relationship so sensitive, so complicated it had to be secreted away in a safe place where no one else was likely to see it. Until the apartment was cleaned out…after Dad died.

I study the letters. Then I remove the rubber band and thumb through the stack. The return addresses are Nice and Marseille. Each of them has E. Renault printed above the return address. I am taken aback by the dates—1945 to 1990. Emilie wrote to Dad from the end of the war forward for at least forty years. I set them aside and pick up the manila envelopes. And I'm startled. Lovely, small watercolors: a boat riding waves, a red-roofed cottage on a shoreline, the sun rising over mountains, several gardens. In the corner, each is signed E. Renault. They are delicate pastels, soft and romantic.

The white envelope contains a handful of black and white photos of a villa, street scenes possibly from Marseille, an older man, and a girl, and color photos of gardens. None of Emilie. The last items are the file folders stapled along the sides. The first also has a painting. I withdraw it carefully and blink, stunned. *It's me.* A painting of me from my college graduation picture. *Oh my God.* Emilie had a photo of me, and she copied it. For Dad. He'd kept it locked away from prying eyes. Since Mother had passed away the summer after I graduated, it's unlikely she'd ever have seen it anyway. And that was a good thing. It occurs to me more and more lately that as a spoiled young woman—who looked a lot like my father, incessantly speaking French—I represented a constant reminder to my mother of what Dad might have given up and might still be missing. Something that my mother could never give him.

The other file folder has a flat object wrapped in yellowed tissue paper, a black-and-white photograph glued to a piece of poster board. A woman holds a paintbrush in one hand, a paint palette in the other, as she smiles at the camera. Her dark hair is piled haphazardly on top of her head, and her bare breasts are visible above a canvas resting on an easel. Her naked thighs appear below the canvas. I turn the picture over. "Nice, 1944" is scribbled in Dad's handwriting. The photo was taken that December. Emilie is striking. Beautiful.

Questions nip at the back of my mind...the envelope that Lloyd showed DJ and me back in March had Emilie's return address as L'Avigne. It was also her daughter Yvette's address. But the letters in the safe had only Nice and Marseille as return addresses. Had Emilie not written to Dad once she moved from Marseille? She had to have written at least one letter...the envelope Dad gave Lloyd. A more pressing question is why was the memoir separate from the items in the safe? When did Dad receive it? Who sent it to him?

I have a few pages to finish before I head home.

36

During the month of June, I was ill and could not keep food down. My head ached, and even Monsieur Zazou was worried. Victoire divided her time between the apartment in Nice and her mother's farm in La Turbie. When she was gone, I had time to think of Daniel and to sort my souvenirs.

Then I received a postcard. It was a picture of Coney Island with beautiful sunbathers on a beach and the ocean behind them. Daniel wrote, "Like Nice. I see you here. Please write to this address." Then signed it "D" as though he might be afraid to write his name. There was no mention of his travel home or family or Margaret. The return address was "Whitman Textiles" in New York.

Victoire came back from La Turbie in July and took me to the doctor. He told me what I already knew. I was pregnant with Daniel's child. Losing weight made it difficult for many women during the war to get pregnant. But by the spring of 1945, I had regained much of my weight. It happened in Paris. I was terrified. What was I going to do? I was too ashamed to tell Monsieur Zazou, and I doubted he noticed my belly was becoming more rounded. Victoire insisted that I write to Daniel and tell him. I picked up a pen, but my hand shook. I could not eat, I could not sleep, and I was angry and sad and happy all at once. I could not even paint. For two weeks, I worried. I wrote to Daniel once but could not bring myself to mention the baby. He had a new life in America. What would he think about a child in France? What would be the honorable thing for him to do? I worked at the shop during the day and walked along the Promenade in the evening to clear my head.

Then I had a dream. I was sitting in a café with Bibi and Guy, and we talked about Monaco before the war. Guy held Bibi's hand and pretended to read her palm.

"You can't imagine what I see," he said.

Bibi yanked her hand from his and called my name. "Make him stop," she said.

Then they both said, "Emilie," over and over.

I awoke, and my pillow was wet. Victoire put her arms around me. "It was a dream," she said.

Days later, I was about to close the shop when the bell above the door jingled, and I thought of the day Daniel stood there. My mind was full of him, and for a moment, I did not really see the figure closing the door. I asked if I could help him, and then I heard Guy's voice. "Emilie." Like in my dream. I gazed into a face I both knew and didn't know. It *was* Guy. I ran to him, and we hugged each other, and I called out for Monsieur Zazou.

Guy's beard and hair were streaked with gray, and the hollows of his face created sharp angles.

"I cannot believe it is you!" I said.

Monsieur Zazou cried and wiped his eyes and patted Guy's back. He brought out a bottle of wine to celebrate. When I asked where he had been, Guy told us his story. He was arrested on the road near Toulon with photographs that he was passing to an underground agent. The Gestapo had followed him for days.

He rubbed his right arm that hung loosely. I touched his right hand, and Guy curled two fingers around my thumb. His arm was broken so many times the bones never healed right. He shrugged. "At least I have a left arm."

Monsieur Zazou and I were stunned at the calm way he described torture. "The bastards," he said. Even with the Allies a few miles away, they still tortured prisoners for names so that they could break the resistance. "German stupidity and arrogance lost the war."

His voice was soft, but I heard rage. I was afraid to ask how he survived. The Germans took prisoners north with them to Lyon and to the French border near Strasbourg. Then they fled and left a prison full of starved, half-dead French *résistants*.

Guy coughed a deep, dry growl. I asked when the Germans had abandoned them, and he said November. Nine months ago.

"Where have you been?" I asked.

"Here and there, Marseille mostly." He touched his jacket sleeve. "It was hard to find work with only one good arm."

"Why didn't you come back to Nice?" I asked.

"I was an empty shell."

"You are still Guy," I said.

He drank his wine and hung his head.

Later that night at the apartment, he sobbed, and I held him. He was so thin I felt his shoulder blades inside his jacket. I knew there would be no peace for Guy ever again. We both survived the war but not without scars. Mine were emotional. Guy's were physical and emotional. Within days he moved into the apartment with Victoire and me. He had no place to go. Most of his family and old friends were dead, and we were his only friends now.

Events happened quickly. Guy returned to the Art Studio to work, and Victoire, with many tears, left for America and promised to write about her life in Ohio. Guy moved into the bedroom with me. At first, we shared the bed like a brother and sister. He cried himself to sleep many nights, and I held him until the shaking ended, and his breathing became slower. Seeing Guy had given me a purpose for living. He needed me, and I needed him. My stomach grew a little every day.

I received a letter from Daniel. He wrote about his father and living with Bert in New York. He was back at work at Whitman Textiles, and he missed me terribly, he said. I missed him too. There was a pain in my chest each time I told myself I had to go on and live my life grateful for the months we had. I answered his letter and wrote of the news in Nice and Monsieur Zazou and Guy but nothing about his baby.

Guy asked me to marry him. It was natural since we had come to depend on each other. When Monsieur Zazou heard about our marriage plans, he announced that he was giving the Art Studio to us as a wedding gift. He said he was too old to own a shop any longer, but I knew he wanted to see Guy and me start our life together with some security.

So, on a day in July, I was no longer Mademoiselle Caronne but Madame Renault. I had always dreamed of a beautiful large wedding, but now with the baby, I was too ashamed to ask Maman and Papa to come from Monaco. Guy insisted that we marry in a simple ceremony at the magistrate's. He wanted no part of a church wedding. Religion had died for him with the war, he said. Monsieur Zazou joined us for a wedding supper in a restaurant by the tribunal, and then we went back to the apartment as husband and wife.

Guy was shy in bed. His bad arm was useless when he made love to me. I had to help him. When he finished, he rolled off me without a word and turned away, embarrassed. I lay there and cried. My dreams of a life with Daniel had ended.

August 8, 1945

News of the bomb was in all the newspapers. Japan had surrendered, and the war in the Pacific was over. Monsieur Zazou was stunned to read of the devastation in Hiroshima and Nagasaki.

"It is the end of the world when a country uses such weapons," he said.

Guy's expression was grim. "The world had no choice."

On August 30, I celebrated my anniversary with Daniel. We met a year ago. I reread the letters I kept locked in a jewelry box. His baby celebrated by kicking and moving. I was growing rounder, but Guy seemed not to notice. He was often preoccupied, and some days he barely realized I lived in the apartment with him. I told myself Guy was probably like many men. He paid no attention to female issues.

I waited until the end of September, and then I broke the news. Over dinner, I timidly told him, "we are going to have a baby." There was a full minute of silence as Guy absorbed what I said. Then he cried and hugged me. Later that night, as we lay in bed, I felt guilty for lying to him. But it was too late for those thoughts. The baby was coming, and it would have a father.

At the end of October, I was nearly six months pregnant. I let Guy believe it was four months. What would I tell him when the baby came "early"? Standing for too long was uncomfortable now, and so I worked fewer hours at the shop. In the apartment, I opened my easel and laid out paper and brushes. I painted.

Though the days were generally good, Guy was often ill with headaches. He refused to see a doctor and was sometimes angry and difficult. He grunted at me when I asked him anything. This was not the Guy I had known. Only when I mentioned the baby did his face light up and his expression soften.

December 25, 1945

It was not a merry Christmas that year. Monsieur Zazou died the week before the holiday. He collapsed at the shop, and his heart stopped beating instantly, they said. The funeral was small and quiet. Guy wiped away tears when he thought no one was looking, but I made no effort to stop mine. I loved the old man. Since Monsieur Zazou had passed away and I was more and more at home, Guy hired Stephania, a friend from art school, to develop film and serve customers. She was happy to have the work, and I was happy to be at home with my painting and my growing belly.

My little angel was born January 28, 1946. I named her Yvette Danielle. Yvette after her grandmother and Danielle, after her father. Guy was so thrilled with her arrival that he was indifferent to her name. She had brown eyes and a thatch of thick brown hair. Daniel's eyes and hair. Yvette was tiny, but her lungs were healthy. She screamed for milk within hours of her birth. It was a difficult labor, and the doctor was not sure we would both survive. I told Guy afterward that she was premature. My heart hurt with gratitude when I watched her sleeping.

Daniel would have loved his daughter. Sometimes I saw Guy give Yvette his thumb, and she wrapped her little fingers around it. He glowed with a tenderness that reminded me of the past.

In February and March, the days passed quickly, and little Yvette grew rapidly. Guy worked long hours and came home only to eat and stare at the baby as if he could not believe he was responsible for this tiny being. I tried to paint, but it seemed that each time I picked up a brush, she cried for milk. I loved to hold her tightly and sing the songs

Maman sang to me as a child. At night Guy and I carried her around the apartment by turns when she fussed. I was amazed that Guy was such a devoted father. I never expected that of him.

On the first of June, I received a letter from Papa. He had never written to me, and I was frightened. If it was about Maman, I wondered why he had not called me. I scanned the sheet of paper quickly. As I read, I understood. The news was too painful to speak aloud. Papa was a proud man, and it would have destroyed him to have me hear this devastating news from his mouth.

Marie was found outside Lyon and accused of collaborating with the enemy. I closed my eyes and saw a photograph on a flyer posted near the Nice train station. A woman with her head shaved stood naked in a town square. A crowd of people laughed and clapped behind her.

I wondered what Marie was doing in Lyon. Was Monsieur Boudreaux taken as well? I knew there were acts of revenge in many towns against French women who had slept with the enemy. They were called *les tondues*, horizontal collaborators.

Yvette screamed from the next room as if she had heard and understood the news.

Marie was dead. She was denounced by a friend and arrested, Papa wrote. The humiliation was too much for her. They found Marie hanging in a rented room. Her head shaved, naked. My body caved in and I crumpled the letter.

She was buried in a cemetery near Lyon in an unmarked grave. Afterward, her personal items and identity card were sent to the local magistrate and then with an explanation to Papa. I tried to write to him for three days, to thank him for his letter, to comfort him and Maman. I knew this would ruin him, to hear that his daughter was a collaborator.

Finally, I packed up Yvette and took the train to Monaco. Maman cried when she opened the door, and Papa stood still and stared at Yvette and me. Then he reached for her and said, "What is her name?"

Last week Guy announced that we were moving to Marseille.

"What about the shop?" I asked.

"I am selling it," he said. "I've had enough of Nice and photography and art."

I was surprised but not upset. There was nothing or no one left in Nice for me. It had become a cemetery. I asked what Guy would do in Marseille? He would find work, he said.

I am ending here. There is no more to tell. There has been too much pain in my life these last years, but there has been goodness and joy as well. I hear Yvette laugh, and she makes me want to live each day. She will not meet Daniel. She will not meet Marie. Yet I will make her life a happy one. She will grow up trusting that Guy is her father.

She is awake now and crying. I must go to her.

37

"I swear Kate I had no idea." Lloyd moves from behind his desk and sits down beside me. He is visibly shaken. "Daniel requested the change in his will but said nothing about a child." He studies his hands. "I thought his will was an act of restitution."

Lloyd had never said anything about Dad that was so personal, so opinionated. "Restitution?"

"I didn't know the details of his relationship with Emilie Renault but I assumed...he wanted to make up for something," he says. "He loved all of you, you know that, but I think a part of him never came back home in 1945."

"What do you mean?"

"I was the first to see your father that summer in June. He didn't want anyone to know he'd come home. It was the strangest thing. He landed at Idlewild Airport at five a.m. I'll never forget that morning. Most fellows were coming home on ships, but he had enough points to leave immediately from France. Everyone in the family was waiting for his return but I was sworn to secrecy. Daniel's telegram firmly stated he wanted no one at the airport but me."

"Was Uncle Bert home?" I ask.

"No. He was still in Germany liberating a concentration camp and recuperating from his wound. Awful stuff," Lloyd says.

I wait for him to continue.

"Daniel looked so different from the last time we'd been together, the winter of '42. When he left for Fort Bragg. I was 4F," Lloyd says. "We had some drinks and I promised to check on your grandfather."

"Was he upset about being drafted? He graduated from Columbia the year before, right?"

"Oh, he wasn't drafted. Your father volunteered. He was eager to get away. Not to fight," Lloyd adds. "He wanted to be a medic so he wouldn't have to carry a gun. Daniel kept saying he wanted to be his own man. When he came home…there was something different about him. Same eyes, same hair, but thin as a whippet. Same but not the same. Relief, anger…" Lloyd pauses. "And grief."

I understand his grief.

"He cried. I guess we both cried. First thing he wanted to do was get a drink." Lloyd laughs.

"At five in the morning?"

"That's what I said. I wondered what he'd told Margaret about his arrival." Lloyd studies a spot over my head. "We went to Luigi's in Little Italy. Worst greasy spoon in Manhattan. Runny eggs, hash browns as hard as a rock, cold toast, and a cheap bottle of whiskey. The standard breakfast at Luigi's."

"Did he mention Emilie?"

"Not that I recall. We talked a little about the winter in Belgium and the Bulge, how it was hell for those guys. Most GIs didn't say much when they got home. They kept a lot inside. I do remember telling him that 'at least you made it home in one piece' and he laughed. Almost bitter, you'd say."

"Poor Dad."

"That's not the half of it. I tried to drive him home, and he wouldn't have any of it.

"'Take me to a hotel,' he said. 'I don't want to see anybody yet.' I tried to convince him to call his father, to let your mother know he'd arrived, but he was so adamant I gave in." Lloyd spread his hands as if to say, "what choice did I have?"

"Who knew all this?" I ask.

"Nobody as far as I know. For the next two weeks, Daniel stayed at the hotel doing I don't know what during the day while I worked. Then in the evening we'd have dinner and go out on the town."

Lloyd folds his hands and places them in his lap.

"We hit clubs and cocktail lounges from the Lower East Side to the Upper West Side. But I couldn't keep up and told him so. After all, I had to work," Lloyd says.

"And Mother?"

"If I said anything, he flew off the handle and went into a tirade. All he wanted to do was drink himself to sleep every night, get up the next day, and do it all over again. Maybe he was having a nervous breakdown, some form of shell shock."

He pauses. "Then one night we met for dinner at the Stork Club—he always ordered the same thing, a rare sirloin, and a baked potato—and I told him I had to end our nightly jaunts. I was falling asleep at the office. He said something like 'Okay, okay, we'll talk about that later.'" Lloyd shook his head. "We ended up in a bar in Hell's Kitchen. Daniel sometimes liked places that were seedy. We had a drink or two and I wanted to leave. I said something like 'let's go get some coffee to clear our heads' but Daniel insisted the night was young. So I took my jacket and stood up to go. I was pretty impatient by now and probably told him he should go home to New Jersey. I didn't want to leave him there."

Lloyd struggles with the memory. "Then this big guy walked all the way down the bar in our direction. I grabbed Daniel, he had his uniform on, he always wore his uniform, and tried to pull him to his feet. Somehow, we accidentally bumped into the big guy. His hands were on Daniel's medals, and he was saying how he was a GI, too. He had just gotten back from Europe. We tried to ignore him, but the guy wouldn't give up."

He bows his head.

"Then he asked Daniel how he liked the women over there and that they loved American soldiers and American money. Daniel shoved him away and the guy went berserk, pushing us and yelling. He was drunk, too." Lloyd stops suddenly. "Then the big guy said something about 'those French whores liking uniforms.'"

"Oh, God."

"Daniel roared out loud and threw a punch. I think he probably broke the guy's nose. There was blood everywhere. He choked Daniel and I had to kick him in the...well, you know, to get Daniel free," Lloyd says.

Dad and Lloyd in a barroom brawl.

"We escaped out a back door, ran about half a dozen blocks until we were safe. I thought I might throw up so I sat down."

"Dad?" I ask.

"Well, Kate, that was something. Daniel stood stock still in the middle of the sidewalk. Howling, you might say."

Lloyd blows his nose.

"The only thing I made out was 'She's not a whore. She's not a whore.'"

The ticking of the wall clock beat a rhythm that matched the throbbing at my temples.

"I put him to bed that night in my apartment. When I got up a few hours later, your father was gone. No note, nothing. I called his hotel and he'd checked out," Lloyd says.

"Where did he go?" I ask.

"I don't know. I ran and searched all over town. Every place we'd been. It was like he'd dropped off the face of the earth. Then in July, Bert showed up. I got a call from him that Daniel was fine and was staying with him."

Lloyd pours a glass of water for me. I take a sip. "When did he see Mother that summer?"

"I'm sorry Kate. The next time I saw your father was in October at his wedding. Daniel and I never spoke about that summer again," he says. "He seemed so conflicted when he came home. He obviously intended to do right by your mother, but…I guess he was in love with Emilie."

"They wrote to each other. It's in the memoir," I say.

Lloyd stares at me. "Well, I knew he heard from her at least once." The envelope Dad had given Lloyd when he changed his will. "But I had no idea about the exact nature of their relationship," he says. "Or about Yvette. The only time he ever mentioned Emilie to me was when he wanted to include her in his will."

The image of Dad's despair generates a dull ache in the pit of my stomach. "You think maybe the will was also about Yvette?" I ask.

"Well, we don't know that your father ever found out about Yvette. It's all conjecture," Lloyd says hastily.

"He had the memoir in the New York apartment," I remind him.

Lloyd sighs deeply. "But we don't know when or how he received it. Your father put the war behind him. He didn't talk about it. He wanted no part of it."

Except for his correspondence with Emilie. "It seems clear that Yvette doesn't know about Dad," I say.

He places his hand on my arm. "Kate, it's better to leave it that way."

My mind is juggling all the information that I've absorbed over the past months, and I see pieces of the puzzle fitting together.

"Lloyd," I begin. "I'm the only one in the family who reads French."

"Yes," he says.

"I inherited the apartment and everything in it. He said I would be the person going through the contents of the place. All of the contents," I say. "Maybe Dad wanted me to find the memoir."

Lloyd searches my face. "And do what with it?"

"I don't know. Contact Yvette? Maybe contact Emilie? We don't know if Dad found out that she died the year before him."

"Kate, that would be opening quite a can of worms," Lloyd says.

"It's unfinished business. I think Yvette deserves to know who her father is, don't you?"

"What if she doesn't want to know?" he asks, raising the crux of the issue.

"It would be the right thing to do," I say. "Have someone in the Whitman family acknowledge her as Dad's daughter."

Lloyd rises, moves to his desk, and touches Dad's framed print. "I don't know what's right and what's not anymore," he says heavily.

"I'd like to meet her." I whisper, "She's my sister."

38

I stretch my legs out until they reach the railing that runs along the Atlantic City boardwalk. I tip my face up to absorb the late afternoon sun. Uncle Bert has recently entered a rehab center as an outpatient and is making good progress; at least he still appears to be on the wagon, and his clothes are clean and neat.

"Here." Bert offers me a piece of saltwater taffy.

"No thanks. Not good for my caps." We strolled up and down the boardwalk for an hour and have sat down to rest. I am astonished at how sociable he is today. When I arrived, he gave me an enthusiastic hug. I didn't have to coax him to leave his apartment, go to a restaurant for lunch, and go out for a walk in the sunshine.

Uncle Bert is the only other link to the summer of 1945 when Dad returned home a different man than the one who left New Jersey in 1942. Lloyd had no idea how much Dad had told Bert about Emilie.

"Uncle Bert, do you remember the summer when Dad came home from the war?"

Bert clears the gravel from his voice. "The summer?"

"1945."

Bert scratches his head and looks out at the ocean. "Yeah," he says.

"Lloyd told me when Dad came back from Europe that summer he stayed in New York and didn't go home. Did you know that?" I ask.

He chews a piece of taffy. "Yeah. Dan..." He stops. His lower lip trembles. "...Dan stayed with me." Bert coughs, and phlegm rumbles in his chest.

"He did?"

"Yeah. He lived with me. I still had my old apartment in Greenwich Village." Bert squints into the summer sun, groping with his recollection.

"When was this?"

"I got back...a few weeks after Dan. The Fourth of July we went up to the roof to see the fireworks." Bert seems surprised at his ability to remember that summer day.

"Yeah? Tell me about it."

"Over the East River. Reminded me of nights in the Hürtgen Forest. Except they were red, white, and blue," he says.

He regards his right hand where the fingers are missing. "Sit in foxholes and watch the sky light up."

"Dad always said you were a hero."

Bert shakes his head vigorously. "Not me. Dan."

"Why did Dad stay in the city that summer?"

His eyes roll up, and he struggles for an answer. "Some guys...felt that way...couldn't face their family." Bert watches three kids running by on the sand, fighting over a beach ball before one of them grabs the ball and throws it toward the water. He clears his throat again. "I kept asking him 'when you gonna go home?' He kept saying 'I'm not ready.'"

Then, he says, one afternoon, he and Dad took the train to New Jersey and had dinner with Mother and Granddad. Uncle Bert

223

remembers fragments from that first evening at the Whitman home—discussion of the wedding, talk of the war ending, and the status of the textile factory.

I hesitate. "How was Mother?"

"Huh?" he asks, confused.

"You know, did they...did she seem happy to see Dad?"

"Well..." Bert says and crosses his arms, tucking the bag of taffy into the crook of his elbow, "I remember a big storm. Electricity went out. Had to eat with candles. Hotter 'n hell."

"And Mother?" I prompt him again.

Bert pops another piece of taffy into his mouth. "Pretty. Always dressed nice."

"Do you remember what they said to each other?"

Bert appears to be studying the waves rolling in on the sand. "Can't remember anything like that."

It's a long shot, relying on Bert's memory for detail that happened sixty years ago.

"One thing I remember," he says unexpectedly.

"You do?"

"Dan gave Margaret a necklace. Beautiful thing...diamond and a ruby."

My feet hit the ground. "I know that necklace. Mother wore it for years."

Bert says, "To make amends, I guess."

We are silent for a minute. I think about what he has said. *Amends.* Then I look him in the eye. "And Emilie?"

"Emilie?"

"Did Dad write to Emilie?" I ask softly. I already know the answer, but I'm hoping for any detail Bert might remember.

Bert dips his head. "Yeah. Couldn't help himself," he says and taps his chest. "Broken heart."

"Did he talk about her much?"

"He didn't like to talk about the war."

I drop Bert off after negotiating the streets around the casinos to stop at a 7-Eleven for coffee and milk for his breakfast. I kiss him and wait on the street until the light goes on in his apartment. Then I pull away from the curb and head for the Atlantic City Expressway with the windows down. I inhale the humid air.

As I fly by the exits on the parkway, the humming of the tires on the road is soothing. Yet something nags at me. Uncle Bert said Dad wrote to Emilie, that "he couldn't help himself."

It was the Christmas Eve of my junior year in high school. A snowstorm had left two-foot drifts surrounding the house, the temperature was below freezing, and the wind howled. The fragrance of baked pies and cookies that were not available for eating until the next day filled the house. I was excited and bored at the same time.

Hannah, our housekeeper, buffed silverware in preparation for Christmas dinner and warned me to stay out of the kitchen; Mother locked the door of the den to keep my prying eyes and fingers away from the mound of gifts waiting to be distributed tomorrow. Dad fiddled with a string of tree lights in the foyer that kept flashing on and off. DJ and Nancy did last-minute shopping, and it was hours before Uncle Bert would appear for the evening. I wandered into the living room with a book and snuggled into the blue brocade sofa, careful to remove my shoes before curling up. I tried to read but drifted off.

I woke up, and it was dark out. How long had I been asleep? An hour? I heard voices that wrenched me from the warmth of my cocoon. Mother and Dad were talking. No, arguing. Strange sounds because I never recalled hearing them raise their voices to each other. I thought I was still dreaming because suddenly there was silence. Then the voices started again, and this time the sounds became words, and the words surged in and out of the living room. My parents were in the hallway outside the door.

Dad said, "Keep your voice down."

"How long?" she asked.

Something about the tone of their speech frightened me. I clasped a sofa pillow to my stomach.

"...searching my coat pockets?"

"...give me the attention you must be showing her..."

"I told you the truth...over..."

"Still writing to her...?"

"...my friend..."

"No more letters...never speak of this again."

Footsteps moved away, and all was quiet.

I had to pretend I hadn't overheard the conversation, so I waited half an hour, crept out of the living room, and ran up the stairs to change my clothes. At dinner, everyone acted normal—Hannah served platters of food, Dad poured wine, Uncle Bert told a story that made everybody laugh, and DJ rolled his eyes. And Mother...Mother gazed serenely on the group around the table.

All traces of the afternoon confrontation had disappeared.

Mother found letters from Emilie. Based on what I found in Dad's safe, they had continued to correspond well after the war. Bert was right. Dad probably couldn't help himself. Mother knew a part of him lived, would always live, in a world separate from hers. And I was the trigger that kept reminding her of that fact.

39

I reread what I've written.

"Dear Yvette,

Thank you again for the box of souvenirs. Since they are remembrances from the time my father spent in France during the war, I will treasure them always."

Now that I know what each one signifies, the souvenirs tell a story that I want to share with Yvette. She is part of my family, after all. I nibble on the end of my pen. If I had her email address, correspondence would be a whole lot simpler, not to mention faster. Even though she has mine, she never sent hers.

Yesterday I drove the two and a half hours home from Atlantic City jousting with myself: should I contact Yvette or should I let it go? I knew the answer long before I swung my car into the driveway. I cannot ignore the memoir and its contents. I have to know if Yvette knew about Dad, and with Dad and Emilie gone, I don't feel as though I am breaking any confidence.

"I wonder if I can impose on you. I plan to be in France this summer on vacation and, if you are willing and available, I would appreciate visiting with you. We have some common interests, and I would like to meet you."

There. Plain and simple and completely untrue. I hadn't made plans to travel to Europe, but saying I had, gave me a reason for asking to get together. Once again, I include my email address and suggest she might email back, sign the note, address and seal the envelope, and go directly to the post office.

I release the brass knocker and listen as metal bangs loudly against metal. It's bizarre, knocking on the door of the house I'd once bounded into at all hours of the day and night, a house I'd once called home.

Nancy greets me warmly, "Hello Kate."

"Hi." I notice a change in her. She wears no make-up, a pair of khakis, and one of DJ's flannel shirts. More casual than usual. Maybe DJ's heart attack has adjusted her outlook on things.

"How is he?" I ask.

A frown wrinkles Nancy's forehead. "The doctor says he's making good progress, but slowing him down, that's the challenge. He's working from home a few hours a day but dying to get back to the office. Still, he's trying to adapt." She laughs lightly. "You know DJ."

"Where is he?"

"On the deck."

Nancy picks up a pitcher of iced tea and escorts me through the house. "DJ? Kate's here." She refills DJ's glass. "Kate?" Nancy gestures with the tea.

"No thanks. I had lunch."

DJ appears healthy—ten pounds lighter than before the heart attack and more relaxed than I'd ever seen him. He sits in a deck chair, barefoot, reading *Business Week*. I bend down to kiss him, and I can't help but glance at his eyes. He is glad to see me.

"How are you feeling?" I ask.

"Not too bad." DJ pulls his legs up and tucks them under the chair.

Nancy moves the *New York Times* off another deck chair, and I settle myself onto the canvas.

"Call me if you need anything," Nancy says and squeezes DJ's shoulder. He watches her walk away.

I'm sensitive to marriages these days. I'd never thought much about DJ and Nancy, but I can see that their bond has remained strong over the years. Theirs has been a durable relationship.

I shut my eyes and inhale the bouquet of early summer. In the stillness of late afternoon, insects buzz around the beds of flowers scattered around the lawn: blue and white irises, brilliant yellow daffodils, dark pink peonies, and Nancy's prized red and coral roses. The colors are magnificent, and the fragrant air soothing.

"Nice out here," I say.

"Dad put a lot of time in on his flowers."

"And Nancy picked up where he left off. She's got a green thumb," I add. "How are the twins?"

"Fine. Nate's got his heart set on Harvard Law, but in the meantime he's joining me at the office."

"The next generation is taking over at Whitman Textiles."

"Wish I could get Drew interested in business. He's planning on staying at NYU to get an M.F.A. I asked him 'what can you do with an M.F.A.?' Teach, I guess. Unless he can sell some of those paintings." DJ takes a drink and studies me over the rim of his glass. "You've seen his paintings?"

"Oh, yeah." I laugh. "Dad enjoyed them."

"There was some attachment between Drew and Dad. Kind of like you and Dad." DJ stares out into the backyard. "Most of the time I drove him crazy."

"That's not true," I say gently. "Of course I had my own problems with Mom." DJ swats at a fly and sips his tea. "I've been thinking about her a lot lately. About her and Dad."

The muscles in his jaw tighten, and I sense he is prepared to defend her.

"I didn't really understand her and what her life was like." There is no need for me to introduce the war into the conversation or to mention Emilie's name. Or the memoir at this point. DJ can read between the lines if he wants. His mouth softens, and he sighs.

"Who understands parents, right? God knows the twins have no idea what Nancy and I go through with them," he says.

"Maybe someday they will."

"Maybe."

"Kids can be pretty self-involved. Ignorant," I say.

DJ turns in his chair and faces me. "I guess that's true."

We can hear the phone ring from inside the house.

"It's probably the office. Nancy took away my cell phone."

Nancy's head appears at the door. "Nate's on the line."

DJ stands and stretches. "Time to get back to work."

I swing my bag over my shoulder, and then, without overthinking it, I place my hands on his shoulders and pull him into an embrace. Very slowly, his arms move around my waist, and we cling to each other. Siblings coming together.

What Remains of Love

40

"Are you taking these?" Cheryl holds up a pair of black pants.

I nod and fold a sweater. Mother knew best...the weather in Europe can be unpredictable in the summer.

"Where are you putting shoes?" Cheryl has a sandal in each hand.

When she heard my plans, she insisted on helping me pack even though I've traveled most summers for the past two decades, minus recent years when Dad was ill, and have always managed to do this myself.

"In the smaller bag." I rearrange some underwear.

"What have you told DJ?" she asks.

"That I'm going away for a bit. He can reach me by cell phone." I stash my camera and a book in the carry-on.

"For two cents I'd pack a bag and go with you," Cheryl says.

"For two cents I'd cash in my ticket to France and head for Hawaii."

"Are you getting cold feet?"

"A little, I guess." I've been uneasy ever since I received the email from Yvette politely agreeing to see me. Perhaps it was my anxiety that caused me to interpret her message as "come if you must, but what would we, total strangers, have to say to each other?"

"Yvette doesn't sound overly...friendly," Cheryl says tactfully.

"I didn't know how to approach her in my letter. What does she know about our parents? I still have no idea how the memoir got into Dad's desk or if she's ever seen it."

"What are you going to say to her?"

I shrug. "Welcome to the family?" We both laugh, but mine is apprehensive. What *was* I going to say to Yvette?

"I have to hand it to you. You have guts, kiddo, confronting your father's past like this. I admire you, Kate," Cheryl says.

I smile my thanks. "Every day's a rollercoaster. Some days I'm driven to get to the truth, most days I simply want to satisfy my enormous curiosity." I sit on the bed and close the lid of my suitcase. "I never saw the kind of passion he had with Emilie in our house, and I never understood so many things about my mother. I want to put my own memories to rest."

Cheryl embraces me. "Godspeed."

41

I maneuver the rental car along the highway, studying the tiny French road signs. The village of L'Avigne, where Yvette lives, sits on the outskirts of Marseille, about twenty minutes from the airport. Despite my many visits to France, I have never gotten used to navigating the roundabouts, and now I keep one eye on the road and one on the signage. Traveling in France was easier in the summer of '82 when we took trains and hitchhiked, and there was no shortage of French men happily offering everything from directions to marriage.

I pull to the side of the road to allow the honking car behind me to pass. It speeds off with the occupant, his mouth moving rapidly, pointing first to me, then to the autoroute. My exit has to be close. The day is warm, and a trickle of perspiration runs down the inside of my blouse as I adjust sunglasses sliding down my nose.

Within the hour, I find the village center, a quiet cluster of off-white stucco houses with red-tiled Mediterranean roofs, and a strip of shops that include a chain grocery store, a bakery, a flower shop, and a photography studio. Nestled next to a pizzeria is L'Avigne's hotel, really a glorified B&B that houses six rooms. Mine is modestly furnished with a bed, free-standing closet, and tiny bathroom.

I don't mind that if I stretch my arms out, I almost touch two opposite walls; the accommodations feel like heaven. I collapse on the bed, ready to plummet into a deep sleep. Nothing, not the non-air-conditioned room, not two angry customers yelling at the management outside the pizzeria, not my fear of facing Yvette for the first time, is going to prevent me from passing out. As consciousness slips away, I remind myself that sleeping during the day of arrival isn't a great idea.

I awake with a start and, for a moment, forget where I am. The room is dark, the only illumination provided by slivers of moonlight visible between the shutters of my bedroom window. I shift my body, all of my limbs dead weight, and close my eyes again, this time dreaming of a rollercoaster. I am flying out of my seat when a disembodied hand yanks me back. I slam on the hard metal bench of the car and cry, "I've got to get out of here!"

This time when I open my eyes, I blink and pull my left arm up to my face. My watch reads three o'clock—nine a.m. here; I've slept fourteen hours straight, except for the brief interruption in the middle of the night.

A half-hour later, I butter my croissant in a minuscule breakfast room off the hotel foyer and pull out Yvette's address written on a slip of paper.

"*Mademoiselle, café?*" asks a woman in a sparkly, spandex top.

"*Oui, merci,*" I answer.

As the server refills my cup, I ask if she knows where Yvette's street is.

She shrugs and points to the lobby.

"*Merci.*" The man at the registration desk offers clear directions, and by eleven, I am ready to set off. I back the car out of the private parking lot, three spaces tucked behind the garbage bins of the pizzeria, and head in the direction of Yvette's house.

Twenty yards past the address, I sit in the air-conditioning sweating profusely and take deep breaths to calm my racing heart. We had confirmed my date of arrival by email, finally, and a meeting time. Eleven thirty a.m. I'd fantasized about this moment, but confronted with the prospect of encountering Yvette face-to-face, I fervently wish she had rejected my request to see her. I glance at the entrance to the villa in the rearview mirror. I put the car in gear and back up the road, stopping at 20 Avenue Le Casson. A high wall, coated with the same beige whitewash that covers every house in the village, surrounds the property, broken only by a heavy wooden gate reinforced by iron, wide enough for the entrance of an automobile.

I open the car door and remove my bag and some gifts I've brought for Yvette—a hand-painted scarf bought at an art fair on campus, a box of delicate jellied candies, and a collection of family photos of Dad, DJ and his family, and myself. I also have the memoir.

Not sure about the pictures, I push them to the bottom of my purse and decide that they might be part of another visit, if there is another visit.

I ring the bell at the edge of the gate and freeze. Ferocious growling is followed by loud barking within the walls. Then I hear a voice.

"*Sh, sh, ma petite Mignonne.*" It is deep and rich but firm.

Seconds later, the barking ends, replaced by a muted whining, and footsteps crunch gravel, one set measured and light and one set wild and rambunctious.

A key turns in the lock, and the gate swings open to reveal a woman and a dog. She is tall, several inches taller than me, and slender, perfectly manicured, in a white cotton blouse and crisply creased jeans. Her light brown hair is short and feathery and flatters her face—heart-shaped with high cheekbones. Like Dad's and mine. A German shepherd leaps at me and then frolics around her legs. She grabs the dog's collar.

"Yvette?"

"Yes," she answers. "*Mignonne, shush*. She is all bark," Yvette says and smiles.

I hesitate slightly. "Thank you for seeing me." I extend my hand, and she takes it, her palm cool and her grasp strong.

"Won't you come in," she says politely in precise but lightly accented English and gestures for me to follow her.

Once inside the villa, Yvette invites me into the living room while she prepares refreshments. "Coffee or tea?" she asks.

"Tea, please." I want to tell her not to go to any trouble, but it's too late. She has already disappeared into the kitchen.

I can hear Yvette putting a kettle on to boil and pulling out plates and silverware. I glance around the living room. It's filled with watercolors of gardens and lush fruit trees, the hills surrounding the villa, and the sun rising over Marseille. Many are similar to the ones I found in Dad's safe. On the mantel above a fireplace, I see several framed photographs. Mignonne stretched to her full height with paws on an older woman's shoulders. Emilie? Fishing boats bobbing in an inlet off the Mediterranean. A leafless, fallen branch resting on the stump of a tree in winter. I recognize Dad's photography.

Finally, there is another picture of the older woman. In it, her hair is white, her shoulders slightly hunched, and her face aged, but with the same eyes I have come to know from the wartime photos.

"My mother, Emilie," Yvette says. She motions to a dining table set off in an alcove of the living room. I join her as she arranges cakes and biscuits and pours hot water over the loose tea.

She serves the tea, and I bite into a pastry. "This is delicious."

"Thank you. Our little bakery in town makes them fresh every day. When I moved here from Paris I was afraid I would have to sacrifice my pastry obsession." Her grin is wide and transforms her features from merely courteous to gracious. She is radiant when she smiles like that.

"Have you lived here long?"

There is a moment's hesitation before Yvette answers. "I came two years ago when my mother fell ill." She sips her tea. "She died eight months later."

"I'm sorry," I say quietly.

"You understand the loss of a parent, yes?" It is more a statement than a question.

"I do."

Mignonne sprawls at her feet, chewing unmercifully on a red rubber ball, the gnawing interrupting the silence. Yvette asks about my vacation in Europe, and I mention my friends in Paris, trying not to sound too evasive. I ask about L'Avigne and the gardens behind the villa, and Yvette inquires about the weather this time of the year in New Jersey. We could have been two friends catching up on each other's news had our parents not shared a past that now bound us together as more than friends.

"Where did you learn English?" I ask.

"I studied at McGill University in Montreal and then at the London School of Economics."

"What did you do in Paris?"

Yvette refills our cups. "International banking and asset management at Le Crédit Lyonnais. And you?"

"I teach at a university in New Jersey. French," I say.

"Yes, I remember you mentioned that in your letter," she says and studies me.

"And here in L'Avigne...?"

Yvette sighs. "In the beginning I telecommuted. With email and fax I could work anywhere in the world. But when Maman worsened, I decided to retire."

Hearing her say "Maman" triggers images from the memoir.

"When Dad was ill, some days it was difficult for me to teach. Impossible to keep my mind on classes."

"You were close to your father."

"Yes."

Yvette leans back in her chair. "I think you are curious about my mother."

Her directness catches me off-guard, and I can only say the truth. "Yes, I am curious. When we found out that Dad left...the gift to your mother, we, naturally, wondered."

"Naturally." Her voice softens.

"I am grateful for the souvenirs."

"I found them among other mementos my mother kept over the years. She was a sentimental person and hated to throw anything away." Yvette smiles. "After she died I found boxes of old clothes and Christmas cards. And paintings. Upstairs there is a room full of her work."

"The watercolors on the mantel," I say.

"From the time she was a girl until a few months before she died."

"Her work is beautiful. My father was a photographer."

"Yes?" she asks, her face a question mark.

"Amateur, but he improved steadily," I add quickly.

We are silent for a moment.

"And your father? Was he an economist or an artist?" I ask lightly, wondering if Yvette knows Guy's history.

She laughs. "Neither. My father was a practical man. He was a mechanic and ran an automotive shop. He was ill often and he died in 1980."

A mechanic? When he rejected art, he became a mechanic.

We finish our tea, and Yvette sits forward. "What would you like to know about my mother?"

What *did* I want to know? "Well, how was her life after the war?"

I notice that Yvette's eyes, staring at me, unwavering, are deep pools of blue. Like Emilie's. While friendly, her observation of me is disconcerting. She taps her spoon gently against the perimeter of the saucer. "Why do you want to know this?"

"I never knew much about Dad's wartime experiences. Since he died, I've become...very interested in his past." Obsessed is more like it. "And there is the will," I say carefully.

"Yes, the will." She frowns.

"I think my father and your mother became very close during the war. She kept souvenirs of times they spent together." I'm acutely aware of the memoir buried deep in my bag. *Close* does not begin to describe their passion.

"My mother knew your father for a very short time," Yvette says. "There were many wartime liaisons." I find the sophisticated dismissiveness in her statement irritating.

"Yvette, did your mother ever mention my father?"

"No. I don't remember her ever speaking of him."

Before I can respond, the phone rings, and she rises immediately to answer it, perhaps grateful for the interruption. I hear the ringing stop, then soft replies, a little laugh. Yvette knows that I'm fluent in

French, and it sounds like she's being careful to keep the conversation private.

I'm in a quandary. How can I plop the memoir on the table and announce that the man Yvette thinks was her father was not? I need to decide how to approach the subject.

The kitchen goes silent, and Yvette appears in the doorway. "That was my daughter. Sorry to interrupt our talk."

"You've been very gracious," I say. "I'd like to repay your hospitality. Could I take you to dinner tonight? Somewhere in town?"

She smiles regretfully. "I am sorry to tell you that dining out in L'Avigne offers few choices."

"Out of town then? Somewhere nearby?"

She sits down and folds her hands in her lap. "Kate, I appreciate your coming to see me. I also appreciate your interest in my mother but there is nothing I can tell you. My mother lived a very ordinary life in Marseille and then here in L'Avigne. She was married to my father for over thirty years. She never said a word about your father."

I reach in my bag, and my hand touches the hard cardboard of the memoir's cover. I can't do it. I cannot hand it to her this way. "I know there may be nothing more you can tell me, but I would still like to take you to dinner."

Yvette hesitates. "My daughter is coming home tonight. She is at university, and I haven't seen her since March. She's moving out of her apartment for the summer and starting to bring things home." She shrugs as if to say, "college kids."

"Then both of you, of course. It would be my pleasure," I say.

She inclines her head. "I planned on having dinner at home tonight. If you would like to join us..."

It is a reluctant invitation.

"Thank you. I would love to meet your daughter, but maybe another time."

I pick up my bag and stand. "Yvette, would you mind finishing our conversation over breakfast? We could eat at my hotel or someplace else if you prefer."

"I know your 'hotel,'" she says. "Why don't you come back here for breakfast. Eva will be leaving in the morning anyway and we can speak again."

I am so grateful my eyes fill, and I nod briskly and turn away. Yvette accompanies me to the door, and before I exit, she takes my hand in both of hers and tells me to have a good day.

I have the afternoon to myself. I stop by the hotel, change into my bathing suit, and pick up sunscreen and a towel. I have water and snacks from the grocery store and am set for a day at the beach. According to my friend behind the registration desk, if I stay on the highway heading south out of town, I will eventually "run into the sea."

I drive for half an hour, following his instructions, through several roundabouts and another small town, and then, as I reach the crest of a hill, the Mediterranean appears. The azure blue of the sky merges with the aqua blue of the sea.

The beach is crowded, so I park in the lot and trudge through the sand to an area vacated by a couple with glowing skin and fashionably small suits. I spread my towel, smear the sunscreen on my arms and legs, and lay back on the sand. The pungent fragrance of saltwater and the sounds of music and voices mingle amiably.

I am slightly uneasy about the upcoming breakfast but determined to complete my task and hand over the memoir. My eyes fly open in surprise. *The memoir needs to stay in L'Avigne with Yvette.* A kind of peace envelops me at this thought, and I allow myself to let go and forget about Yvette and the book and tomorrow's visit. I am curious about her daughter—my niece. Maybe at breakfast, Yvette will open up a little more and talk about Emilie, about growing up with her in Marseille and living in L'Avigne together. I am uncomfortable making a melodramatic announcement that Dad is her father; I can simply give her the memoir and let her find out for herself. It can be a peace offering from the past.

Where have I heard that before? The heat slows my thinking, and I feel lazy as the burning sun seers my skin leaving it damp. I remember. Uncle Bert said Dad gave Mother an engagement gift to make amends.

I flip over onto my stomach and allow my back to cope with the fierce rays for a while. The sun beats on my shoulders, and I hear someone say, "a peace offering."

In March 1981, I spent spring semester of my junior year in Paris, living with the Chival family and attending the Sorbonne. I was walking along the Left Bank with Mother. The sun was hot, unusual since it had been a chilly spring. I unbuttoned my jacket and tilted my face upward. Mother warned me that I would catch a cold if I didn't keep my coat closed and a scarf around my neck. I ignored her advice. I was twenty-one that day and old enough to make decisions about such trivial things for myself.

I was surprised that she was here. She had finished her most recent round of chemotherapy only two months before. But the doctors had given her the okay to travel, and she was determined to come to France. "You have to take advantage of opportunities when they present themselves," she'd said. I wasn't exactly sure what "opportunities" she was referring to, but I prepared myself for the arguments that I was certain would arise. To my astonishment, Mother seemed calmer and less uptight than usual.

She asked me what I wanted to do to celebrate my birthday, and I stalled. I met Marcel, a very cute guy, in class a few weeks earlier, and we made plans to have dinner and go dancing tonight. I hadn't accounted for Mother. She'd arranged to be in Paris for a week; two days were spent shopping, two were spent sightseeing, and the last three days were to be spent with me. We'd sat in cafés, taken the Bateaux Mouche down the Seine—even though I told her boat trips were for tourists—and stood together in line to await the daily opening of the Louvre. Tomorrow was her last day.

She announced that she didn't like Paris very much. The people were not friendly, no one would speak English, the money was confusing, and the food was too rich. I argued fiercely in its defense. I loved all things French, so here we were, side by side meandering along the Seine with Mother still resisting the charms of the city. I couldn't understand her.

"Why did you come if you hate it so much?" I asked.

"To see you, of course. To make sure you were eating properly and taking care of yourself," she said.

"I'm fine. This is Paris, the best food in the universe, the best cafés, the best shopping, the best—"

"I get the picture," she said and laughed. "I felt that way about New York when I was your age."

"You did?" It wasn't often she shared her feelings.

I immediately felt guilty about my birthday plans. "So about tonight..."

"I thought we would have dinner at that little place near the Sorbonne that you like. And why don't you invite your friend."

"My friend?"

"The young man you were talking with yesterday," she said.

I bumped into Marcel at the *pâtisserie* but neglected to introduce him to Mother. It didn't matter; she picked up on him anyway.

"Okay. I'll ask him," I said. "Thanks for taking us to dinner."

"It's a peace offering, Kate," she said. "This trip is about making amends." She tucked her arm in mine.

42

I swing the heavy wooden shutters on my windows open, drinking in the warm Mediterranean air. My skin is rosy from yesterday on the beach, and I dress hurriedly. I want to be on time—ten-thirty—for breakfast. I've been turning over the memory of that day in Paris. Mother's words are like a splash of cold water, bracing, startling. Piecing together clues—Mother's comments about making amends, the Customs stamp in her passport—I'm convinced that she went to Marseille to see Emilie. What I wouldn't give to have witnessed that meeting!

I arrive at Yvette's villa bearing gifts of pastries and flowers. She welcomes me graciously, accepts the presents, and escorts me to the patio that opens off the living room through wide double doors. Yvette excuses herself to finish breakfast preparations and urges me to help myself to the coffee pot. The table is arranged simply but elegantly, like Yvette herself. Heavy white crockery rests next to polished silverware.

I move around the patio and inhale the perfume of the flowers, and then decide to take Yvette up on her suggestion. I pour myself a cup of coffee and have barely put it to my lips when I hear a flurry of noise and Mignonne barking excitedly.

"*Bonjour*," says a light, musical voice. "*Comment allez-vous?*"

I swing my head around. "*Bien, merci, et vous?*"

An extraordinarily striking young woman with large violet eyes, jet black hair, and a long, thin face approaches and holds out her hand. "I am Eva."

"Hello Eva. I'm Kate." I shake her hand.

"I speak English when I can. But not with Maman." Her dark eyes twinkle. "Maman says she spoke enough English in school."

"You both speak beautifully."

She cocks her head and studies me. "Maman says you are a French professor."

"Yes. I fell in love with your language when I was a girl."

Eva claps her hands delightedly and kisses me on both cheeks.

"I hope I'm not intruding on your visit with your mother..." I say.

"*C'est rien*. I am leaving after breakfast, but I will be home in two weeks for the rest of the summer."

"It's so nice to meet you."

"Me too," Eva says with a grin.

Yvette appears at that moment with two platters of food. "Eva, please?" Eva darts away and then returns with another. "Let's sit."

I examine Yvette as I sit at the indicated place setting. She has brushed her hair off her forehead. Her blouse is now a rich maroon, and the jeans are replaced by a flowered skirt. A thick gold chain with a single garnet encircles her neck. Her birthstone.

"Everything smells delicious," I say, placing a napkin on my lap.

"The egg casserole is my mother's recipe. Eva's favorite."

Eva hands me a platter of baked tomatoes garnished with bits of basil. "From Maman's garden."

We pass around the rest of the food: bread, pastries, cones of goat cheese so fresh they barely hold their shape.

I am ravenous. It's been two days since I've eaten anything resembling a home-cooked meal, and I can't remember when food tasted this good. Eva chats easily and provides a talking tour of the garden, describing the peach, fig, and cherry trees, the terrace of vegetables, including the tomatoes, and pots of herbs scattered around the patio. Every imaginable plant and flower thrives in the south of France.

Yvette says little, apparently content to let Eva take charge of the conversation. I ask encouraging questions and generally allow breakfast to proceed pleasantly. Eva doesn't seem curious about my motivation for appearing in their home.

When she takes a break to catch up on eating, I ask, "Where do you study?"

"In Marseille. At the art academy," she says.

"That's wonderful. How many more—?"

Eva grimaces. "Two more years. I lost time when I transferred from the art school in Monaco."

"Oh?"

"I wanted to study there because that is where *grand-mère* went to school." Eva pouts a little. "Maman wanted me to be closer to home."

Yvette glances at us and shrugs. "You are my only family now," she says simply.

Eva looks as though she has heard this argument before.

"I might visit Monaco. I intend to drive along the coast and spend a few days in Nice," I say.

"Oh, I haven't been to Nice for a year," said Eva. "I can't wait to go back."

Yvette lifts the coffee pot. "Kate?"

I shake my head, already beyond my caffeine limit.

"Do you have a family?" Eva asks.

I catch a glimpse of Yvette wiping her mouth and folding her napkin on her lap.

"I have two brothers. My older brother DJ lives in New Jersey with his wife and sons. Twins. Billy, my other brother lives in Alaska." I smile. "He likes to wander. We don't see him very much."

"I would love to have a twin," Eva says.

Yvette smiles indulgently. "Two of you?"

Eva waves her hand dismissing her mother's comment. "And children?" Eva asks.

Yvette raises her eyebrows at her daughter for broaching such a personal subject? "No, no children."

"I would love to go to the States," Eva says. "My friends have been to New York and Los Angeles."

"Yes, you should come to America," I say. "Did you always want to paint?"

"*Mais oui!*" Eva says enthusiastically. "Like *grand-mère.*"

"I've seen her paintings," I say. "In the living room."

"The living room, dining room, bedrooms. *Grand-mère* painted watercolors of everything. They are so delicate. They are like her." Eva puts her fork down.

Yvette places a hand on Eva's arm. "She misses her *grand-mère.* We both miss her."

There is silence for a moment, then Mignonne barks and whines.

Eva rises. "I will go." She enters the house, and I can hear her low voice and a door opening and closing.

"She is a lovely young woman," I say.

"Yes, she is. Very sensitive."

I pick up a plate. "May I...?"

"No, I will clear later," she says. "Can I get you anything else?"

"Breakfast was lovely. Thank you."

Eva appears in the entranceway, Mignonne licking her hand and prancing around her legs. "Maman, I have to leave. My ride is here," she says in French.

Yvette crosses to her and kisses her good-bye. "*Au revoir.*"

Eva waves in my direction. "Good-bye, Kate. It was a pleasure meeting you." She takes a step toward me.

I rise. "It was wonderful to meet you, too." Eva kisses me and bounces off.

We wait until her footsteps can no longer be heard. A door closes, an engine revs, and the patio is quiet.

Yvette clears her throat and politely inquires about my travel plans. Again, I tell her that I intend to drive to Nice and a few of the other coastal villages. I don't add that I especially want to see the places Emilie mentions in the memoir.

Though the day is hot, I shiver and pull my sweater protectively around my middle.

"Yvette, could we..."

She frowns. "You would like to ask more questions about my mother?"

I trace a pattern on the tablecloth. "I know this must feel...intrusive," I say haltingly. "I would still like to understand more about my father and your mother."

"Kate, I'm not sure what else I can tell you."

I waver. "My father and your mother wrote to each other after the war. He remembered her in his will. I think they shared more than...a casual wartime liaison. I want to understand my father's past. Your mother was an important part of it."

Yvette is quiet, watching me carefully.

"I found this picture among your mother's souvenirs." I withdraw the photo of Dad and Emilie on the Promenade from my purse. I extend it to Yvette. She has seen it if she sorted through Emilie's box of mementos. But I'm not certain she was that curious about her mother's past.

She takes the picture and examines it, then lays it down on the table.

"What they shared during the war...I don't know...it doesn't change their marriages. My father loved my mother and I'm sure Emilie...your mother loved your father."

"Kate, what are you saying?" Yvette asks.

"I know I am a stranger to you and Eva, and I realize just because my father left a gift to your mother I have no right to assume...anything or to trespass on your lives." Am I making any sense? Get to the point.

"Yes?"

I hesitate, knowing that for better or for worse, when I hand the memoir to Yvette, her life will shift dramatically. Eva's, too.

"After my father died, I cleaned out his office and, like you, I found things."

"What sort of things?"

I reach in my purse and press my fingers along the edges of the book. "I found this in a locked drawer." I place it on the table next to the picture. "It is your mother's memoir. She wrote about her life from 1944 to 1946." I push it several inches across the table toward Yvette.

She stares at me. "How did your father...?" She touches the binding.

"I'm not sure."

She is wary. "You've read it, of course."

"Yes. I read it. I'd like you to read it, too."

Suddenly I'm weary. Laying down the burden of Dad's and Emilie's past. Yvette has not moved since I produced the memoir. Her gaze is fixed on the cover.

"I'm leaving tomorrow to go to Nice. I want to see the places your mother describes. If you want to...talk...or see me..." I let the rest of the sentence drift off. "Thank you for breakfast."

Yvette looks up at me, her eyes wide and full of questions. "You are welcome."

"I can see my way to the door." Before she is able to protest, I snap up my bag and exit the house.

Once outside, I breathe easier. I have completed my job in L'Avigne and am desperately hoping to hear from Yvette tonight or tomorrow. In the meantime, I'll explore the town, then return to the hotel, pack my bags, and prepare to head to Nice.

43

I awoke at nine, showered and dressed, and ate my breakfast of coffee and rolls. Now I am surveying the mess of my open suitcase. When I arrived in L'Avigne less than forty-eight hours ago, completely exhausted, I rifled through my luggage for toiletries and sleepwear, causing an eruption of clothing. I have to repack everything before I leave for Nice.

A knock on the door abruptly stops my work. "*Oui?*" Is the hotel maid already inquiring about my checking out?

"Kate?" Yvette's voice is slightly muffled.

A wave of panic hits me. I have no idea how she reacted to the memoir, and I don't want to say anything that will make this moment more difficult for her than it probably already is. I stall. "Just a minute." I make an effort to push the open suitcase and clothes off to one side of the bed.

I cross to the door, my hand grasps the knob firmly, and I face her. Her appearance—beige slacks and matching top, espadrilles, and a bright red sweater draped casually around her shoulders—is much the same as yesterday: attractive and together. She could pass for a model. But her eyes tell another story. Dark circles suggest little sleep, and traces of puffiness hint at tears. In her hand, she holds the memoir.

252

"May we speak?" she asks.

I manage to find my voice. "Of course." I've been waiting for this moment for weeks. Still, my room is in a state of chaos. "Could we meet downstairs in the café?"

We sit opposite one another at a small table in a corner of the breakfast room. The breakfast service is over; however coffee is available. I don't want any, but it gives me something to do, setting up cups and sugar and milk for the two of us, and allows me to study Yvette. She was quiet on the way downstairs to the café and seems vulnerable and almost helpless.

"Thank you," she says when I finally sit. She rubs the handle of the coffee cup. I wait; when she says nothing, I break the silence. "You read the memoir?"

"Yes."

"I'm sure it must be…a shock. I'm sorry. I didn't know how else to tell you."

"I knew Daniel Whitman was my father," she says.

I set my coffee cup on the saucer, stunned. "How? When?"

She sighs. "Before my mother died, she gave me a letter."

"She told you?" I ask.

Yvette leans back in the chair. "Not in so many words. She said my father was not Guy Renault but an American soldier stationed near Nice during the war."

"She said his name?"

Yvette shakes her head. "My mother felt there was no point in my knowing who he was. But she did not anticipate his generosity."

"It was the will that gave him away."

She falters. "Yes. When I received the letter from his lawyer, I knew Daniel Whitman must be the soldier."

After all the angst of the last months, I'm frustrated that Yvette is only now admitting the truth. "Why did you deny knowing anything in your letters to me?"

She is shocked at the vehemence of my question. "What difference would it make to you if I knew now? You wanted to know about my mother and your father and there was nothing I could tell you. Besides, I was angry that my mother waited all of these years to tell me. I never had the chance to...to find out about Daniel Whitman. As it was, Maman was so ill when she gave me the letter, she could barely speak. There was no opportunity for me to understand and accept this huge change in my life." Yvette pushes her coffee cup away.

Even as adults, we are children, I think, still capable of being frightened and hurt.

"You refused the gift in my father's will," I say softly.

"It was meant for Maman." Yvette stares at the wall behind me. "I thought my biological father had abandoned me."

"I'm sorry, Yvette."

"I had hoped that you would not pursue our parents' past. It would be easier to forget."

"You sent me the souvenirs," I say in my own defense.

"I thought you might be satisfied to see the objects." She smiles at me. "I was wrong."

"I would have been if I hadn't found the memoir."

Yvette puts the book on the table between us.

"Thank you for coming. It is good that I read Maman's memoir and I see some things clearer now. At first, I thought it was simply a brief wartime affair. Now I know Daniel never knew about me," she says. She gently pushes the memoir toward me.

I shake my head. "No. It belongs to you. Maybe someday Eva..."

Yvette closes her eyes, nods. Then fiddles with her car keys. "Would you like to have dinner this evening?" I am pleased, but I pause. "You are going to Nice, yes?" she asks.

"I want to see the places where Dad was during the war," I say.

"The places in the memoir."

"Your mother's writing, and the souvenirs you sent, are like a road map of the time he spent with her. The story is so vivid, I feel as if I know Victoire and Monsieur Zazou and your father. Guy."

"I see," she says.

She sits up straighter suddenly and thrusts her chin upward as though she has made a difficult decision. "May I come with you?" she asks in a small voice.

I am taken aback. This is one request I had not anticipated. My eyes blur. "Of course. That would be very nice."

44

A little before two, I sit in the car by the gate of Yvette's villa. She said she'd be right out. Though I'm grateful for the opportunity to know my half-sister better, I wonder how it will be to spend a few days with her. We are still nearly strangers.

At exactly two o'clock, Yvette appears, an overnight tote bag in hand, and I drive the car down the road that runs past the villa, negotiating two roundabouts, and find, with Yvette's help, the A8 that will take us into Nice. I struggle to keep up with the flow of traffic, noting the tiny signs that fly by announcing the exits to Toulon, St. Tropez, and Cannes. Yvette sits with her hands folded in her lap.

It is late afternoon when we turn off the coast highway and follow signs for Nice. I'm excited when I see the arrow directing us onto the Promenade des Anglais. Though I had taken the train to Nice several times over the years, it had always given me the impression of being just another French metropolis. Now it feels like familiar territory. Despite it being the tourist season, I managed to change my reservation from one room to two at the hotel, not far from the Negresco.

"When was the last time you were in Nice?" I ask.

Yvette stares out the window. "We passed through Nice when I was seven for my grandfather's funeral. Then a couple of times for business, but we mostly stayed in the hotel."

"So you haven't really seen the city?" I ask, amazed.

She twists in her seat and looks at me. "No. Maman called Nice *la cimetière*. A city full of dead people. Like many things she said, I never really understood what she meant until I read her memoir."

We check into the hotel and disappear into our respective rooms to unpack and rest for an hour. I fling open the shutters and soak up the sight of the Mediterranean. Colorful crowds dot the rocky beach and the long stretch of boardwalk. I am restless and can hardly wait to set foot on the Promenade.

I had made dinner reservations at a restaurant in the Negresco, a fitting beginning to our tour of Nice, as it had played a role in Emilie's story of the city so many years ago. When I announce our destination to Yvette in the lobby of the hotel, she nods. "Good."

I order champagne, and we feast. Niçoise salad followed by fish baked in fennel leaves, tender julienne vegetables, and a dessert that stood eight inches in the air, a spiral pastry filled with egg custard that nearly reached my chin.

"*C'est formidable!*" says Yvette.

It is challenging to find our way with each other. Conversation in the car had been limited to directions, impersonal comments on the towns we passed, and French and American politics. Contrary to given wisdom, politics was a safe topic. Sooner or later, we will have to shift focus to Dad and Emilie and the war.

"Did your mother hear from Victoire after she moved to America?" I ask.

"Oh, yes. Victoire visited every year or so to see my mother. Until about 2000 when Jimmy passed away and she was too frail to travel alone. She always came by our house in Marseille. And then L'Avigne later."

"Was she happy in America?" I ask.

"Happy enough. It was hard with so many new people and places. She wanted to be in France, but…" Yvette shrugs.

"Jimmy's life was in the U.S."

"Yes."

"Did they have children?" I ask tentatively.

Yvette laughs a full, throaty chuckle. *"Mais oui!* Six. I cannot even remember all their names. Sometimes several of them would come to France with her. Most of them had curly blond hair and dimples like Victoire." When the waiter brings more coffee, Yvette waits until he has refilled our cups. "I believe Victoire and Jimmy had fifteen grandchildren. She is gone now, too."

It is after ten when we step from the restaurant into the lobby of the hotel, and I pause to take in the whole area. "I can imagine how this must have looked in 1945."

We exit the hotel and cross the Promenade, which, even at this hour, is crowded with joggers, rollerbladers, and cyclists. The Mediterranean stretches out endlessly before us, and on a private beach, which is now closed, a sign advertises admission to La Plage, beach umbrellas, and chairs for twenty Euros. Though it is dark, there are still bathers scattered about the free beach, sitting on the bank of smooth stones.

"Dad and Emilie—" I stop and glance at Yvette. I don't want to be too familiar too soon, but her face is a question mark.

"The souvenir pebbles came from here."

We continue our walk down the Promenade and, after twenty minutes, find ourselves on the Quai des États-Unis overlooking the harbor. The image of the explosion on the docks shortly before the

Allies entered Nice is still burned into my mind. The port is now home to yachts and fishing vessels moored in the inky water.

We retrace our steps back to the hotel and Yvette is about to say good night, but I don't want the evening to end yet.

"Let's have a drink," I say, before she can escape, and we seat ourselves at an empty table in the rear of the bar that offers a modicum of privacy and order champagne cocktails.

"Yvette, why did you decide to come with me?"

"I am not sure. To see my mother's life through your eyes? To see what you see when you think of your father?"

I hadn't counted on her monitoring my responses.

She smiles at the waiter who delivers our drinks, and I sip my cocktail, enjoying the bubbles sliding up into my nose.

"Do you mind if I ask a question?" She toys with the champagne flute, rolling the stem between her fingers.

"Of course not," I say quickly.

"You know quite a bit about my mother from reading her memoir, at least her life during the war. But I know very little about your father."

"True," I say. "What would you like to know?"

She glances at a couple across the bar who whisper in each other's ears. "What kind of man was he?" The question is innocent enough, yet I realize how fraught with danger my answer might be. Though we are sisters, he had raised me; he had no part in her life. Still, she deserves an honest answer.

"My father was a kind man. He loved his children and his wife. He was good to us. In his last years he enjoyed himself so much with his photography and grandchildren. I miss his loving, generous way of making me feel like I was the most important person in the room." I stop. "I thought I knew him well, but ever since his will...and the memoir...I'm not sure how much I really did know him. Dad's life seemed so conventional. Now, knowing about Emilie...and you..."

"The will was out of character?" Yvette sits forward and appears more interested in Dad than she had since my arrival in L'Avigne.

"His relationship with Emilie seemed out of character. The passion, the throw-caution-to-the-wind, the secrecy," I say.

She studies me curiously. "How was he with your mother?"

"They had a good marriage, were cordial with each other. But what he had with Emilie...I don't know. I think a part of him never got over it." There is a moment of quiet. "What about your mother and Guy?"

"They were compatible. There was love, yes, and my father worked hard to support us. But he was a solitary man. Sometimes I think he enjoyed his dogs more than Maman and me." She finishes her glass of champagne.

"He was an artist," I say.

"I was surprised to learn that."

"But Guy never found out that...?"

"That I was not his biological child? No," she says emphatically. "As it turned out, I was to be his only child. The war left him damaged and angry. His wasn't the happiest of lives, but he did his best." She pauses. "He was a good father and I loved him."

I let the words settle between us.

"Your mother never spoke of the war or her life in Nice?" I ask, repeating the same question I had asked in a letter weeks ago and yesterday in Yvette's home.

She puts her head back. "Once. One day when I was about ten we went to the cinema. I loved the movies but my father thought they were a waste of time and money. Never mind, Maman said, we'll go, the two of us. I cannot remember the name of the movie...a love story.

I was enthralled. Halfway through the film, I looked at her and she was crying. 'What's wrong?' I whispered. She said, 'It reminds me.' 'Of what?' 'Of my other life.' I was startled. What other life? Then a woman in the seat next to me said 'Shush' and I kept quiet." Yvette closes her eyes. "I'd forgotten about that night until I read the memoir."

"Did she ever tell you what she meant?"

"After the movie was over and we walked home, she put her arm around me, and said 'I was in a movie once.' I thought she was teasing me. 'Maman, you were in a film?' She laughed and did a little dance step, and I didn't believe this was my Maman. I pressed her for an explanation, but we had arrived at the house, and my father was waiting for us, angry that we were out this late. She must have forgotten about the conversation because she never mentioned it again." Yvette grins at me. "That was some story, yes? She and Victoire and the riot on the movie lot. *Les Enfants du Paradis*."

"I watched it again recently, searching for your mother in the crowd scenes. The movie has taken on a new meaning," I say.

"When I was a child, I wanted to ask Victoire about the scar on her cheek but Maman insisted I say nothing. And of course she never explained the incident," Yvette says.

"It was fortunate she met Jimmy."

"Yes, and that he married her."

She may not have intended the reproach, but, nonetheless, the message is clear: unlike Dad.

I felt protective of my parents. "I don't know if Dad wanted to go through with the marriage to my mother, but he felt it was the right thing to do."

"Daniel's life was in America with your mother. How different things might have been…"

"If he had stayed in France or brought Emilie home."

"Yes."

We let the tinkling of glass and the soft conversations of patrons fill in the space between us.

Yvette stands up. "It's getting late."

I signal the waiter for the check. She reaches inside her purse, and I interrupt her. "I'll take care of it."

"Thank you. Good night," she says.

I am rummaging in my wallet for Euros when I hear her walk back.

"I have been meaning to ask you. How did the memoir come to be in your father's possession?"

"I don't know," I say. "I really don't know."

Yvette accepts my answer, and I watch her walk out of the bar and move toward the elevators.

We meet early for breakfast, as pre-arranged, in the hotel restaurant. I eat an American breakfast of ham, eggs, potatoes, rolls, and coffee; Yvette sips a *café au lait*. No wonder she's so thin. We intend to spend the day traveling in and around Nice, to see the places Emilie wrote about.

I cruise past the Place Masséna, crowded with visitors and overflowing with tropical flowers and fountains, and pull the car to the curb opposite No. 14 Avenue Félix Faure. Monsieur Boudreaux's former residence looks as I have imagined it, a brick row house with neatly painted door and window sashes.

"I wonder what happened to him," I say.

"It is possible he met the fate of other collaborators," Yvette says. "Many were tried and punished."

And many were punished without the benefit of a trial, like Marie.

262

As if she read my thoughts, Yvette says, "It was unfortunate about my aunt Marie. Until I read the memoir, I assumed she had been killed in the war fighting with the resistance."

"Your mother told you that?"

"Not outright, but she implied that Marie died a hero's death," she says.

I am astonished.

"My mother avoided the truth," she says without bitterness or sarcasm. It's a statement of fact.

A mile away, Monsieur Zazou's Art Studio on Rue Berlioz is now a glass and steel modern bank.

"My father rarely spoke gently about anyone and could be very harsh at times. But according to the memoir, he saw Monsieur Zazou as a father," Yvette says.

We drive past the location of the bakery on Rue de Rivoli, where Emilie spent weeks in the cold, damp bedroom at the top of the stairs. It is now an upscale coffee bar. Finally, we find the apartment on Rue Saint François de Paule where so much of Emilie's story took place: nursing Victoire after the movie riot; fighting with Jean; spending time with Dad. I glance sideways, wondering what Yvette is thinking.

We stand across the street and watch as a family of four departs the building, father and son bouncing a soccer ball back and forth while mother and daughter link arms and share an ice cream cone.

"A happy family. *Bien*," Yvette says.

We stop for lunch at a sidewalk café around the corner from the apartment and eat *croques monsieurs* and witness the parade of life pass by. Tourists, businessmen, students, old men, and women. On a bright, sunny day such as this, it is difficult to envision the terror that permeated the city while Emilie lived here.

"Kate, another drink?" Yvette asks.

We had a glass of white wine each, and I'm already feeling a little too relaxed. "Thanks, but no, I won't be able to drive. Maybe later?"

Yvette agrees. During the course of the morning, we allowed ourselves to open up a bit. We exchanged divorce stories, and Yvette revealed that her ex-husband was a moocher constantly begging for loans. I shared tales of Terry's prowess in the kitchen. It was fun to have "girl talk," sister talk, really.

I slowly ease the car into traffic on the Promenade and drive east over the coast road.

"Have you been back to Monaco?" I ask.

"Not since my grandparents died. And Eva moved to Marseille to study."

Yvette slides her eyes in my direction. "I wanted her closer to home. Her father says I baby her too much." She gazes out the window. "She is my only child."

She reads the road signs and points out the approximate location of the dispensary where Emilie first met Dad. Flashy condos dot the landscape on both sides of the road.

Further along the low Corniche, we take a turnoff and drive up the hill into Eze. We decide to get out and stretch our legs by climbing the steps upward, leading to the wall that surrounds the city. From this vantage point, we can see far into the Mediterranean, as Dad and Emilie might have sixty years ago.

"Gorgeous," I say.

"Mmm," Yvette agrees.

At a café on the beach, not far from where we assume Le Marin had been located, we drink another glass of white wine. I can see Dad and Emilie dancing on the patio.

"She knew then that she was in love. Even though she had doubts."

"My father loved her so much, Yvette. I know she said he wrote to her in 1945 and 1946. That's in the memoir. But they kept up a correspondence for forty years."

Yvette is surprised. "How do you know?"

"I found a packet of letters in my father's safe. In his apartment in New York City."

"Did your mother know?" Yvette asks.

I get a flash of that Christmas Eve when I overheard my parents arguing. "My mother found a letter from Emilie in my father's coat pocket."

"What did she say? What did she think?"

"I don't know for sure," I say.

"She must have been a forgiving person."

I would never have described Mother that way. Of course, she had come to see me in Paris and make peace, she had said. To me? To Emilie too?

"She did not know that her husband had a daughter in France, yes?"

"True. At least I haven't found any evidence that she knew." Dad's correspondence with Emilie was one thing; a child with her would have been an altogether different matter.

"I still do not understand why Maman sent her memoir to Daniel, to someone who could not read French," Yvette says.

"Safekeeping." I stare at Yvette. "Your mother knew I majored in French."

"How?"

"She painted my college graduation photo. I'm sure Dad would have told her."

"So Maman hoped you would read it? That you would know about me?"

265

"Maybe this wasn't only about our parents but about us."

We sit in silence for a moment and then finish our drinks and return to the car. The sun is dropping lower in the sky, sunset an hour away. I find a parking spot on the Promenade near the entrance to the public beach. I had suggested that it might be nice to leave Emilie's pebbles here, to leave a little bit of our parents in Nice, where they had shared so much.

Yvette hooks her arm in mine to steady herself as we walk across the stones until we reach the edge of the water. Whitecaps roll in and splash foam onto our feet.

I hold out the pebbles that Dad and Emilie had picked up half a century ago and offer them to Yvette. She picks one. We throw them into the waves and watch them skip over the water.

"Who knows, they could wash up on a beach somewhere in the U.S."

"A person does not really die when someone remembers them," Yvette says.

She turns to me, and I reach for her, and we remain on the beach, arms wrapped around each other. Sometimes things and people have a way of traveling a long distance before coming back to the place where they began.

45

By three o'clock the next day, we're back in L'Avigne, and I've moved into a guest bedroom on the second floor of the villa to spend my last night. Yvette insisted that the small hotel in town had seen the last of me. The room is simple but comfortable. A bed covered with a hand-made quilt, a well-worn dresser, nightstand, and rocker. Sketches and watercolors cover a wall across from the mirrored chest of drawers. Eva was right—Emilie's work is everywhere.

Opposite my room is an airy painting studio with a drafting table, easels, and dozens of canvases and paintings. I poke my head in and see an unfinished watercolor of the sun rising over the hills behind the villa, still on an easel.

"It was the last painting Maman worked on," Yvette says behind me.

I gesture at the room. "I hope I'm not intruding."

"Of course not. I cannot bear to put it away."

"Why should you?"

"I feel her presence in here," Yvette says.

"She was certainly prolific."

"Especially the last twenty years. Whenever she faced a crisis, she painted. It was her way of dealing with catastrophes, like the night my

267

father died she painted from midnight until dawn. Or when I went into labor prematurely shortly before Eva was born. Even my divorce," she says ruefully.

How do I ease my way through crises? There was a time when I drank more than I should have, even a time when I would have exercised like crazy. With Dad, I poured all my grief into Emilie and Yvette.

"I need to go into the village. Would you like to come with me?" she asks.

"I'd love to."

As Yvette backs her Audi out of the driveway, I can hear Mignonne yelping from the rear of the house, put out at being left behind. In the center of L'Avigne, she leads me through a grocery store, picking items off the shelves: a box of crackers, another quart of ice cream, a tube of spaghetti sauce that, according to Yvette, is not half bad squeezed onto pasta.

At the bakery, we wait patiently with other customers while fresh bread is browning. When the loaves are finally stacked upright in a large basket, Yvette chooses two and sets them in her cart, thanking the baker over the din of fresh dough being shoved into the oven. At the *boucherie*, I hang back while Yvette confers with the butcher about cuts of veal, chicken thighs, and a slab of beef that I do not recognize.

Outside the shop on the street, with the late afternoon sun warm on our faces and the light changing intensity, we walk to the car silently, companionably. I'm more relaxed than I've been in weeks, in a place I belong with someone who understands me.

"I can see why you stayed in L'Avigne after your mother died. It's magnificent."

"I had the villa to take care of. I planned to go back to Paris, but Eva was beginning art school and I needed to be near her. She was very close to Maman and took her death badly."

"Did you ever have any desire to paint?"

"The artist gene skipped a generation," she says. "I thought about resuming my work after Maman died. But I became used to the slow life here. I miss Paris, but I love my gardens, and flowers, and the sea."

"Do you know if your father ever went back to photography?" I ask.

"Not as far as I know. He seemed to have no interest in art, in lightness, and feelings. His world was too dark by then," she says. "He found comfort in his dogs."

Once at the villa, I reorganize my suitcase and find a skirt, a lightweight sleeveless blouse, and a sweater since the nights have been cool. I offer to help with dinner, but Yvette is emphatic; she likes to cook alone.

The German shepherd sits at the foot of the stairs leading to the second floor and whines. *"Shush, Mignonne! Viens!"* Yvette's voice floats up to my room as she coaxes the dog to follow her.

At seven, I wander downstairs, bypass the kitchen, except for inhaling the sharp tang of hot oil, and walk out to the patio. The table is laid, and the wine stands adjacent to a basket of fresh bread and a plate of tomatoes still warm from the sun. How can I be so hungry?

The sweet fragrance of tropical flowers permeates the air. On the other side of a tall hedge that forms the perimeter of Yvette's property, specks of light from flickering candles are visible through the shrubbery. Voices, intermittent laughter, and the tinkling of dishes and silverware mark the dinner hour.

Yvette appears with a platter of meat and a bowl of green beans. *"C'est tout!"* She fills the wine glasses. "From the vineyard in L'Avigne."

I see veal cutlets smothered in a cream sauce.

She passes the tomatoes and bread. "Kate, do you like to cook?"

I spear a green bean and pop it into my mouth. "I cook well enough. Remember, it was my ex-husband who could work miracles in the kitchen."

Yvette cocked an eyebrow. "Yes. And you divorced him?"

I laugh out loud. "Hard to believe, right?"

"So why did you divorce him?" she asks sincerely.

I let my mind meander back to the final year of my marriage. "We fell apart. We were good friends, but the excitement, the passion left. And then so did he." Not to mention his straying and my own indiscretion with the salesman years ago.

"Passion," she says and cuts a bit of veal. "Someone said, 'passion leaves an imprint on the soul forever.'"

"Honestly? I'm not sure I even know what passion is. It's more than good sex. We had that for a time," I say. Yvette puts down her knife and fork and studies me. "That burning need to be with someone, to see them, touch them, the I-can't-live-without-them thing. Always thinking about them, day and night. No. Never been there," I say, and then I ask, "Have you?"

Yvette blinks. "Once, when I was nineteen."

"And your husband?"

She waves her hand dismissively. "Definitely not."

I lift my glass, and she lifts hers, and we clink. "Here's to some passion in our lives," I say.

"Like our parents," she whispers.

Maybe it's the wine, or maybe it's the realization that Yvette has said "our parents," but I feel light-headed. "Like our parents."

"For thirty-five years Maman was married to Papa," Yvette says, "and she had only nine months with Daniel. Remarkable. Even when she no longer saw him, he was with her. Nearly sixty years."

"Dad let go of his passion and surrendered to a life that I don't think completely satisfied him."

"I am happy you are here," she says and touches my fingers.

I curl my hand around hers.

After dinner, I share the pictures I brought from New Jersey, and Yvette withdraws a worn family album from a bookshelf adjacent to the fireplace. She slowly flips the pages and points out photos of her grandparents, Armand and Camille, and of Emilie and Marie in happier times at their home in Monaco.

"All gone. My family is very small now," she says. "Eva and myself."

I pause and feel the words before I say them. "And us."

She glances up from the album. "*Oui, tu es ma soeur.*"

My vision of the black and white prints in the album floats as if the past is washed away to leave room for a new present. "And you are my sister."

Yvette is gradually filling a part of the aching void left by Dad's passing.

The alarm goes off at eight, and I awake with a slight headache. After the dinner wine, Yvette and I indulged in cognac. I throw back the coverlet, swing my legs over the edge of the bed, and open the shutters that allow a flood of sunlight to saturate the room. From the balcony, I can see behind the villa and into the hills surrounding Marseille. A blanket of red-tiled roofs against a bright blue sky.

Mignonne begins to bark outright.

"*Silence!*"

I put on a robe, shove my feet into flip-flops, and descend to the first floor. "*Bonjour, Mignonne,*" I say, digging my fingers into the fur at the nape of her neck. Mignonne cocks her head for a moment and then, satisfied, leads me to the kitchen.

Yvette, also in robe and slippers, is already at work, making coffee and opening a jar of homemade peach preserves. We share breakfast, spreading jam on toast, and downing second cups of coffee. The previous night has opened a floodgate of conversation, and I share my experience of Dad's last year. Yvette confides that there was a time when she was estranged from Emilie: she hadn't approved of Yvette's elopement. They made up when Yvette got pregnant because she felt her child needed grandparents.

"What did Guy think of your husband?" I ask.

"He supported everything I did, even my stupid decisions. I could do no wrong as far as he was concerned," she says.

"That sounds familiar," I say.

"Maman and I were too much alike in some ways."

Mom and I were opposites.

Then I check my watch. I have two hours to shower and dress before I must leave for the Marseille airport.

Upstairs, I resist the impulse to push down on my suitcase to zip it shut; that would endanger some of the gifts I am toting back to New Jersey. Instead, I flip the lid open once more and grab an armful of clothing, rearranging this, sorting that, until the bag closes with a minimum of effort.

"Kate, the paintings," Yvette calls from the floor below.

"Yes. Thanks."

She suggested I look through Emilie's watercolor collection to find some paintings to take home for myself and DJ. On one wall of the studio, files stand in a vertical holder, each containing at least a dozen watercolors. I search the files: the hills surrounding Marseille, fishing boats, goats grazing on the hills, flowers and more flowers, and paintings of villages—Grasse, Vence, and Cannes.

I start to pull out a watercolor of the fishing boats when a black and white picture catches my attention. At the back of the holder, in the last file, there is a photograph whose stark light and dark contrast sharply with the soft pastels of the paintings.

I remove it from its hiding place. It is the same photograph I'd found in Dad's safe in New York. Emilie, magnetically beautiful, posing behind a canvas. She is mesmerizing. No wonder Dad fell in love.

I roll my bag down the stairs, nearly catching Mignonne's tail in the wheels since she insists on jumping and pawing my suitcase until Yvette reprimands her.

"Do you have everything?" she asks.

"I think so. I will treasure the paintings." I stoop down and grab Mignonne's head. "Good-bye, you lovely. I'm already thinking I need a dog."

"I know one you could have," Yvette says wryly and adjusts a blue and green silk scarf that she had tied around her neck.

I bend forward to kiss her good-bye and freeze. I stare at her necklace, speechless. I must have turned white because Yvette looks alarmed. "Kate? What's the matter?"

"Where did you get that?" is all I can get out.

Yvette touches her throat. "From Maman."

It is a diamond and ruby pendant on a gold chain, identical to the piece of jewelry that Mother had worn for decades until a year or so before she died. The same necklace that Dad had given her as an engagement present the summer he returned from Europe. "To make amends," Uncle Bert had said.

"When?" I stammer.

Yvette checks the wall clock. "Kate, your flight?"

"I have time. I need to know about the necklace. It belonged to my mother," I say.

"What are you talking about?" she asks.

"I know this sounds crazy, but my father gave my mother that necklace in 1945."

Yvette is puzzled and takes my arm. "Come. Sit down before you fall down," she says and leads me to the dining room table.

"The last days before Maman passed, she was in the hospital and tried to talk but she was very weak. Three days before she died, she was slipping into and out of consciousness. At one point she told me to find an envelope she'd left for me in her bureau. I was not to open it, simply to get it."

I wait for her to speak again.

"The last day, she told me the envelope contained a letter she wanted me to read after she died and also there was a special piece of jewelry that she wanted me to have."

"And that was it? That's all she said?"

"I wondered about the necklace, where it had come from and why it was not with the rest of her jewelry. The letter told me about Daniel."

"My mother came to Marseille in 1981," I say.

Yvette touches the pendant and gazes at me, confused.

"I found her passport. She visited me in Paris that spring. But she flew into Marseille."

The room is still, save for the sound of Mignonne's snoring and her occasional shift from one position to another.

"We didn't always get along, but that trip was the best time we'd ever shared." I breathe deeply. "She knew about your mother and that she and Dad had corresponded over the years. I think she wanted to...talk with Emilie."

Yvette is quiet, watching me. "I was living in Paris then."

Finally, my eyes meet hers. She unclasps the chain, holds the jewelry up to the light, and then hands it to me. "I want you to have it."

"I can't take this, Yvette. It was your mother's gift to you."

"Shush," she says as if commanding Mignonne to settle down. She fastens the chain around my neck then turns me to face her. "First your mother wore this, and then my mother, and then me. Now it will go home with you."

I hug Yvette and then kiss her good-bye, tears flowing freely. "Thank you."

"Your mother was a special person," she says.

"I am beginning to find out how special."

46

It is fall, and the leaves are changing. Everything around me is changing. My autumn mantel decoration—red and gold leaves, orange gourds, and dried multi-colored cobs of corn—is a perfect match for this time of year. Next to it is a photograph I found in a shoebox in the attic of the Whitman home. It's an informal picture of my parents on their wedding day.

After visiting L'Avigne, I dug around in ancient trunks and dusty cardboard boxes, excavating memorabilia from my family's past. There were wonderful photos of my brothers and me at all ages, playing in the sand on beaches, graduating from one school or another. Given Dad's reluctance to be the subject of photography, I was happy to find pictures of him and Mom sitting at a club in Manhattan with Lloyd and his wife Arlene and celebrating their twenty-fifth anniversary. They look as happy as any two people had a right to be. I'd pulled the wedding day snapshot from the pile and had it framed.

In it, my parents are at a banquet table, the table linen decorated with half-empty glasses, an ashtray, and a dark stain. Dad stares out as though searching for someone, Mother smiles broadly as she glances sideways at her new husband, and their tightly clasped hands suggest a unity that hints at the solid, strong bond that was to last nearly forty years. It's a study in commitment. Responsibility to their marriage and family claimed primacy over their individual desires and issues. There are no simple conclusions to my parent's story, I think, as I stroke the diamond and ruby necklace that I wear most days.

I have an asparagus casserole—one of Terry's old recipes—and I push the doorbell. I can hear the chimes reverberate inside the foyer of the Whitman home as I breathe in the autumn air. Next to me, Eva fidgets and balances a covered platter with DJ's favorite hors d'oeuvre: caviar and cream cheese on toast.

"Are you nervous?" I ask.

"*Non*," she says and grins. "I am excited!"

Nancy opens the door and takes us in. "Hello, Kate." She kisses me and extends her hand to Eva. "Hello."

"Nancy, this is Yvette's daughter, Eva."

Eva beams and kisses Nancy. "I am happy to meet you."

Behind Nancy, Drew, his girlfriend Molly, a pretty redhead, and DJ appear. "Come on in," Drew says and ushers Eva past Nancy and me. "Dad, this is Eva."

DJ awkwardly offers his hand, and she springs forward, shyly kissing him European-style on both cheeks. He says nothing but looks pleased. I refrain from using the words "niece" and "cousin" during introductions. Better to save the intimacies for later.

"Everybody, make yourselves comfortable." Nancy takes my casserole, and we move into the living room.

DJ's slim new appearance is attractive and removes a few years. He drops into an easy chair. According to Nancy, his new health program is doing wonders for his heart but taking a toll on his mood.

"Where's Nate?" I ask.

"Working late. Whitman Textiles can't get along without him now, right Dad?" Drew teases.

"He reminds me of me," DJ grumbles.

"Drew and Molly, will you get drinks? There's a bottle of white wine in the refrigerator and red wine on the counter. What would you like Eva?" Nancy asks.

Drew slips an arm around Eva's shoulders. "I'll take care of her," he says, and the three of them disappear into the kitchen.

"She's very sweet," Nancy says.

"Yes. A lovely young woman," I add. DJ remains quiet.

I survey the room. "I like what you've done with the colors in here. Hunter green, yes?" I unwrap the caviar and cream cheese and set it on the coffee table.

Nancy nods. "It's not too dark, is it?" She frowns.

"Suits the room perfectly. Can I help with dinner?" I ask.

"Everything's under control."

DJ leans forward, glancing at Nancy to get approval before he picks up a piece of toast.

"It's okay for one night," she says.

Good for Nancy.

She watches me sit down beside DJ. "There's a timer going off in the kitchen." She disappears as well.

"I talked with Uncle Bert yesterday. He's adjusting to assisted living. Said he's making friends and likes poker night." DJ shrugs. "That was nice of you to get him into Springdale."

"I guess everyone deserves a second chance."

That covers a few people. When I came home from L'Avigne with the necklace and the story of Mom's visit with Emilie, my brother was silent, grappling with the events and people of our parents' pasts.

Eventually, he was more receptive, and we talked about Dad, Mom, Emilie, and Yvette. And Eva. It was a lot for both of us to absorb.

"The old man had himself some kind of war," he said.

I agreed. His response made me feel optimistic.

Drew, Molly, and Eva reappear with glasses, wine, and a vodka martini for DJ. "Mom said dinner's ready, so everyone come sit." He escorts Molly and Eva to the table, and I hang back with DJ.

As he bends to pop another hors d'oeuvre into his mouth, I touch his arm. "Thanks."

"Did you know that Drew's going to have an exhibit of his paintings in Hoboken? A group of NYU students have put it together," says Nancy and hands the meat plate to DJ.

"Congratulations," I say, and pat Drew on the back.

Drew pours wine for all of us but his father. "He had his one drink already," Nancy says and fills his glass with water.

"Nate is studying for the LSAT," Drew says.

"That's what your dad said." I pass the asparagus casserole to Eva, who daintily spears a few and hands it to Nancy, who smiles warmly at her.

"We're so pleased," she says.

DJ takes a bite of potato and grimaces. "Yeah, we're pleased. I'll be working another ten years."

Out of the corner of my eye, I observe Eva. She shifts her focus from speaker to speaker following the conversation. When I heard from Yvette that Eva accepted my offer of a visit to New Jersey, I was thrilled but had some misgivings. Even more when Nancy suggested this get-together. I can see that I worried for nothing.

"He wants Harvard Law, unless he gets married. He and Angie..." Drew entwined two fingers. "It's been five years."

Angie, a high school English teacher, is good for Nate. Warm and funny. A great counterbalance to Nate's serious side.

"Eva, there's a Whitman family tradition. Always a crisis at a wedding," I say. She looks at me with interest. "On my wedding day the florist forgot my bouquet and they had to take the bridesmaids' flowers and make a kind of temporary arrangement out of them. When I tried to hand them off to the maid of honor, the whole thing fell apart and there were roses and carnations all over the floor. Everybody panicked and the ushers were on their hands and knees trying to rescue the day."

Eva grins, and everyone laughs.

"Yeah, my favorite is Dad's story," Drew says. "He tripped coming up the steps of the church and tore a hole in his trousers. He had to change pants with Grandpa. He wore the ones with the hole."

"Okay, okay," DJ says and shakes his head. "Anyway you weren't there. So I was a little nervous."

"A little?" Nancy's eyebrows arch.

I giggle. "I remember Dad whipping off his trousers in the vestibule behind a screen and claiming that no one paid any attention to the father of the groom. Mother was beside herself."

The mention of "Dad" and "Grandpa" raises a specter that could introduce a level of discomfort. Instead, the memories fill the space around us and warm the atmosphere.

Drew says easily, "Eva, you don't know what kind of a goofy family you're getting into."

Seconds pass while DJ, Nancy, and I process his comment, but the next generation takes it in stride. Molly agrees with Drew, and Eva grins again, her pleasure at being included in the conversation and the family clear.

"I'd like to make a toast," I say. They raise glasses. "To all of us here and those who can't be." I glance at Eva, and she nods.

We tell stories until ten. Then DJ heads upstairs, I offer to help clean up, but Nancy says no, Molly and Drew will lend a hand and excuses Eva and me to view the family album together. It's brown leather and has photos of DJ and Billy and me running under a water sprinkler, sledding down a snowy hill, and blowing out candles on birthday cakes. Mom is holding the twins on a vacation at the Jersey shore. As I turn the pages, Eva studies each picture carefully as though collectively they hold answers to a mystery. She is fascinated to discover her relatives and eagerly hangs on every word of explanation, every bit of family lore.

"You are lucky, Kate," Eva says.

"Why?"

"So many people in your family," she says wistfully.

"I am lucky." I put my hand on hers.

"I love this house, too."

"So do I." Memories rise up. The blazing fireplace radiating blasts of hot air, the slightly sweet aroma of furniture polish, the tapping of shoes on the parquet floors, and Billy chasing me from one room to the next. I think of it now with affection.

Eva takes the album and points to a picture of Bert dressed as Santa Claus. "*Qui est-ce?*"

"Our Uncle Bert. Dad's brother."

"Is he alive?" she asks.

I laugh. "Oh, yeah. In fact, your Grandmother Emilie met him in Paris at the end of the war."

Eva closes her eyes and drops her head onto the back of the sofa. "Maman told me about *grand-mère* in Paris after the war. I can see her there."

"She was about your age."

Eva shakes her head. *"Incroyable."*

Drew and Molly walk in. "Ready Eva? We're going to hang at my place."

The carriage house is now "Drew's place." Dad would have enjoyed that.

"I'll drop Eva off later."

Eva closes the album and kisses me good night. *"Au revoir, tante Kate,"* she says, and a lump rises in my throat. Since she has discovered the relationship between her grandmother and Dad, I am "Aunt Kate."

"Not too late. We're going to the museum tomorrow." An art student from France could not leave New York without seeing the Museum of Modern Art.

"No problem."

I kiss Drew and Molly good night, and he reminds me that the three of them are partying in the city Saturday and staying over at my apartment.

I am a trifle nervous. I keep telling myself to let go; after all, I lived in the city at their ages.

On Sunday evening, her last night, Eva and I have a quiet dinner at home. After we eat, Eva insists on doing the dishes.

I kick off my shoes, collapse on the sofa, and hear her loading the dishwasher and rinsing the broiling pan. "Eva, come in here. I'll get it tomorrow."

"One minute."

Ten minutes later, she bounds energetically into the living room.

"Aren't you tired? I hear you didn't get to sleep until three this morning," I say and yawn. Nancy's report, via Drew, confirmed that the threesome had gone clubbing to a handful of nightspots in the Village. East and West.

Eva waves it away. *"C'est rien."*

"Come sit." I pat the cushion beside me.

Eva folds herself into the sofa and curls her legs under her. We sit shoulder to shoulder until she changes her position and rests her head against me affectionately.

"I like your family," she says.

"Thanks. But it's your family, too."

"Oui."

"Did you call your mother today and confirm your arrival?"

"I will tomorrow morning. I have so much to tell her about the dinner and New York and the apartment. I like the apartment," she says, and her eyes twinkle.

I put my arm on the back of the sofa, and Eva slips further into my shoulder. "What will you tell her? About all of us?"

Eva smirks. "That we are a goofy family."

I laugh.

"I think *grand-père* Daniel was a good man who loved you and your mother. And I think you all loved him very much," she announces seriously.

Her remarkably simple assessment brings me up short. "You got all that from this visit?"

"Mais oui," she says as if amazed that I even question her.

She burrows deeper into the couch and twists her head to look at me shyly. "I would like to study in New York when I finish the academy in Marseille."

"You should talk it over with your mother." I don't want to encourage something that Yvette might not agree to.

"I will. You studied at the Sorbonne."

"Yes, I did. It was a wonderful time."

"So I would like to do what you did. Is that okay, *tante* Kate?" she asks.

I drape my arm lightly around hers. "More than okay."

DJ is right. Dad *did* have himself some kind of war. Yvette and Eva are living proof. I wonder if he could have imagined how his will would lead to the revelations of his and Emilie's past. The Whitmans and the Merints are coming to terms with the legacy of our parents' choices, and I am grateful to Emilie for telling her story. It's possible she had no idea who would read her memoir or view the souvenirs she kept of the war. Yet, her memoir has allowed me to see both Dad and Mom in a new light.

I kiss the top of Eva's head. I am beginning to collect my own souvenirs.

Acknowledgments

This book began its life in late 1997 when I visited a small village in the south of France and met the people who would make this story a reality. I am grateful every day for that visit, and later ones, that provided the inspiration and emotional core of this novel. I am so appreciative of early editorial feedback from the wonderful writer Christina Baker Kline, who was the first person to tell me I had a novel. I am especially grateful for the detailed editing of the amazing Paul Dinas, who made me a better writer and made the book what it is today. Thanks also to the supportive Elaine Ash for her efforts on my behalf and to my great friend, the late Grace McCormack, for her cheerleading as she read early chapters.

I am grateful to the folks at Between the Lines Publishing for seeing the possibilities in this book, especially Deb Alix, Siân Helyg, Abby Macenka, Jace Martell, Morgan Bliadd, and Cherie Fox. Your enthusiasm is infectious and your assistance invaluable.

I owe a deep debt of gratitude to my sisters, my mother, friends, and mentors who listened to me tell, over and over again, the spine of the story and supported its circuitous journey. I am thankful for the family members who shared the beginning of the journey with the first trip to France—Denise Trauth, Eileen Trauth, John Huffman, my beloved late mother Martha Trauth, and my dear late aunt Rita Trauth—and who provided encouragement from the beginning to the end, offering enthusiastic interest in the project. Thanks to Jeanette Trauth for her supportive reading of an early draft, to Patty Trauth, who told me to "put myself in the novel," and to Kate Trauth for her steady reassurance and patient encouragement. Most of all, I am grateful to my late sister Charlene Harvey, my in-house French expert, for her delightful curiosity about this story, her translating duties, and her contribution to my understanding of French culture. I felt her sitting on my shoulder throughout. I am blessed to be a member of such a loving and generous family who has always believed in my writing. You are my role models.

A special thanks to my late uncle Lee Trauth whose World War II journal provided details of his experience in Paris after VE Day. His personal story was invaluable.

Many thanks to the friends who listened good-naturedly to my storytelling, especially Lori Katterhenry, Patty Michaels, Jane Peterson, Susan Kerner, Eileen Skarecki, and Diane Zaremba. Thanks also to my group of advanced readers for your time and energy.

Finally, I am most grateful for the unwavering encouragement of Elaine, my tireless champion and insightful beta reader. This book would not have happened without her patience, sense of humor, and steady love. Thank you.

Questions for Discussion

When Kate takes a trip to Europe with girlfriends after graduation, she ignores her parents' demand that she stay in touch and let them know if she changes her itinerary. She doesn't and must pay the consequences. Have you ever made decisions that forced you to confront painful consequences?

Kate has a complicated relationship with her parents and very different connections with her father and mother. What is the basis for each? What is/was the nature of your relationship with your parents?

Have you explored your parents' backgrounds or pasts and discovered secrets? What did you do about it? What were the consequences?

Does your family have secrets? Have any come to light?

Can you identify with Kate's relationship and conflicts with her brother DJ?

Do any members of your family have stories of World War II that they've shared or that have been passed down from one generation to the next?

Suzanne Trauth is a novelist, an award-winning playwright and screenwriter, and the author of the Dodie O'Dell mystery series—*Show Time, Time Out, Running out of Time, Just in Time, No More Time*, and *Killing Time*—in addition to plays and screenplays. A former theatre professor, she is a member of Mystery Writers of America and Sisters in Crime. She lives in Woodland Park, New Jersey.

Visit her website: www.suzannetrauth.com
Connect on Facebook: https://www.facebook.com/SuzanneTrauth

9 781950 502981